We are Wormwood

Autumn Christian

First Published July 2013 by
Never Sleep Again Press

Original Photograph by Bailey Elizabeth of
www.baileyelizabeth.com
Cover Design by Janice Duke of
www.janiceduke.com

Dedication

To Lux, who showed me her demon, and took out her revenge by loving me.

We are Wormwood

Part One:
Dry Rot

One

A TINY GOLDEN BEETLE wriggled through the window and into my eye as I slept. They'd been coming all week - the beetles, the roly-polies, the spiders - searching for the way into our house, shimmying, wriggling, and weaving nests. When I woke, I felt the beetle squirming underneath my eyelid, its filmy wings fluttering and scraping. It made a small noise, an almost non-noise. Sh. Sh. Momma must've opened the window when I fell asleep. The oversized curtains hung across my bed and, in the dark, they looked like limp birds with wings of red velvet. I rubbed my eye but the beetle wouldn't come out. I turned on the lamp beside my bed. Moths rushed in the open window and fluttered around me, against my lips, crowning my head. The beetle wouldn't come out.

I ran to Momma's bedroom, crossing the hallway shimmering with little slices of moonlight. She was awake, sitting up in her bed amidst her magic relics and candles, reading a book, plaiting her blonde Scandinavian hair. Momma never slept. Not when the moon was full. She saw me running down the hallway and held her arms out to me. She batted the moths away from my face. I pointed to my eye, tearing, blinking frantically.

Momma held me on her lap, trying to extract the beetle, saying the bugs were thick because the Wormwood star was high in the sky. I couldn't see it, but it shimmered bright and bitter. Wormwood meant this would be a year of poison. The insects knew this as the eye of the mad star beat hot on their backs.

Momma held me still. She said warriors like us knew how to endure pain better than anyone. She held my eyelids open. The golden beetle crawled onto my Momma's finger. I told her to kill it or it'd be back again; she released it on her windowsill where it flew away.

I was six years old, spilling out of her lap, but she cradled me as she rocked back and forth. Warriors stayed close. We were once Vikings who rode dragon-headed boats across the ocean, across the ice. We replaced our flesh with metal to endure the cold and slew creatures others couldn't even have nightmares about, but still we loved better than anyone else. Around campfires, many a story was told about us and the monsters that loomed in the dark, quivering in fear at the mention of our names. She said, "We will always kill dragons together."

Later we crept downstairs, Momma holding a votive candle and a gazelle skull.

"Do you need that skull?" I asked Momma in a quiet voice.

"Shh, baby," she said. "I'm going to give you a treat."

On the staircase, a spider furiously wove a web. I wanted to tear the spider's web down, because its fingers, thin, like the threads of a wicker chair, were in my bad dreams. It carried a mark on its back like a pirate's skull. Momma told me it only needed a home. Give it this corner of the universe. I pressed my back against the banister so I wouldn't have to touch the web. She laughed, shaking her blonde hair that could've been the ruin of the Vikings. If she'd been born a few centuries earlier, her likeness would have been a mermaid-figurehead for their ships.

In the kitchen she opened the window above the sink, turned on the stove, and started to make us hot chocolate. I stood on my tiptoes and turned on the lights. Roaches with silver feelers skittered away. I swear I heard them shriek. Momma didn't notice. She was humming, weaving her fingers through her hair.

"Turn the light off. We'll dance by candlelight," she said.

I turned the light off. Her skin was split, honey in candlelight, powder in moonlight. I climbed up onto the countertop and curled my toes so the roaches wouldn't scurry across my bare feet; she laughed.

"You've forgotten," she said, "that you once slew a wolf pup of the great beast Fenrir. I know when you remember you won't be afraid of insects anymore."

I inhaled and I could smell the milk-breath and musky fur of a wolf. I saw myself in that den, with a silver axe, wrestling the pup. His paw trapped my hair on the floor. I slew him and wore his pelt as a cloak. There was a time when I believed that anything Momma said was true.

We drank the hot chocolate together in candlelight and moonlight. She rested her head in my lap as if she was the child and I the parent. In order to be a sorceress you have to learn to not sleep. The full moon recharges you like a battery. You see the shimmer in everything, so you can pull the thin, magic threads that connected everything and change the world.

"Drink your hot chocolate, baby, the milk will make you strong. One day I'll bring a goat into our backyard. I'll feed her warm hay and feed you her milk. You'll be able to lift six hundred pounds. A thousand. You could lift a truck if you wanted; you'd be stronger than the strongest person in the world because you're not of this world. Stronger than Thor. You should go to bed, baby, you're falling asleep."

"I'm not tired, I want a story," I said, nodding off, the drained cup of hot chocolate dangling in my uncurling fingers.

She kissed my forehead, took the cup from my hands, and sent me upstairs. A story for another time.

In my bedroom a Fiddleback spun a web in my doorjamb. Its poisonous bite could eat a hole through skin. Ants scurried across the floor, carrying off droplets of honey. A scorpion clacked around my feet. I might've once killed a wolf pup, born in mythology, but I never had to deal with anything like this.

I ran back to tell Momma that I wouldn't sleep until they were all dead. Halfway down the stairs, I heard the glass votive holder smash against the wall. I stopped and listened; silence. I leaned over the side of the railing to try and see Momma, but there was only an open kitchen door and candlelight piercing the entryway. I crept down the stairs, treading lightly so the steps wouldn't creak. Holding my breath, I crossed the light and entered the kitchen.

Momma wasn't there. Someone else stood by the kitchen sink heaving, the gazelle skull tied around her head. Someone else with bleach and blood oozing from her chewed fingertips. Cockroaches smashed in the sink. She turned to me with Momma's body, but with the eyes of The Exorcist, eyes like scratches of lightning.

The Exorcist didn't smell like Momma. She smelled like antiseptic, like the sour fake smell of lemons and bad magic. A rosary of powdered bleach ringed her neck. Her eyes were reddened by popped blood vessels. I wondered if she still had Momma's face underneath the mask, or a void where a human face once was.

"She's here," Momma said.

She pressed her lips to her mouth and in between grit and blood-smashed teeth whispered the name.

Nightcatcher. The Nightcatcher's been here.

I grabbed my cup of hot chocolate from the counter. It was sticky and covered in bleach. She grabbed it out of my hand and tossed it away in the trash bag at her feet.

“There was poison in the food,” she said.

There was poison in the tap water. Poison on the doorknobs. Poison in the teacups, on the window latch, in the sunlight, and in the pill bottles on the countertop. Invisible poison that could not be seen, touched, or smelled. Poison that would make tongues unravel, bones rot, arms fall off, and turn a face into a dog's face.

Maybe I only imagined the walls throbbing, trying to squeeze in on us, but I still couldn’t breathe. The Exorcist flung bleach onto the ants on the windowsill. She grabbed a broom and rushed past me to the staircase where she broke the spider's web apart. When the spider tried to flee, she stomped on it, leaving a black and red smear between her toes.

The shadows were alive; the house was alive and it was squeezing in on me. A chill followed The Exorcist like a ghost spot. There was a monster that lived in her skin and wanted to poison us, a monster that not even Vikings could kill. The Exorcist turned toward me but I knew I couldn't look into her eyes. Even if she came to protect us from The Nightcatcher and the poison, those eyes would sear me, burn me, and even kill me. I turned toward the front door as she touched my shoulder; her hair was screaming, the air was screaming. I grabbed the doorknob, turned it, and ran onto the lawn then past the lawn. She called my name and told me to stay inside. Wormwood was out. I ignored her and ran towards the woods.

It was almost winter. The grass tilted to one side, brown and withered. The trees were skinny and as cold as lightning rods. The moon hid behind clouds, casting everything into darkness. I did not see Wormwood in the sky. Momma said it was a small, green star, just above Mars. If you could drink it, it would taste like cedar.

I reached the edge of the neighborhood where the small woods lived. I climbed over the barbed wire fence and the "Do Not Enter" sign protecting the woods, hiking my dress up over my hips so that the hem wouldn't catch on the barbs. I thought I felt The Nightcatcher's shadow. She chilled the air and all stories could be real. I fell on the other side of the fence and stood up, my arms throbbing.

I ran into the woods. The branches and leaves hid the stars away. I had been here several times before, but never at night, and never while shadows pursued me that I thought wanted to eat me alive. I delved further into the place where the dirt was dark and burnt. In the center of a grove, I found a hollowed out dead tree once struck by lightning. It had a mouth like a door. I knelt down and crawled inside.

In the darkness she reached out and touched my shoulder.

"This is my hiding place," she whispered.

Even then, when I first heard her speak, I thought that fangs and rattlers would want to borrow her voice.

"I can't leave," I whispered. "Something's out there. Please don't make me."

I felt a stirring underneath me, like the earth had begun to crawl. Then a pungent smell like wet feathers. I pressed my head against the damp old wood. Her hand slid down my shoulder and touched my palm.

"All right," she said after a period of silence. "You can stay."

I looked up. Her eyes were dark and shiny. Like Wormwood, I thought. Poison. She sat cross-legged with her knees spread, and in the lap of her skirt lay hundreds of glittering and squirming roly-polies, spiders, and golden beetles.

"You..."

I tried to say more, but my tongue turned webbed and dry. I panted softly. She spoke my name.

“Lily.”

The bugs in her lap shone like living crystal. She smiled, her teeth full of feathers, and touched my cheek.

Then she opened her mouth and made a vociferous noise, a clacking insect noise.

“Ke-ke-ke-ke.”

I ran.

Two

BEFORE THE EXORCIST came, Momma used to be a professional storyteller. She called herself Saga, the goddess of storytelling, she who drank from golden cups with Odin. She carried a magic staff, wore a robe sewn with stars, and told stories for children in libraries and huge sterile cafeterias. Sometimes I would go with her and watch with the other children as she read to them from her Wolf-Book, a tome bound with black fur.

"...And the princess awoke when she heard the thud underneath her bed. She bolted upright and before the beast could flee, seized him by the tail. 'Let me go, let me go,' the beast pleaded. But the princess refused to release him until he danced with her."

Momma was not a writer. She wasn't born to sit down because lightning coursed through her and kept her dancing. She made up stories on the spot - hunters, demons, beasts, and new gods who flew across frozen oceans – nobody but she and I knew the pages of the Wolf-Book were blank.

As she performed, I watched those bored, wriggling children become still and listen with rapt attention. She had a different voice for each character, from the deep-throated growl for the troll's wife, to a soft, dream-high voice for the ghost girl. Even Saga, her storytelling persona, spoke in a husky voice like an ancient codex buried within a queen's tomb.

"...She did not want to be a princess, she wanted to be a night girl. Wild girl. And when the priest married her, the new husband's cloaks and garments were lifted to find, not the baron the princess's father had promised, but the beast that hid underneath her bed. She fled with the beast to the underworld kingdom, where they lived out their lives in dark and beautiful wonder."

She finished her stories with a flourish, then bowed so low that her robe touched the floor. The children applauded. The teachers always wanted to ask her, "Where did you get your training?" "Where did you hear that story?" "Who are you really?"

"A sorcerer never reveals her secrets," my Momma said with her hand pressed against her nose, and the children laughed.

Then she swept me up in the whirlwind of her starry robe and we fled. She often took me out afterwards to eat cheap Italian food, and sticky, thick caramel milkshakes. As I ate, she leaned over the table and pushed the hair out of my face. She spoke.

"You don't know this, yet, but when you grow older, you'll dye your hair a bright red because it's the closest you'll ever feel to being on fire. You'll fall in love with the ocean because the boys won't be enough."

"I'm never falling in love," I said.

"You'll be a beautiful woman," she said, continuing on as if I hadn't spoken, as if I was another character in her stories, "once your face grows into those spark-devil eyes. You'll topple cities."

During that time it was easy to forget that she took pills to keep her from going insane — Risperdal, Haldol, antipsychotic drugs with names that sounded like those of old Southern gentlemen. One time, when I was still an infant, she'd been in a mental hospital. She laughed about it now, mimicking her Trichotillomania, how she pulled her hairs out one by one. She told me about the nurses with fat, frowning lips who injected her with sedatives when she started to scream.

"You need to practice your coping mechanisms," she said, mocking their sweet-sick voices, "Have you accepted Jesus Christ as your personal savior?"

She told me about how they attached her to machines that she thought were singing her lullabies in the night, via tiny voices rattling through electrical nodes. How she told other patients she was their deliverance; a robot-god imbued with a divine message. One woman fell trembling in front of her, in dazed worship, and had to be carted away by frantic, chittering nurses.

"I'm better now," Momma said. "There was no way I'd stay for long in a place like that."

I should've seen the warning signs. Her pills disappeared from the kitchen counter. She started staying up at night, unable to sleep, even when the moon wasn't full. Once, during a reading, her hands shook as she gripped the wolf book and a seizure passed across her face. For a moment, only a moment, she forgot her story. I was the only one who noticed, but on the ride back home, she sat listless, like her head was barren.

"The best storytellers die young before they learn how to forget," she said.

Before, she used to let me roam everywhere by myself, telling me warriors learned to forge their own paths. If mother's stayed too close, they created children that were chained and fearful. Yet now, she started to hover, pulling me into her robe.

"Don't stay out too late. Monsters eat the best children," she said in a hushed, crackling voice.

One night I awoke to find her sitting on the windowsill near my bed, with the window cracked open and the cool night air blowing through. It was quiet. She held her breath and stretched out her claw-cracked hands.

"Momma?"

I sat up and pulled my blankets around me. She let her star-sewn robe fall to the floor; underneath she wore a stained nightgown, exposing her scratched collarbones. Her eyes reflected like animal eyes in the light, and when she spoke, her tongue bled.

"Did you know, on the night you were born all my father's horses died? Their necks caught in the barbed wire fence behind the barn. Their legs chewed by wolves."

I drew my legs up underneath the blanket. The room had grown small, too small, and the window bared at me like an angry wolf's mouth.

"I want you to know where we came from, baby."

I thought if I moved the window would chew me apart.

"We were once great hunters, and we can be again. This world isn't meant for us. I've seen the place where your great-grandmother tread cloven-hoofed over the grass. She had eyes like wet diamonds and she sang in a language forgotten, so beautiful it would cause her prey to lay down, paralyzed, in the grass for her to kill. She killed a great snake, a python, who fed on virgin's blood and had terrorized a village for hundreds of years; its skin became her crown. They worshipped her as a goddess."

Momma rose from the windowsill and moved toward me. I suddenly didn't want her to touch me, the way she rubbed her fingers together, violently, until her nails broke. She must've seen me seize up, and stopped at the foot of the bed.

"Are you listening? Because this isn't a story."

"I'm listening," I whispered.

"When I was pregnant I knew you were a girl, because of how fiercely you kicked. You are my little huntress. When you were inside me, I was followed by fire. When I left the hospital after a sonogram, half of the building burned to the ground. I started to have dreams of you and the lives you lived before.

"Would you like to know? Would you like to know who you once were?"

"No," I said.

I didn't dare raise my voice. Was this my Momma who stood before me, speaking in this dark language, in a voice like boiling water?

She reached for me, as if to smooth the hair from my face, but then suddenly stopped. Her body shook as if electrified. She stood paralyzed for a second. Two.

“Momma?

“Oh god, you hear that? She’s gotten into the refrigerator,” she said.

She tore out of the room and down the stairs. I heard the refrigerator door as she slammed it against the wall. I heard the food hitting the floor as she threw it out, then the bottles, then the water purifier. She screamed, an inhuman wail that went on and on.

The next morning I crept downstairs expecting to find a murder scene, the wolf Fenrir's fur in the window jam and my momma's severed hand on the kitchen tiles. But there was only Momma, humming and cooking French toast. She wore her robe of stars and her Wolf-Book sat on the counter beside her. There was no food on the floor, no broken glass. Everything had been cleared away.

She tried to hand me a plate of French toast, but I didn't take it. I searched her for battle scars, missing fingers. Nothing. I started to tremble.

"Are you not feeling well?" she asked, setting the plate on the counter.

She pulled me to her, smoothing my hair, feeling my temple.

"You feel fine. But it's been too long since we've had a sick day together. I'll cancel."

She whisked her Wolf-Book away. We ate breakfast outside on the porch, in sunlight. Everything seemed so far away. My hands out of proportion to my body, the glass of orange juice a thousand years away. She told me it was a lovely morning, a fine morning, and the flowers were beginning to bloom. She and I would go to the fields, out in the woods, and pick them together. We could weave garlands for our heads.

Maybe last night had been a dream.

But the next night she was back at my windowsill with her eyes ringed red. She ripped out blank pages from her Wolf Book and scattered them across my bedroom floor.

"The Nightcatcher knows we're here," she said. "The Wormwood star led her to us. I don't have much time."

"Momma? Are you still taking your medicine?" I asked.

She sat down on the edge of my bed, took both of my hands and clasped them between hers.

"In my dreams, you were the daughter of a witch, and the two of you lived in a cottage out in the woods. She taught you to walk between reality and dreams. The village folk nearby called you deer-girl, because of how silent and quick you were. Nobody could catch you, or see you, if you didn't want them to. Every day you were becoming less and less human. You made your own hunting bow from a great black cedar. You could strike a deer in the heart and kill it instantly. You wore the blood and bones of a stag so the does would follow you, believing you to be one of them. Once a king came into the village, demanding your hand in marriage, your soul, because you were beautiful and powerful. With an arrow, you struck the crown from his head. You forced him to kneel before you and promise never to bother you again.

"When you came of age, The Nightcatcher arrived in the village looking for you. She is made of night and eats the stars for nourishment."

"She's evil," I said, despite my effort to ignore her, the story taking hold of me.

"Not evil, but selfish and powerful. You would know her by the cities she ruined that sat upon her shoulders, and by the river that ushers from her mouth whenever she speaks. The Wormwood star belongs to her, her emissary, and it poisons the earth at her command. It took all the gods to drive her from the sky, so she made her home in the underground place, between hell and earth. In the hush place. The night sky used to be so much brighter in the old days. That is, until she took half of the stars and brought them down into the hush place with her to light the walls. She captured heroes and great hunters and made them slaves. To play with. To amuse her. That's why she came looking for you."

"But she didn't get me," I said.

Tell me she didn't get me.

"You could best a king with your strength, but not The Nightcatcher. She collected rooms and rooms of heroes to enslave as her pets. She played with gods like they were children. She hunted you in your own forest, like you hunted the stag. She was fast upon you. She twisted your dream world so that it no longer belonged to you. It became a labyrinth of nightmares. She took the ground from underneath you. There was no escape."

"That's it?" I said.

"No, baby. Because you are clever, as well as strong. Just as The Nightcatcher was upon you, you cut your shadow from your body. It grew into the shape of a girl, your dark-half with night for hair and eyes. The Nightcatcher seized the shadow, and you were free."

When Momma finished her story, a great and empty noise roared in my head. My momma's eyes were like swirling plates. I felt hot, a fever slamming into my skin.

"It's taken a thousand years, baby, but she's back for us. And you've only got one shadow."

I shivered in her stare and waited for the moon to collapse.

***

She insisted that I go with her to her next storytelling. I sat in the front row of a sloped auditorium, next to the teachers. She crossed the brightly lit stage holding her Wolf-Book and magic staff.

She wore the gazelle skull to hide her face.

"Once there was a girl, the daughter of a gravedigger, who was known for her ability to talk to the dead. She used to sit in the piles of bones and whisper to them for long hours until they gave up all their secrets. It was even rumored that, in the nighttime, that special time when the sky was dark and the moon gone, she assembled the bones and, together, they danced in the graveyards. She fell in love with a boy with blue eyes like cloud light, with dancing sparks for fingertips. She taught him how to speak to the dead. "Be quiet," she said, "and they will sit on gravestones. The trick is to be quiet."

Momma lurched forward. She was trembling all over, and her eyes were red and raw underneath the mask.

"Do you know why we tell stories?" she asked the children.

She no longer spoke like Saga, the storyteller, wise and calm. No, this was a new voice. An older voice, that spoke from the bone, that shifted underneath the dirt with blisters on its tongue.

The teacher sitting next to me squirmed in her seat. She had nails ready to chew away. She whispered to the man next to her. I wanted to run up to the stage, drag Momma away, and pull the mask off her face. I could scream at her, “You are not my mother. I want the voices back that I remember.”

But I stayed where I was, and Momma continued speaking.

"Plato once said that storytelling was a sin because it mocked true creation. Stories would lead people away from wisdom. But Plato was an old fool who spit on the backs of his slaves and called it philosophy. Stories are the essence of human experience. They teach us where we've come from and who we can be. Storytellers are not only here to entertain, but to give you a chance in the fight for reproduction. Through stories you learn to avoid eating the blue mushrooms. To pray to the right gods."

The children’s silence was like a whip.

"It's why you feel so cheated when a story ends badly. What was supposed to become a guide for you to successfully route through life, has become a dead-end. A husk. It isn't just the story that dies, but you who dies with it.

“So what happened to the little girl and the boy who fell in love in the cemetery? They who danced with the dead? Should I give you a comfortable evil to fight? Perhaps a jealous suitor, with mined coal for a heart? A bitter grave-digging father, who buries the boy in a crypt so that the girl must free him?"

No, I mouthed. No. I don't know what you're planning but nothing good could ever come from that deepening voice, that skull mask.

"You shouldn't trust a comfortable story. You should know by now that only the heroes get to win, and even then, one day they will come across a force so great and so vast that they're consumed by it. I want you to know that the boy brought together the bones of a dead thing to dance with him in the moonlight. But it was not a dead thing at all; it was an old god with a mouth of crystals. With hands forged in the fires underneath the Great Mountain that burned anything they touched.

"Every story you will ever be told will be a story of possession. Every story will be about a love that you throw a chain around to keep, and the thing that can steal her away. The boy was not ready to confront the world of the dead, and he could do nothing to fight back. The old god touched him and burned him alive. The girl felt him die, and awoke with a start in her bed. She ran across the meadows and fields to the cemetery. She tried to bargain with the god. She was reduced to one long shivering scream. 'I will do anything you want to bring him back.' The god laughed. 'I am older than the DNA that was formed at the beginning of the universe to sew together your fingers. You have nothing I want.' Then the god threw her in an open grave and buried her alive."

My mother finished her story with a flourished bow. The children stared with unblinking eyes, not daring to speak. Not even to cough. The teachers applauded with prim, quiet little claps as they herded the children out of the auditorium and back to their classes. My mother stepped off the stage.

The principal touched her on the shoulder.

"May I speak with you?" she said.

The principal was an older woman with collapsing cheeks and a crisp floral dress, the kind of woman who'd never tear pages out of a Wolf-Book, who would, in fact, never own such a thing as a Wolf-Book.

My momma's eyes were dazed. She pressed her hands into the hollow of her throat. The principal ushered her aside and they stood at the corner of the hallway. The principal spoke in a hushed, racing voice. My mother nodded and smiled. When Momma came to get me, she grinned wide enough to split her head.

"I'm not allowed back anymore," she said.

There was no caramel ice cream on the way back home, no fortunes shared over milkshakes. No prophecies on my hair color or forbidden loves. Only the long silence and her long smile.

How quick, it seemed, that one moment she could be the bright storyteller in front of an audience of rapt children, possessed by the voices of her characters, and the next she was the dirty savior with the bedraggled hair, dripping water across the kitchen floor after she tried to drown herself in the pool.

How quick that one moment Momma could be telling me my fortune, giving me dragons to fight, feeding me caramel ice-cream; and the next, scratching her face off as she perched, bird-like, on a wooden rocking chair. She could be stroking my hair telling me that blue looks best on me because blue matches the color of my eyes, then the next she'd speak in a hollow throated voice, "Do not call me mother, I am The Exorcist. Do not cry. You must be strong to survive this night."

Three

DADDY TOOK HER TO the hospital where they bleached all the color out of her. They replaced her blood with antiseptic and took away her robe of stars, her magic staff, and Wolf-Book.

"What happened to Momma?" I asked.

"She stopped taking her medicine," Daddy said.

What I meant was, where has Momma gone? They pumped her full of sedatives until her eyes were UFOs. They gave her paper slippers and told her they were glass, that when the medicine started working again, she would be a queen. The first time I was allowed to visit her in the hospital, I watched her shuffle down the hall toward me with her slippers crumpling. These delicate steps, as if the hospital walls were made of paper, as if she too was made of paper.

She sat down beside me while the nurses watched from the doorway. She opened her mouth enough so that I could see the scar on her tongue, in the place where she'd try to sever it, giving herself a forked devil's tongue. We couldn't speak. Words were fat and sluggish, too big to fit in our mouths. I wanted to hold her, but maybe she would collapse. Maybe I'd squeeze her shoulders and find that she'd transformed into a morphine drip.

With Daddy, on the car-ride home, I curled up in the back seat and cried.

"She's never coming back home," I said. "They took away the most important parts of her and she's never coming back home."

I don't remember much about Daddy. He was a businessman, I think, someone important - because I never saw him except at the end of the day or during the emergency times when Momma went insane. He always seemed to be wearing a gray suit, crisp and uncomfortable, though his hair was always black and wild. He had a dark laugh. He told me once he was too young to be a father, told me to call him Lex instead of Daddy, though I never did. He refused to discipline me for staying up too late, for screaming, for being stubborn.

"Little demon," he called me, and laughed his dark laugh.

Momma came back from the hospital listless and thin. Her skin was pale. Daddy fed her pills with a spoon and stroked her throat until she swallowed. He stayed up with her at night as she sat in the rocking chair in the corner of the room. He taped her hands when she tried to scratch her wrists.

All of the color drained out of my Daddy's face, just as it went out of Momma's. One night he bleached his hair in the bathroom and stood in front of the mirror with his hands burning.

"I'm bad!" I said, desperate for him to laugh or pinch me. "I'm a devil! I put black hair dye in the toothpaste!"

He shook his head and leaned close to the mirror. He prodded the bottom of his eyes.

"You see those? Crow's feet."

"Daddy!"

"Lex, baby. Lex."

He picked up his razor and shaved off all his hair. His fried, bleached locks fell in the sink. The humming of the razor ached in the back of my jaw. Momma appeared in the doorway beside me.

"Daddy?" she said.

"I'm not ready for this," he said, and he set the razor down and walked out.

I followed him outside into the garage as Momma cried in the bathtub. He pulled his car keys out of his pocket and unlocked the driver's door.

"You can't! I'm bad! I'm bad!" I called after him.

"Oh Lily," he said, "I'm so sorry."

He wrote the number of the psychologist on the inside of my skirt. He picked me up as I cried and he kissed me.

He said, "Schizophrenia made your mother into a rabid horse. Remember when she calls you a little monster that she still loves you."

He left.

I sat on the cold concrete floor of the garage for a long time after that, shivering, staring out down the driveway, across the street. Nobody ever told me this could happen. Phaedra's parents divorced, but that happened across the street, not here. Nobody ever told me before, that I'd have to sit in moments like this without noise or distraction, waiting with a big yawn in my stomach. I didn't know how.

My teeth ached. My hands ached. I waited for him to return. I thought if he knew how cold I was, how I lay my bare legs on the concrete until I couldn't feel them anymore, then he'd come back for me. I could summon him to me with my pain.

But he didn't come, and then I only wanted Momma to come. She would pick me up and tell me that my eyes were brushfire and that I needed to drink my milk to get strong. But then Momma didn't get me; I got too cold so I went into the kitchen. I found cold macaroni in the refrigerator and I made myself a bowl. I set the bowl on the counter and the spoon beside it.

I couldn't eat it. There were needles in my stomach and if I ate I knew they'd all spill out of me.

Four

THE NEXT MORNING MOMMA came into my room to wake me. It wasn't yet sunrise and gray spots of light lay across the bed. Her face was streaked and sad from crying.

"Get up, baby," she said, "I've found Arachne and she's sick."

I held out my arms and Momma lifted me out of bed. She threw me my pink pullover, and whispered, "Hurry" when she handed me my shoes. They were the ones without laces, because I had yet to learn how to tie my shoes.

Then she picked me up and we went out into the cold.

The bald-headed sun sat above the train tracks. We entered the abandoned lot in front of the woods. This was back when its owners were still trying to sell it, so the grass was clean and trim, quivering with dew.

She lifted me over the barbed wire, and then she climbed after me. She shook when she grasped the barbed wire, and her legs, so thin and splintered, quivered in her frost-tipped boots. I thought she'd disappear inside of her parka.

She took me into the woods. And though it was cold, little blue flowers, azaleas I think, grew underneath the trees forming a carpet. Such pretty little blue flowers.

"There she is," Momma said.

I stopped.

"I don't see anything."

She took my hand in her own, pointed it toward the flowers, and said, "There. See her there?"

Something in the flowers stirred.

I saw her then, black and spindly limbed, as she emerged from the rustling flowers. Someone wounded her. A black arrow stuck out of her side, breaking the skin. And, though her body was that of a monstrous spider, she had the face of a young girl.

Her expression was slack. A black viscous line of spit dribbled down her chin.

"Momma," I whispered.

She lifted me up in her arms. I buried my face in her shoulder as she brought me toward the creature. I closed my eyes tight and promised myself I wouldn't look.

I wouldn't look. I wouldn't look. My heart squirmed. Oh God, don't let me look.

But I couldn't stop myself. I lifted my head and looked as the monstrous spider with the human face coughed and sighed. She stirred in the grass and the downy ends of her legs squirmed. She had soft, black hair.

"She's hurt. Who did this to her?" I asked Momma. "She's just a baby."

Momma set me down in the flowers. I took several steps back, tripped. I crushed the azaleas underneath me.

"A god did this to her," Momma said.

Arachne opened her mouth to suck in air. In. Out. Her bloodless lips dripping black. When she moved she stained the flowers black. A sticky web wrapped around her hair and crystallized over her eyes.

"Why?" was all I could think to say.

"I don't know," she said.

Momma tried to move Arachne, but the baby monster screamed with pain. She shook and trembled. I sat in the flowers feeling my eyes drop out. I couldn't turn away again. I couldn't close my eyes. Arachne quivered and gasped, her mouth opening as if to speak but she was unable to.

Eventually Momma gave up trying to move Arachne. She wiped the blood spilling from the spider's mouth with her dress. Then she sat down in the flowers beside me, huddled in her parka, and buried her head between her knees. It's the last time I remembered Momma crying.

Arachne reached for me.

Her bristly black spider limb touched my palm. Gently, slowly, I closed my fist around it, so small in my hand, and it trembled. Arachne looked at me, opened her mouth, closed it, and opened it again. Her eyes were the color of the azaleas.

Then she died.

For the longest time I wouldn't let go of her, even when she stopped trembling. Momma cried into her sleeves. I didn't remember letting go, but Arachne's arm, limp and drying, slipped down into the flowers.

Momma took me home and I remembered opening and closing my hands; they were black. They were black where Arachne touched me. Later I searched for her, nothing left except the crushed flowers where I fell. Maybe I was becoming schizophrenic like my mother. The disease's acid had started to eat its way into my brain.

But I remembered my hands were black where she touched me. I remembered the black on my mother's dress that never washed out.

Part Two:

Colic Poison Pyro Baby

Five

WHEN I WAS FOURTEEN years old the cats in the neighborhood started losing their eyes. My friend Phaedra owned a cat named Miss Margot - a lean spitting thing that'd writhe and scratch whenever I tried to pick her up. Miss Margot went missing for a night and came back in the morning with her eyes gone, two soft shelled-out places in her head. She never bit again after that.

We blamed Charlie for stealing the cat's eyes. Charlie because of his chubby body, pale quivering lips, black glassy eyes, and hands too big for the rest of his body. His parents were behavioral scientists who thought John B. Watson should've won the Nobel Prize for teaching his son to be afraid of rats. When Charlie was an infant his parents rattled his crib so he couldn't sleep. They rang loud bells in his ears so he wouldn't touch the flowers. When he got too close to a stuffed teddy bear he called Little B, they set it on fire to study his coping mechanisms.

That's fucking science for you.

By the time he was fourteen years old, Charlie couldn't sleep for more than an hour without rolling out of his bed and sleepwalking out of his house. Sometimes he rapped on windows and jiggled doorknobs, calling out for Little B. Other times he sat in the middle of my lawn, reading an invisible book, chain smoking his sister's cigarettes, and laughing at text that no one else could read.

"Everyone knows it was you," Phaedra said to him.

She picked up Miss Margot who'd grown listless. Soft. Phaedra fed her tuna from her open palm. Charlie jerked his head as if someone startled him awake from a long sleep.

"How could you?" Phaedra asked.

"I don't know why. How can I when I'm asleep?"

The eyeless cats wandered the neighborhood: the Calico with silky fur and red leather collar, the pregnant brunette, and the pair of orange colored twins with fat beige nails. One by one they came back from the woods, meowing and panting. That is, all of them except for my black cat Pluto.

Pluto came to me because of Miss Catherine. Miss Catherine called me a dirty little loveless thing; she didn't like the mud crusted underneath my fingernails, my urchin hair, my jacket that smelled like weed. Once I skipped school to smoke with her gardener in her backyard. He didn't speak any English except for the words "hello" and "drugs". Miss

Catherine came outside with a rose between her teeth, little puncture marks on her lip, uttering some incantation meant to revive her dead husband.

"You used to be such a nice girl, before your father left," she said when she caught me.

I sneered and crushed the joint between my fingers.

"You can't even apologize? Get out of here before I call the police on you! And this is the last time I'm hiring someone from PrimCare."

That night I went back to her garden with an armful of summer fireworks and set her rose bushes on fire. While the flowers burned, the black cat rushed out from behind the garden shed, smoke in her whiskers. I caught her in my arms. She scratched ribbons into my bare skin, but I held fast. She mewed, hissed, and spit but I covered her in my jacket and took her home. I locked her in the laundry room and slid some moist tuna and water under the door.

I kept her that way for a few days, waiting for her to quiet down. But every time I turned the doorknob she hissed. Then Momma, on one of her better days, let her out and told me to let her smell the back of my hand.

"Speak softly to her," Momma said. "Shh."

Momma crouched with her hand held out in front of her. The cat crept toward her with tentative steps, her pink nose like a cool, floating pearl. She touched Momma's fingers with her whiskers.

"Her name is Pluto," Momma said.

As though on cue, Charlie, sleepwalking again, appeared on my lawn. He walked with halting, jerky, hypnotic steps as if his feet were about to pop off. His clumsy troll-like shadow followed behind him. Just like his hands, the shadow seemed too big for his body.

He lurched to my window and pressed his face to the glass.

"Little B," he called out, "Little B."

Pluto hissed at him as I wrapped her in the sheets.

"Little B," he called out once more.

Charlie rapped on the glass. Once. Twice.

"Leave my cat alone!" I said.

I held tight to her in the night. I knew that, whatever waited outside in the dark, even if it was a fat, depressed, adolescent boy like Charlie, was waiting for the chance to grab Pluto; waiting to tear her eyes out and leave her blind and stumbling.

In the morning Momma came to me with skin flushed and bleach burning her gums. She smelled of blood and tin.

"You're leaving again," I said.

"I'm going to Alaska," she said. "I'm going to start a colony there, to build Skuldelev warships and take over the United States."

She threw on her selkie skin and smiled. I knew that smile. It meant she'd left her body, OBE, gone to wrestle the moon.

"Fine," I said. "Have fun."

When she left I screamed. I kicked a hole in her bedroom door. I smashed the living room lamp against the floor, broke the coffee pot and dumped the kitchen drawers out onto the tiles. I smashed wine bottles against the wall, and overturned the kitchen table, which shattered the flower vase that had been on top. I strewed flower stems and dirt across the floor, the windowsills, and the chairs, and then ripped open bags of flour and sugar and over the carpet.

Charlie found me outside huddled on the curb with Pluto in my arms, my arms covered elbow-deep in flour. He came to me with his mother's funereal veil pressed across his face and a book of ancient mythology in his hands.

"They're going to lock you up one of these days," Charlie said.

"Well, you look ridiculous," I said.

He outstretched his hands against the veil.

"Nobody can see your face when you're dead. When I get to the spirit world, I'll ask Persephone for a kiss."

I pressed my face into Pluto's fur and sighed.

"Do you want to walk with me?" he asked.

"Not when you're wearing that."

He didn't move. I remembered when we were eight his mother tied a snake to his wrist and told him it was poisonous. When we were ten, he ran screaming into my yard because his father taught him to fear the cottontail that lived in the mulberry bushes.

"Wait here," I said.

I ran inside and grabbed Momma's car keys. I never knew why she thought she'd be able to get to Alaska without her car, and I didn't care. I went back outside, unlocked the car door, and got into the driver's seat

"Get inside," I said, pulling the seat up so I could reach the pedals, "and hold Pluto for me."

I drove out of the neighborhood with Charlie, past the grocery store, then down Main Street. We lived in a small, murky town with crumbling buildings and withering trees. An insect-ridden, rotting town. The trains poisoned the ground. The factories poisoned the sky. As a child I remembered blue flowers and lush grass growing here. Now there was nothing left but whipped-back trees and the ashes of Miss Catherine's roses.

I drove onto the highway and sped away from town. Charlie, underneath his mother's funereal veil, sat beside me for a long time without speaking, stroking Pluto's thick black fur.

"You're not a cat killer," I said.

He pressed Pluto into his chest.

"Do you have any weed?" he asked.

"No. Miss Catherine fired her gardener."

"Want a cigarette then?"

He handed me one from the pack in his pocket. I stuck it in the side of my mouth.

"Keep driving, I'll light it for you."

He pulled out a lighter, flicked it on and brought it to the tip of my cigarette. I inhaled and started to cough. The cigarette dropped down onto the floorboards. I tried to stamp it out with my foot and the car swerved. A black-flamed, hell-on-wheels Cadillac cussed at us as it careened past.

I pulled over into the grass, retrieved the cigarette from the floorboards, and threw it out the window. Charlie exhaled. He'd been holding his breath.

"Hey, you said you wanted to get to the spirit world, right?" I said.

He laughed. A pale, shuddering kind of sound. I couldn't remember a time before when I'd heard him laugh. Misery child. Dead teddy bear connoisseur.

I kissed him through the veil.

I grasped his cheeks, his hair. I smeared flour over his skin. It wasn't the first time I'd kissed anyone, you know. There'd been the gardener with the cracked-chasm lips, whispering "drugs" in my ear like a love story. And the boy from the nearby high school that I'd revenge-kissed for calling me ugly. But never like this. Not with the heat and the veil between us. Not with his eyes rolling up in his head as if he was dreaming; not with the blood draining from my face; and not with my flour-encased hands turning us into ghosts. My hands felt like bear traps. If I weren't careful I'd break my own bones.

I leaned back into my seat and wiped at my mouth. Charlie, panting, pulled the veil back over his face. I drove back home.

I pulled into the driveway and turned off the ignition. I took Pluto out of his arms and she snuggled into the crook of my arm. Everything seemed quiet, in a painful way, away from the blistering noise of the highway. There was no engine to cross the space between the two of us.

Charlie held his hands up in front of his face, the fingers outstretched.

"Trying to figure out if your hands are still attached?" I asked.

Speaking felt like breaking a sacred thing.

"I'm trying to wake up." He said. "It's how you know if you're dreaming."

"Your hands tell you all that?"

"In a dream you never know where your hands could be."

He stretched his fingers further, further. I touched his wrist. His hand was so taut I thought the veins might burst.

"The woods," I said. "Tomorrow."

All romance happened in the woods. Yes, we could be alive together, climbing up trees and rolling in the grass. I'd toss off that veil. Only the dead and boring, like our parents, made dates in coffee shops and fancy Italian restaurants. Pass the wine, baby, no sex until I've eaten my fill of garlic bread.

We'd be alone there.

The next night as I headed for the woods, I thought of the story that I'd tell him. A ghost story, about a demon that I once met in these woods. It would be almost comical, I thought, to get him to believe that I met a girl who hissed like an insect. "And did you know," I would say, "that I found her in the hollowed out trunk of a dead tree? She opened the folds of her dress and showed me the shining spiders she kept? She was playing hide-and-seek with me."

And when he trembled, I would laugh and say, "Don't be afraid, she doesn't exist. It was only a story. It was only a dream."

In the woods I found the demon with him.

She hung upside down from the trees dangling a teddy bear from one arm. Teasing him, taunting him. Charlie reached out toward the bear, his eyes those of the sleepwalker.

"Little B," he called out. "Little B."

She'd grown as I'd grown in the last few years, except she was taller, leaner. Her dark hair fell across her eyes, twisted and dripping. A spider crawled from her hand into Charlie's hair.

She tilted her head back toward me and opened her eyes. Those wormwood eyes.

And just as I did when I was six years old, I ran.

"Little B!" Charlie called, his voice a metallic echo.

I only stopped when I heard a familiar meow behind me. I stood at the mouth of the woods, near the barbed wire. A wet nose touched the back of my leg.

"Pluto?"

She meowed again, a soft, weak sound. I picked her up from the ground. Blood trickled down her eye sockets and stained her snout.

The demon replaced her eyes with wormwood, shining stars.

Six

I DID NOT TELL ANYONE about the demon that stole Charlie from me; I already knew what they'd say.

"Little girl, those are not demon eyes inside of your cat's head. That is not a spider-headed child dying in the weeds. Schizophrenic - just like your mother. We should've seen this coming."

I'd be crawling across the floor in hospital ties, spit on the cusp of my lips, eyes gurgling like a fountain, my mouth full of soft pills.

Charlie didn't mention the demon hanging upside down from the tree with his teddy bear, but then again, he never remembered what happened in his sleep. He could barely keep his eyes open in those days, even when he walked barefoot across a carpet of sharp stones in his backyard.

"I'll be a Houdini," he said as the stones cut into his feet. "I'll be a Sufi mystic, transcending pain."

Maybe he believed he could transcend the pain, even when he started to walk like a cripple, bow-legged, wincing with every step. I asked him why he no longer read from the book of mythology and why he no longer pressed his mother's funereal veil against his mouth. "Lost them," he said. In a place he couldn't remember.

In the woods.

He took his shirt off. Streaks of sweat shimmered on his back and his pale, chubby body quivered over the stones. When the stones no longer hurt, he moved on to hot coals.

"I'm going to need you to light the coals for me," he said.

I nodded, crouching in the grass, matchsticks in my hands. I only ever saw the whites of his eyes since the pupils always rolled back into his head. Maybe when we kissed, flour on my hands, black mesh on his lips, he'd been asleep. Maybe he didn't remember anything.

He stepped off the stones.

"I have a gift for you," he said.

He gave me a pomegranate and showed me how to open it, revealing the red glowing seeds inside. I ate one.

"Hades gave Persephone a pomegranate," Charlie said, "and when she ate it, she had to stay with him forever."

"I know the story," I said.

"Those are the seeds of hell. Now you'll never again need the sun to see."

The more he sleepwalked, the more his voice cracked, as if speaking to me from inside a collapsed cavern.

I gripped the pomegranate in both hands. I saw the demon's spider crawling on his neck. Her hair unraveling from the trees, her hips the hips of a witch.

"Now," he said, retrieving a bag of charcoal from the patio, "I think I'm ready."

I whispered, "Okay," but I knew that, even if he reached Nirvana through bare feet on burning coals, it wouldn't save him. He belonged to her. She who bewitched him with Little B. She who plucked out my cat's eyes. She who made him reach out for her in the dark.

***

Momma came back home a few days later with her selkie skin shredded and her hair in knots.

"Lily!" she called, "What have you done to the walls? My lamp?"

I kept my hands at my sides. They still smelled of lighter fluid and charcoal. Momma ricocheted through the kitchen, smearing flour on her arms and face, flying through broken glass, flowers, and spilled wine. Scraps of her selkie skin fell to the tiles.

"Baby, are you angry with me?" she asked.

I stepped barefoot on broken glass, and it sliced into my heel. I stiffened.

"Why don't you look at me?" She asked.

I didn't want to tell her it was because I thought poison would drip from her eyes to mine.

"Look at me."

Why did my mother have to be a warrior chartered with keeping the moon and sun from crashing into each other? Why did she have to plant an acid seed in my brain, my sister Schizophrenia?

"Baby," she said. "Oh, baby."

Her mad red hair shot up to the ceiling. She danced in mid-air like Jesus.

"Stop calling me that," I said.

I felt dizzy and dry-mouthed, but why?

"You're bleeding everywhere."

Ah, yes, that was why. Paralyzed from the waist down. My blood congealed in between my toes.

Momma caught me before I fell.

She set me down on a kitchen chair. She spoke but I heard only a ringing in my ears. She knelt and pulled the glass out of my foot, a big, bloody shard of glass. From the looks of it, a piece of Momma's special Saint-Aignan wine I smashed, spraying it up the walls.

"There it is," Momma said. "My Lily's devil smile."

I wanted to ask if she knew Charlie's parents were behavioral scientists - and by the way, can you tell that we kissed in your car and the smoke smell will never come off the leather seats? And have you seen Pluto lately?

I lolled my head back, curled my toes. Pluto jumped up onto my lap. Momma saw her wormwood eyes, the blood on her snout, and stroked her black fur.

"Someone's looking out for you," she said.

I imagined the demon, luring the cats of the neighborhood into the woods, one by one. It was she who tore their eyes out and asked, "Do you know a girl named Lily?" until she met the one who mewed a soft, "Yes." My black Pluto.

At night Charlie chased the demon through the streets as she taunted him with his teddy bear, laughing, always a step ahead. She lured him onto my lawn and ran circles around him in the grass, the teddy bear held over her head. Charlie ran after her with the soles of his bare feet blackened from walking across burning coals until his legs gave out. He collapsed in the grass outside, panting up froth, clutching at the sky. He cried for Little B. Always Little B.

I threw off my blankets and ran toward the door to go save him, but the demon slammed her hands against my window. The force reverberated through my house. I fell backwards into bed, clutching at the sheets.

She pressed her mouth against the window. She wore the funereal veil, and bit down on the top of the teddy bear's head.

I dreamt, sometimes, that she opened the latch and came into my room, pale skin wrecking the light, wormwood about to collapse. But instead of screaming, I opened my arms to welcome her into my bed. And instead of destroying me with fang teeth, she curled up against me, shivering, trying to warm herself underneath the sheets.

Pluto jumped into my arms. The window rattled and I held tight to her. Charlie continued to foam and writhe in the grass, but I couldn't hear him over the hiss in my ears. A swelling noise, louder than the blood in my throat, louder and louder.

She whispered. Let me in, baby girl. Let me
In.

Seven

CHARLIE PROGRESSED FROM walking across hot coals to self-flagellation. While muttering incantations, he beat himself with a cat-o-nine-tails crafted in shop class of bits of leather and shards of glass. The kids at school called him "suicide boy" while giving him wristbands to hide his cuts. To Charlie, they were mute, because his brain was frying from sleep without rest. The teachers referred him to a counselor; he fell asleep on the counselor's desk when asked if he had a "safe home environment." Her recommendation to the teachers was to move him to a desk in the back and let him sleep. Hidden in the back row, he scratched at his wrists with a broken piece of glass. As his appetite waned, he lay in my lap, underneath the bleachers, whispering of mythology.

"After Persephone ate the pomegranate, she could never go home again," Charlie said. "Well, except to visit her mother."

"Why would she want to do that?" I asked, only half-listening.

Thinking: I want to build a time machine. I want to climb inside and go back before they set your teddy bear on fire. I'll bring it to you unsinged so you can sleep again.

"The god Zeus was in love with a beautiful woman, named Leda, so he turned into a swan and raped her."

He pressed his chin into my knee and coughed. I kept expecting him to choke out glass. It was only spring, but we were already well on our way to becoming insane that year. I still hoarded matchsticks and firecrackers. Charlie kept hitting himself in an attempt to transcend the pain. Phaedra started tending to carnivorous plants. As for Momma? Well, she was the same as she'd always been. The last time I'd seen her, she held a sword underneath her tongue. When The Nightcatcher came around again all she'd have to do was open her mouth and cut off The Nightcatcher's head. With it, she'd grow a tree, and from that tree, feed the entire world. Nobody would ever go hungry again.

"Once, a god of poison came out of the hush place, and poisoned an entire town," Charlie said.

"That isn't in your mythology books," I whispered.

He coughed again. There it was, a chunk of glass from his cat-o-nine tails, spit and saliva in my palm.

Phaedra told me to leave him. That I was addicted to the pain that broken people caused. She said all fourteen-year-olds were, but I don't think she paid much attention. She smuggled Venus Flytraps in her backpack and whispered Bukowski poetry to them. She whispered to me with her nose in the mouth of Venus' prickly hairs.

"And besides," she said, "he kills cats."

"No he doesn't," I said.

She didn't hear me as she started whispering frenzied Bukowski poetry under her breath again, rubbing the Venus's hairs with the tip of her finger.

Summer came and school let out. Charlie took me to the river outside of town. His scars flushed red in the heat. His thin cotton t-shirt and swim shorts couldn't hide the whip burns and scars webbing his skin.

We stood on the bridge and looked down into the water. Even in summer's sunshine, the water below lay dark and churning.

"I used to come here alone," he said. "I held my hands over the water until I didn't know where I began and the water ended."

When I stared down at the murk, I knew Charlie didn't take me here to swim. I crossed my arms over my chest and felt my Momma's two sizes too big bikini underneath my clothes.

"I used to think it didn't have a bottom," he said, and then nodded off in the middle of the sentence, his head dipping against his chin.

Nobody would think of swimming in that murky blackness. Nobody except someone who'd been there before.

Sleep deprivation could cause dizziness, hallucinations, aching, paranoia, stunted growth, self-flagellation with a cat-o-nine tails, and sleep chasing a demon across your girlfriend's yard. Maybe it could cause you to kiss her by the side of the river, like you'll never kiss her again, pushing grit and sand into her mouth with your tongue. Maybe you'd stand up, knees shaking, point to the highest tree and say, "Think I can jump from all the way up there?"

I watched Charlie climb the tree above the river until it arched like an arthritic spine, until he couldn't climb any higher without breaking branches. I should have told him to stop, but I guess I wanted to know if he'd actually do it. If he'd really jump.

I sat down on the edge of the bridge where the concrete scraped against the bottom of my legs.

"Think I can touch the bottom?" he asked.

He could've been a pale animal snarled in the branches. Maybe another year of sleepwalking and he'd forget human speech and speak only in hisses. He grasped a thick branch in one hand and leaned out over the water.

He held his hand out, light swelling between his fingers.

She snuck up behind me and whispered in my ear.

"Ke-ke-ke-ke-ke."

"Charlie!" I called out.

He jumped from the tree. For a moment he seemed to hang suspended in midair. He outstretched his hands like wings and his fingers scraped the underside of the sun. His wounds were no longer wounds, but sparks of light, gold and glittering. The light suffused him in magic that replaced his pale, flabby skin and insomniac eyes with a heavenly glow, a falling star, chariot fire, a single shining image of a god before he plunged downwards.

He disappeared into the turbid water.

I rushed to the edge of the bridge, calling his name though I knew he couldn't hear me.

Though I knew he wouldn't resurface.

He wanted to jump. He'd wanted to jump since his parents set fire to Little B, long before he made his first cat-o-nine tails or took his first walk across burning coals. Every moment led up to this; his moment to wear the sun like a crown.

I couldn't feel my fingers, my throat. My head throbbed. I opened my mouth but I couldn't breathe.

The demon behind me held the folds of her white dress out like wings. She tossed her head back, thick black hair, her mouth open in a rictus.

"Ke-ke-ke-ke."

I stood before her, vulnerable and shivering.

"You can still jump in and save him," she said.

But I saw the dark waters below. Heavy, so heavy, the thick blackness enough to crush me. The river whispered, "Hush, hush, suffocating is so easy." I held my hand over the water. I couldn't tell where my hand ended and the river began.

The demon lifted up the bottom of her dress, her pale thighs so white I thought her bones must be on the outside. She revealed her jutting hips, her small black panties, her skinny, scratched ribcage.

She discarded her dress on the bridge and jumped into the river.

Sometimes I imagine the two of them, Charlie and the demon, sinking downward through miles and miles of water. His hair in her hands like a leash, his head between her palms, his scars kissed by blind fish.

They never found his body.

Eight

AT SCHOOL THE BOYS called me black widow and baby killer. Terrance Fleur said I pushed Charlie into the river because there was no loyalty among weirdoes. He knew I kept a stash of matches in my coat pocket; I lit them and threw them at the teacher's back when I got bored. According to Terrance, with his buckteeth and dirty, ginger-colored face, this meant I was capable of anything.

Some nameless jock pushed me against the lockers and lifted up my skirt. He asked me with his fat, bruised mouth dripping tobacco spit, my hair pulled taut, if I liked to fuck corpses.

"Do you want to find out?" I asked, my voice soft, cheek against the cool metal lockers.

He let me go, but that didn't keep him from tongue-lashing me in the hallways, leaning over to whisper, "Suck my dick?" in math class.

My English professor made me stay late after class. I assumed to lecture me about not reading the Great Gatsby, or to send me to the principal because I'd burned a hole through his favorite leather jacket. Instead, he suggested counseling.

"I'm over it," I said.

"We're not talking about Charlie."

"Then what are we talking about?"

"I'm talking about you."

"I try to avoid that."

"Exactly what I'm talking about. This kind of unacceptable behavior," he said, "your antisocial tendencies."

If only I had a goddamn cigarette. I'd blow smoke into his mouth until his lungs burst.

"I don't want you coming back to class until your behavior improves."

His face was like a horse's face, lean and panicked, with eyes too big for his head. I took a step towards him. He reached for the phone on his desk, ready to call for help. A teacher like him never had an adolescent daughter.

"I'll think about it," I said.

I blew him a kiss and left.

I knew that, instead of helping me, he wanted to bind me in chains, take me to the bridge of the river, and command the river to give Charlie back and take me in his place.

Charlie's parents didn't invite me to the funeral. Behavioral scientists, so inconsiderate. The morning of his funeral service, I sat on the church steps in a velvet-black dress stolen from my mother. In my arms I held a bouquet of tiny blue flowers I picked in the woods for Charlie.

I leaned my head against the thick church walls and listened to the preacher speak. I couldn't make out any his words behind the door, but they were probably something like:

"She could have saved him, but she didn't. She'll burn in hell for this. There's no special place for daughters of schizophrenics, God didn't account for that one. But don't you worry, my little lambs, we can throw her in with the fornicators."

The organ music started to play and the pallbearers, holding an empty casket, dragged themselves out of the double doors of the church. The rest of the mourners followed behind, including Charlie's frazzle-haired parents who pretended not to see me. Charlie's six-year-old cousin picked up a rock and threw it at me. It narrowly missed my head.

"Go away!" he said, and threw another rock.

It struck me in the stomach. I dropped the flowers and ran.

I searched for her in the woods. Around me insects buzzed and fireflies lit up in the damp gray morning. I tore my hands trying to climb into the skins of trees. I expected to find her in the hollow of a trunk, like an unborn fetus. Or hiding with a child that resembled me, while crystallized bugs squirmed in her lap.

"Where are you?" I called out.

I beat my fists against the trees. I sat down in the dirt in Momma's good velvet, tore at the grass, and tore at my skin. The trees were unimpressed and too old to shudder at my tantrum. The noise of the woods noise continued, clicking and clacking.

Laughing.

I often stayed at Phaedra's house after Charlie's death. She let me throw knives at her old boy-band posters; I got to be a pretty good shot. I could drink her mother's vodka as long as I filled the empty space with water afterwards.

On her bed she clutched a book between her knees called "Beautiful Killers: Carnivorous Plants of the World." She cradled a Venus Flytrap in her arms.

Phaedra was somewhat of a legend in town. She ran from the cops by crossing a muddy creek, in Valentino heels, branches in her hair, and weed in her purse. She looked the epitome of a gothic Americana princess; her eyes like Oklahoma Dust Bowls, her cheeks Great Depression sharp. And she ran faster than any boy, even in Valentino heels and a torn dress.

I always knew her as the girl who grew up faster than the rest of us. She sat with boys in the back of her mother's Volkswagen in her muddy heels, naked from the waist up, smoking a cigarette that turned her teeth the color of spit. She made the boys dress up in her skirts and lipstick before she went down on them. She whispered grim and romantically cliché things in between their legs. Things like, "Each heartbeat brings us closer to death," or "This is the last chance we'll ever have to be truly alive."

From a young age, Phaedra's mother, like mine, had done a disappearing act. Whereas my mother was insane and refused to believe it, Phaedra's mother couldn't get enough of being crazy. For the majority of her adult life, she lounged in doctor's waiting rooms and therapists' couches. For years she lay upside down in bed, high on codeine and clonazepam, watching foreign films.

"Dear, bring me a headache pill," Phaedra said, mocking her mother. "Bring me that 'Singing in the Rain' DVD. Bring me a hit of acid."

Phaedra's mom used to be a fashion designer in Paris. Or maybe she once had a dream that she was a fashion designer in Paris, I couldn't quite remember. Phaedra insisted she remembered being backstage during Fashion Week as a child, while her mother fitted sixteen-year-old anemic girls with dresses made from razor blades.

"The sicker the better, that's what she used to say," said Phaedra. "Real beauty is a reptile. My momma used to nurse me while they snorted cocaine. The designers and the hairstylists and the models, they all did blow together. Momma turned into a monster on cocaine. Her hair stood up on end. Put the models in dresses two sizes too small and bloodied their backs."

Phaedra snorted.

"And now she thinks she's so righteous. She's grown up. Matured, right? Whatever. She just can't afford blow anymore. She caught me once in my room with some Russian exchange student. She wanted me to go to therapy, just because I made him wear a dress before we fucked. You know, the shiny silver one? He looked good in it. Anyways, can you believe her? Go to therapy? Like Hell!"

"They always want you to go to therapy," I said.

Shortly after the Russian exchange student ordeal, Phaedra met her true love: a Venus Flytrap with moist little mouths, planted in a red glazed pot and purchased for a dollar at a farmer's market. She shut the boys out of her room. She stopped smoking in the backseat of cars and reciting gothic faux philosophy to devote more time tending the plants. They were monstrous plants with unhinged jaws that waited for insects to land on their velvet lips. They lined her desk and windowsill. She slept with them in her bed.

"Why the plants" I asked her.

"I don't know," she said. "They're pretty."

Of course, I thought, the gothic Americana princess would think of the moist, carnal, wet innards of a carnivorous plant as pretty.

Soon the common Venus Flytrap wasn't good enough for her. She wanted the big leafy demons of plants that ate deer and jaguar, the roped, sweet smelling bellflowers that housed stomachfulls of half-digested children. She dreamed of owning the legendary Madagascar Man-Eating Tree, a roped veiny myth of a tree with serpents for limbs that tore off people's heads and digested them whole. One of these days I would find her being eaten alive.

But seeing that would be better than going to school to have children throw rocks at me, or having my teachers tell me that Schizophrenia was like the modern Greek cannibal's curse. In five years time, they said, I'd be eating my mother like Tantalus ate his son. I'd butcher her, cook her in a stew, and then try to feed her to Zeus.

That myth, of course, I'd learned about from Charlie and his books.

I dreamed of him sometimes, shivering wet on the edge of my bed. His chubby pale skin turned blue. Not dead, but trapped in Hades with a silent, lipless mouth. A sleepwalker on the ground and a sleepwalker underneath the water.

I dreamed of the pomegranate he fed to me, and sometimes when I awoke in the middle of the night, I thought he came back from the river and slipped it underneath my sheets.

"Ke-ke-ke-ke-ke."

"Phaedra, something's after me."

She turned the glossy page of Beautiful Killers.

"There's this girl," I said, and then paused, "well, I've never told anyone this. I don't really know where to begin."

I scratched at my knees, but I didn't feel it.

"I've known her for a long time."

For once Phaedra set her book down. I continued.

"She tormented Charlie. She made him chase her. It was like a game to her. But I think she was only trying to get to me through him."

"Yeah, well. Good riddance."

"Forget it," I said.

I went home and Momma found me in the kitchen with my head in my hands, tears ebbing at my eyelids. She said, "Baby girl, warriors don't cry," and held her arms out toward me.

"Someone left this for you," she said.

In her arms she held a stuffed teddy bear. A pink ribbon around its neck. Ears singed.

Nine

THAT NIGHT I WENT to the woods and found her dead tree. It shuddered as I spilled gasoline over its hollowed out trunk. The insects screamed when I wedged the fireworks inside. A fat, silver beetle landed on the back of my hand. The rest of the insects - centipedes, spiders, and roly-polies - scurried away across my feet.

I knelt in the dirt and struck the first match. I threw it on the ground but it didn't catch. The silver beetle crawled up my arm. My neck. It had the demon's eyes lodged in its back. I lit a second match.

The tree burned slowly at first. The fire started at the base, where the wood was the soggiest. The tree burned so slow and pale, I thought the fire might die out. I knelt and blew on it. The roots, poking out of the ground like grafted bones, caught fire as well, curled inwards and turned blue.

The flames shot up the trunk. It seared an angry face on the wood and climbed higher. I took a step back, nearly tripping in the dark.

I didn't want to look away and miss anything.

I stood in the hunched shadow of the tree as the trunk split apart. I threw my head back and spots burst in my eyes as the limbs burned. The fire unrolled them like scrolls and they crashed to the ground at my feet.

The fireworks went off and the tree exploded, showering me in silver sparks. They struck my face, my arms. The heat felt good. I could've been blinded, but I didn't care, I was crazed by Phaedra's vodka and Mommy's schizophrenia that night. I wanted the demon to come screeching out of the woods so I could spit in her eyes and rub dirt in her face. I'd laugh as I spun her around by her thick black hair, taunting her, "Do you remember when I crawled in here to find you? I hope you burn with what's left."

This was your real funeral, Charlie. This was the best I could do.

The beetle crawled onto my face. I slapped it away. In my peripheral vision I saw her silhouette appear. She held the funereal veil, and when I turned towards her, she threw it over my face. I tore it away and it fell into the fire.

CRACK. The branches broke and crumbled. A wounded moan escaped from the demon's throat.

She ran through the trees; I chased after her. Branches reached out to grab me, like in a bad fairy-tale. I twisted my ankle in the dirt. Sparks flew off my fingers. I grabbed her hair but it hissed like a rattler, so I let go. I chased her to the edge of the woods and she leapt across the barbed wire.

She fled down the street, into my yard, and then climbed up the side of the house to my mother's bedroom window. She pressed a finger to her lips, as if to say "Shh," then climbed through my window.

I tore the door open, ran into the kitchen, and grabbed a paring knife. Upstairs, Momma screamed. I ran to the top of the stairs and burst into her room with smoke in my hair and fireworks on my tongue. A storm of ash and flowers blew through the room. She sat at her vanity with the demon hunched over her, whispering as she set something down in front of her.

A dead bird.

Momma wept with the gazelle skull cradled in her arms.

"Fucking creep," I said.

I lunged at the demon. She snatched the knife away from me as if with no effort at all. Momma continued to weep, not even looking up from her vanity. The demon chased me into the hallway.

I ran toward the stairs, but before I could go down a single step, her hair hissed behind me. I hesitated for only a moment, but that was too long. The demon threw me against the wall and pinned me with her throat.

"Our tree," she whispered.

"Life's a bitch, bitch," I said.

I forced a smile.

She poised the knife at my face, her pupils growing, growing. Her eyes were bigger than a twin cosmos. Momma started screaming again. "Poison." Screamed. "POISON."

I'd never seen the demon's face this close before. I expected a gnashing vampire, a howling dog, a face with Moscow and bitter winters written in the veins. Not this soft and wounded girl; not unlike Baby Arachne dying in the flowers, mouth puckered, breathing quietly as her eyes grew.

She dropped the knife at my feet.

"Calm down," she said.

She opened her hand and blew ash and sparks into my face.

"I could be your slave."

***

The demon fled and Momma stopped screaming. She sat at her vanity, tying on her gazelle skull mask with ash and branches in her hair.

"Baby girl," The Exorcist said, "go play outside."

I went outside so my mother could play dress-up and clean the house until she bled. I expected the demon to wait for me in the dark, maybe with a blade on her tongue and my mother's skin in her teeth, but she was gone.

A police siren wailed, and a fire truck sped past. The sky over the woods appeared dark orange. A column of smoke billowed upwards.

Surely they'd be after me soon. They'd find the empty quart of gasoline beside the burning tree. They'd smell the ash and smoke in my hair and pluck the matches out of my pocket.

I ran toward the river. I ran as if a shadow pursued me. Maybe this was how Charlie felt when he sleepwalked - sleeping but not sleeping - amorphous shapes charging at him in the periphery of his vision. A dark, disembodied claw. A demon. Nothing at all. The back matter going black in the brain.

Maybe if I looked down I'd see a cat-o-nine tails gripped in my hand. Thwack! Blood in my ears.

I passed through the tall weeds to the bridge where the river ran purple. I leaned against the side of the bridge and tossed the matches.

My cigarettes and my lighter had to go too. There couldn't be any evidence on me. I fumbled in my jacket until I found them.

I tossed them into the water, shaking. I couldn't help but think of the time Charlie and I smoked together in my mother's car, thinking we were so dangerous. I couldn't give him that bouquet of blue flowers at his funeral; a pack of cigarettes was more fitting anyway.

I leaned over the edge of the bridge, almost expecting his voice to bubble up to the surface. The demon said I could've jumped in to save him. Yes, I could've saved him.

A roaring noise swelled in my ears. I wondered if Momma ever came down here to speak to the gods, to The Nightcatcher. You could hear anything you wanted in the noise of this place. I leaned closer to the water as the wind sucked my hair down.

I could've saved him.

But baby, you don't understand, it's pitch down there.

Ten

IT WAS MY SIXTEENTH birthday and the librarian was in love with me. He recommended I read Bukowski because, in spite of him being a misogynistic asshole, he was a brilliant writer. I told him there was no "in spite of". Bukowski hated women and was therefore probably a terrible fuck, which made him a terrible writer.

It was my sixteenth birthday and my science teacher asked me, "What do you want to be when you grow up?"

I told him a biologist and he said, "You have to pass science class to be a scientist."

I don't remember his name anymore. Mr. Sands or Mr. Sick or some other sort of noun with an "S", a kind of name that made me taste everything sour if I said it. He had a face to match his sour name, and sour, yellow-nailed hands. After class I tore up my science textbook in the hallway and threw it in the trashcan; I promised myself I'd never go back to school again.

It was my sixteenth birthday and my mother did not bring me a present or bake me a cake. Instead she took me into her bedroom where she lay out her half-melted ceramic sculptures she wanted to sell in Mexico. She told me they were sculptures of dead men with their faces being eaten by sea monsters.

"Before I met your father, I was an artist," she said, and when she smiled, I saw she was wearing her purple lipstick. She'd gone mad again.

She touched my face.

"You're not looking well, baby," she said.

"Do you remember what day it is?" I asked her.

"Wednesday," my mother said, dancing the scissor electric with one of her melted sculptures.

"Yeah," I said, voice soft, "Wednesday."

It was my sixteenth birthday and the only person to come visit me was Phaedra, who gave me a Venus Flytrap she named Terrance.

"Take care of him, he's a shy one," Phaedra said, and then she left.

It was my sixteenth birthday and, on my dresser beside my newly acquired carnivorous plant, I lined up forty benzodiazepines I'd bought from a fourteen-year-old drug dealer. But by the time I'd set them all out, the thought of having to swallow them seemed more tedious than it was worth. So I grabbed Pluto, turned off the lights, and crawled into bed.

The lights flickered on.

"Happy Birthday," the demon said.

The demon sat in a rocking chair beside the window, hair lush and spilling from her shoulders, one thin leg draped over the chair's wooden arm. She smoked a cigarette she stole from the pack on my windowsill as the chair creeeaked.

"I brought you a present," she said.

She motioned toward the bureau, where she'd laid out a dress.

It was not a dress made of silk or cotton, but of insects; butterflies, spiders, and roly-polies, stitched together and gleaming more delicately than lace. Such a dress must've taken months to sew. I imagined the demon going through the woods with a killing jar, capturing insects and smothering them. I saw her sitting in a burnt out husk of a tree, sewing them together with her antenna-like fingers, singing softly to herself by rubbing her legs together.

"Put it on," she said.

I pointed toward the door.

"Get out," I said.

She lifted her head and wormwood took me.

It was as if she'd reached into my skull with phantom limbs and set it on fire. I sat back down on my bed, trembling. My hand dropped to my side and my head tilted back. I was at once boneless and bloodless. Warmth spread throughout my body.

The demon held her hand toward my cat. Pluto jumped from my lap to hers. She buried her face in Pluto's thick fur. She whispered to her in half-language and Pluto purred.

I'd had this dream so many times. My cat and the demon conspiring against me, the demon scratching at my window. In my dreams, wherever she touched me she paralyzed me, and inside, I cried for help.

Yet now with it happening, all I could think was:

Thank God.

Thank God this will soon be over.

The demon opened her hand and, from her palm, spilled chewed up, withered pomegranate seeds.

She repeated her command with smoke spilling out of her mouth.

"Put.

It.

On."

The smoke enveloped me. I became a bubble of warm honey. For the first time in days, my headache went away and the pressure behind my eyes disappeared. I was no longer Lily, sixteen-year-old screw-up, child murderer. I was a glowing vessel, soft and malleable.

She hypnotized me. Her voice had hypnotized me.

I stood up, swimming. Everything seemed so easy. The air pooled around me like still water, the dull colors of the room became vibrant. I slipped out of my clothes and the air cooled on my skin, pulling at the tiny hairs on my arms.

The demon dressed me. I pulled my hair in front of me, and she laced up the back of the dress. Her nails tapped against my spine, clicking like mandibles, as she pulled against the laces.

“You are beautiful,” she said.

In the mirror, the insects were bigger than me, more real than me. The spiders at my throat were engorged and brilliant with colors. I didn’t look like the grubby urchin that Miss Catherine chased out of her rose garden, or like the schoolgirl with burnt fingers the science teacher said would never amount to anything.

"I look like you," I said, my voice a whisper.

We went into the street and Pluto followed. I walked on the hot pavement in my bare feet as the dress swayed, butterflies rubbing against my skin.

We went into the abandoned lot and she lifted the train of my dress so that I could climb over the barbed wire fence. Even though I’d climbed that fence a thousand times, more than a thousand, I cut my bare foot on a barb.

I felt the pain as a far away thing, a sensation that didn’t pierce the warmth surrounding my body. Even pain could be a safe thing, a golden thing.

I bled and we kept going.

We followed a light through the woods, a fairy light that flickered and hovered like something alive. The woods stretched out further than they ever had before, railroad tracks and factory smoke rings, gone. We walked across the burnt remains of her tree.

Pluto mewed at my feet. Her wormwood eyes shone more fiercely than I'd ever seen them shine before.

At the end of the tunnel we came to a dining table in a clearing. The fairy light floated in the center of the table. Up close, I saw it for what it was: an orb of fireflies stitched together and tethered to the table.

"Won't you sit down?" the demon said, and directed me toward a carved bone chair.

I melted into the chair. I don't know why I'd never been here before. I belonged in this chair.

The demon lifted up a glass of what appeared to be red wine. It shone brighter than the fireflies, mottled and glowing.

"Have a drink," she said.

She had to place the glass in my hands and close my fingers around the stem.

"Happy birthday to me," I said, the words bubbling up like foam; I drank.

The wine was thick and sweet, congealing on my tongue. She took the glass away. My hands fell to my sides. I wanted to slide down into the dirt and grass and roll around. I wanted to know what it felt like to press my mouth against the moist dew and have it tickle my lips. But the demon touched my chin, bid me to look, and I stayed in my chair.

On the table, the demon laid out cuts of meat with eyes, cakes made out of skin, and jellied currants made out of glowing metal. Black crabs still quivered in their sauces. The demon carved for me a slice of something red and sticky, pulsing, and placed it on my plate.

"Is this like fairyland?" I asked, "I eat the food and I can never go home?"

“Lily, please shut up,” the demon said. She placed a fork, carved from animal bone, into my hand.

Yes, it always belonged there.

Maybe if I managed to get home this night I would find Mother on one of the days she could still speak. I would say, "Momma, think back to when you were pregnant with me. Think as hard as you can. Did you notice anything strange? Perhaps during the ultrasound the doctor noticed that, along with me, you were housing a star from Revelation in your uterus.

And when I was born, did the doctors have to cut a dark little parasitic twin away from my bones, and did you let her slither off into the dark? Is this where my shadow has been all these years?

No, no particular reason why I'm asking. I'm just curious, Momma."

The demon placed the bone knife in my other hand.

Out in the woods, beyond the clearing, the grass rustled.

Something's out there, but I didn't care. I only wanted to eat the food filling the table in front of me. I knew, going down my throat, it would fill me with a pulsating light. Yet I couldn't manage to use the fork and knife, not with my muscles turning into fuzz and my face melting into soft candy.

The demon leaned toward me, the table creaking underneath her. Her skin glowed in the light of the sewn-together fireflies. She touched my bottom lip and pressed a pulsing red fruit into my mouth. I swallowed; it coated my stomach with musical notes.

Some little girls get stolen by the king of the underworld. I got a demon, smiling at me with fireflies stuck in her teeth.

I smelled an acrid scent, like oil. The grass rustled once more and Pluto bolted from underneath my legs. I lost control of the muscles in my hands and dropped the knife and fork onto the ground.

"It's The Nightcatcher, isn't it?" I asked.

A fawn emerged from the grass trembling and wet.

I tried to call out for Pluto, but my tongue wouldn't fit into my mouth.

The fawn crept underneath the table. She rested her head at my feet, and licked with her rough-sewn tongue at the blood pouring from my barbed-wire wound. The demon placed a piece of fruit in my mouth, but I couldn't swallow.

The demon crawled across the table, knocking over dishes, batting the ball of fireflies away. She weaved her hands through my hair. I coughed and bones and fruit spilled out of my mouth.

The fawn licked and licked my bleeding foot. The demon turned my head toward the trees.

"I don't want to look," I said as she pinched my cheek, my jaw. "Don't let me look."

But just as I did with Baby Arachne, dying in the flowers years and years ago, I looked.

The trees burned away. The ground trembled. This must've been what my mother saw when she went mad. The sky tore apart and ancient woodlands clawed its way out of the dirt, pushing itself through a million years of strata and stone. It toppled the woods and the town. It ringed the sky with ice. It showered me in flowers and black mud.

"Welcome home, Lily."

Home. My forest. It was real. It was here and swallowing me.

The fawn bit my foot.

My limbs snapped back into place. The ancient woods disappeared. The fawn bolted. The fruit spilled out of my mouth and I hauled myself to my feet, choking. The demon jumped off the table.

"What's wrong?" she asked.

"Stay away from me."

"Did you not like the dinner?"

"Stay away!"

The ball of fireflies hummed in my face. I slapped it away and it exploded in a shower of light. The demon uttered a low whine.

I gathered the dead-thing dress in my hands and ran down the tunnel of trees.

She didn't pursue me, but there was something else in the woods that night. Something watching me. Its machinating heart bore down on me.

The dress started moving. The butterflies squirmed and fluttered, showering me with melanin dust. The beetles clicked. The spiders squirmed at my throat. The moths fluttered, heave with panic. I crouched in the dirt and groped for the laces on my back to untie myself, but I couldn't reach.

The woods tilted, the grass and the dirt turned into a sky, bearing its weight down on me.

I grabbed for the collar of the dress and tore it away, showering the ground with thread, lace, and insects. They fluttered and flailed and scurried away.

Eleven

I DIDN'T SEE the demon for several years after that, and in those years, I went mad.

Part Three:
The Artist

Twelve

WHEN I WAS TWENTY, I met the artist with electric lights in his hair and butcher shop blood on his clothes. Phaedra and I showed up at his house because a man promised her a carnivorous pitcher plant. A Sarracenia rubra plant with sweet-veined red skin and pretty black hair.

"He probably just wants to fuck me," Phaedra said, "but I saw it on Facebook. The plant, I mean. It's real. He even time-stamped it."

We'd driven almost an hour out of town for the plant and found ourselves outside a broken house crushed by kudzu. Dance music from inside pulsed underneath the tires of Phaedra's car. The artist sat on the front lawn with a mason jar full of port wine, his clothes frayed and splattered, surrounded by blood portraits of skinless women.

A blue-haired girl with bleeding wrists posed as his model in the wet grass. Light cords snaked down her throat, her wrists, and his wine glass. He tugged on the light cords, telling her to turn over on her back.

"Wait here," Phaedra said as she walked up to the porch.

Boys sat on the darkened porch under a kitchen window lined with empty whiskey bottles. College boys, from the looks of it, skinny intellectuals who drank because it was the closest thing they could get to enlightenment. I overheard the words "Nietzsche" and "Dostoevsky". Typical. The longer I looked at them, the less human they became.

Phaedra disappeared inside the house.

The artist took another sip of wine. Flies stuck in the blood on his clothes.

"I know you," he said to me, the lights straining against his face. "My sister went to school with you. You were the murderer."

"You'd like that, I'm sure."

"What was your name?"

I wanted to say Lily bloodsucker. Lily schizophrenia. Lily stay away from me because I'll eat your head.

I shrugged and headed toward the house.

The boys' silhouettes twisted and transformed out of proportion, like their heads should've snapped off of their necks. Their shadow hands shrunk into their sleeves. They ignored me when I climbed the porch steps and continued speaking amongst themselves. Their voices were loud enough to penetrate through the music coming from inside.

"Just postulate for a minute, that there is a negative and positive balance to the world," one of them said.

"Black and white thinking. That's going to get you into trouble."

"Postulate? Stop being so goddamn pompous."

"Most of us have equal negative and positive aspects. But, what if someone enters the world, and their balance is all negative?"

"The entire world is thrown off."

"Their lives become a hell, and they plunge the earth into hell."

"Oh, please. Be original for once."

I went inside and the door slammed shut behind me.

I expected to find a party, but I found only an empty living room. In the corner of the room, the speaker, partially hidden by a couch, blared music.

"Phaedra?" I called, but I couldn't hear myself speak.

I walked across the room and ripped out the speaker cords. The house went silent. I couldn't even hear the boys talking outside.

"Phaedra?" I called again.

"You're not supposed to be here."

In the kitchen a teenage girl with dirty blonde dreadlocks hunched over glow-in-the-dark teacups, a glowing green bottle clasped between her knees.

"I'm looking for my friend," I said.

"She already left."

"She only came in here a moment ago."

"She'll be back soon."

"Did she go down the hall?" I asked.

The girl held a teacup out toward me.

"I poured you some tea," she said. "You should thank me. You know you aren't supposed to be in here yet."

"You said that already."

"Wait with me, she'll be back."

She continued holding the teacup toward me, her arm unwavering. I sighed.

I crouched beside her and took the cup.

"What's in this?"

"You like absinthe, don't you?"

I didn't know, but I drank all of it anyways. It tasted like acidic licorice, and I fought to keep from coughing.

The girl's body warped like the boy's shadows. Her dreadlocks rippled like water. Her pupils swelled, and I felt mine swelling as well.

She ran her hands across my neck, my collarbone. She kissed my temple.

"Will you tell me a story?" she asked. "The boys are so boring."

"I don't have any stories."

I ran my fingers up and down her arms. Somehow, I couldn't stop myself.

"Not everyone has a story, but I can tell by looking at you that you do."

"What did you put in my drink?" I asked, kissing the palms of her hands.

"I just wanted some company. And a story."

I was about to protest again. There were no stories inside of me. I wanted to say, "I'm a hollowed out girl, and I have to be in order to survive. I don't even know a poem. My mother was a storyteller and it ruined her." But, then the story came.

I pulled her by the dreads and whispered. "Once there was an ugly witch. She was so ugly that they cast her out of the village and made her live in the woods. She stole a child from a nursery and raised her as her own. She taught the child how to make her foul-smelling potions and how to kill animals, so together, they went mad. The child began to think she was a goddess, and that she could talk to trees. Why, she even killed a deer and wore its blood and bone because she thought it would give her magic powers. The townspeople were really quite concerned for this girl, living in filth. Once a boy came to the woods, asking the girl for her hand in marriage. He felt sorry for her, and wanted to cure her. In response she bit him and he ran away, never to bother her again."

"When the girl came of age the authorities came after her for killing the livestock and being a general nuisance. 'Mad, just like her mother, the witch,' they said. 'We'll lock her away so she won't bother us again.' The ugly witch convinced the girl that a great and terrible monster was chasing her and, if it caught her, she would be devoured instantly. So the girl picked up her deer skull and her hunting bow and ran screaming through the woods. The authorities were in hot pursuit, their dogs yapping at her ankles. In order to protect herself, she cut off her arm with the hunting knife in her pocket. The dogs, yowling and yipping, grabbed it and carried it off.

"The girl crawled into a hole and hid. To this day she lives there, trembling and scared. She convinced herself she was a rabbit, and nibbles on berries and grass. Because there are sometimes just better things than facing the truth."

The girl laughed, the sound refracting like light.

"You talk like an old person," she said, and kissed me on the cheek.

The music started blaring from the living room again. The girl grasped my hands, desperate, speaking fast, trying to tell me something important, but I couldn't hear any of her words.

"I'm sorry," I mouthed.

Back in the living room the music chiseled holes into my cheeks. I tried unplugging the speaker, but I couldn't find the cord. I went down the hallway. Broken pieces of mirror were glued to the walls. The ceiling was covered in mold and women's underwear. I called again for Phaedra.

At the end of the hallway I came to a room. I went inside and shut the door. I fumbled for a light switch, and when I touched it, a soft red light flooded the room.

Paintings lined the walls, glowing red and gold, as if illuminated from within. They were deeply textured, crackled like skin. I held my hand out toward one of the paintings and my hand glowed red, the patterns swirling and dancing across my skin.

When the artist entered the room, I knew I hadn't been searching for Phaedra, but for him.

"It's blood," he said, as if expecting to find me here.

He shut the door.

"Of course," I said, feeling dizzy. "What else would it be?"

"My friend works at a butcher's shop, he lets me take gallons of it."

He tripped over a chair, nearly knocking over one of his paintings. Blood smeared the back of his shirt as well as the front. He'd been rolling in it. He pulled out a bottle of gin hidden underneath a red coat on his desk and drank.

"I heat it, mix it with metal. Whatever I can find. Sometimes copper, sometimes gold. Wholesale shops. That's how I make them glow when the lights are turned on."

He turned to me with eyes shining and drunk.

"But you're not the kind of girl that cares about things like that," he said.

"They wouldn't let me be a scientist. So I dropped out of school."

"I heard what you did to that Charlie kid."

He pulled a switchblade out of his pocket. My body tensed. Maybe this would end in a cliché, him coming at me with the knife and splattering my blood across the canvas. Butcher shop; likely story.

Instead he pulled a bag of powder - drugs - out of his pocket.

"Have you ever done molly before?" he asked, setting the bottle of gin down.

"Of course," I said, though, of course, I hadn't.

I wasn't about to admit that I was a drug neophyte to this hulking husk; admit that the most I'd ever done was bad weed and housewives' pills.

He dipped his knife into the bag and snorted off the tip. He tilted his head back and squeezed his nose. He didn't offer me any, only put the bag and knife away and started drinking again. When he lowered the bottle he was staring at me, eyes like stingers.

"Are you lost?" he asked me.

"I was looking for my friend."

"Right. It's obvious you don't give a damn about anything important."

"I never said that."

"Oh, then you have an opinion? You like the paintings?"

"No "

He wheeled toward me with paint in his eyes, paint in his spit.

"Then get out! Get out of my house! I didn't invite you here! I know girls like you. I've fucked a thousand girls like you. Little boring, punk girls with ratty hair who think they have everything figured out."

His body sucked up the gravity of the room.

"So you killed a boy. Do you think I care? This isn't middle school, sister. You're going to have more to deal with than little lady teachers and prepubescent children. You think you're tough? You're nothing more than a spoiled child."

He lurched toward me, splattering me with paint, blood, and gin.

"I can't even imagine being that ignorant," he said.

I spit in his face.

I expected him to lunge forward and hit me. His fingers quivered and his eyes twitched. I flinched, waiting for a blow.

He touched his chin and smeared blue paint across his face. His smile was toxic.

"I'm going to destroy you," he said softly.

He pointed toward the door.

"Now get out," he said.

He slammed the door shut behind me. Dark shadows of creatures seemed to flit through the mirrors glued to the wall. Recorded thunder replaced the sound of dance music. I ran out of the house with my eyes closed, past the now empty porch, onto the lawn, weaving through the blood portraits.

They were like women that had lain down to die after being ripped away from their hair, teeth, and faces. I imagined them trying to move without skin, their exposed muscles grasping at the weeds.

I couldn't see the house. I couldn't see the sidewalk. I could be lost in the lawn forever. I only saw the grass smoking like coals and the women trying to pull themselves out of electric lights. What the hell had been in that absinthe?

The blue-haired girl with bleeding wrists writhed in the grass, lights in her hair, lights on her wrists.

"I know you," I said, "but I don't know from where."

From behind Phaedra snapped her fingers as if beckoning a dog.

"Where the hell have you been?" she said. "Come on."

"Where's your plant?" I asked.

"Just a two dollar Venus and a four inch dick. Let's go."

There were crosses etched into the blue-haired girl's throat.

"Lily!"

Phaedra dragged me to her car.

As we drove away, the blue-haired girl stood up, holding the lights in front of her body, lights swelling in the rearview mirror, until her body disappeared.

That night I dreamed of Charlie jumping into the river. I knew how this dream ended, yet I couldn't stop myself from running to the edge of the bridge and looking down.

But this time, when I turned away from the water I did not find the demon in her wet white dress. I found the artist doused in blood, rotting meat hanging from his hair, his face covered in flies.

I ran to him and he caught me in his arms. He pulled me into his hissing, rotting embrace.

I tried to cry, but what came out of my mouth was an insect noise.

"Shh," he said. "Everything's going to be okay. I am a sick man. Everything's going to be okay."

I clung to him.

Thirteen

I SOUGHT HIM out because of a dream. Because of a stupid fucking dream. I found out his name was Cignus like the northern constellation. Cignus like the swan. I showed up at his art show in a wine bar downtown and found he'd imprisoned my likeness in one of his blood paintings. He'd exaggerated all of my features. My eyes were like those of a mad crow, my hair dark and struck through with electricity.

He appeared at my side, no longer in his blood-spattered dream suit, spitting out flies. He wore a neat gray jacket and, except for his bloodshot eyes and the darkened circles on his face, he looked the part of the gentleman. Like a Cignus, not The Artist.

"Sort of a resemblance, isn't there?" he said, indicating the painting.

He headed toward the wine bar.

I shouldn't have come, but my head didn't know it yet. I was sicker than anyone knew. It would have been better for my mental health to stay home with Momma as she gathered wood for a Viking ship. For months she went to the scrapyard in the morning and came back carrying twisted boards, her fingernails bloodied and filled with splinters.

Better to see that every morning, than see myself trapped in grit and blood, framed and mounted above a bar, with a $500 price tag and a title of "The Hunted."

Maybe the demon visited the artist like she visited Charlie, dressed up in my skirts and sweaters to disguise herself. I hadn't seen her since the night she took me to the entrance of the ancient woods, yet I knew she still followed me everywhere. She whispered glossolalia underneath party noise. I saw her in Pluto's eyes. And here, she'd shown up in a painting to taunt me. Silly bitch. I'm sure that, in hell, that could be called a kind of romance. I imagined her draped over red velvet cloth, pale thighs opened, spider for a cunt, as the artist pressed her face into butcher shop blood.

Cignus came back from the bar and held out a glass of wine.

I hesitated. I expected him to haul me out of the bar, screaming, not offer me a drink.

"Take it," he said. "Don't romance it."

I took the glass. Took a careful sip.

"Good?" he asked.

I nodded.

"I figured you would like it, it's a Riesling. It's what the girls with unsophisticated palates drink."

He motioned toward the back door.

"Come," he said. "I need a smoke."

On the back porch we lit cigarettes together. He inhaled like he couldn't catch his breath.

He'd just insulted me, and then commanded me to follow him outside like he owned me. And all I could think was, he looked better in blood and dead flies than primped for galleries and wine. Those crazy eyes couldn't be buttoned up in a clean gray suit. I sat on the railing and leaned my head back, gazing at constellations. Maybe Cignus the swan lived up there, but Momma never taught me to find any stars but Wormwood.

He spoke my name like a curse.

"Lily, that painting. Do you think it flatters you?"

"I don't think your paintings could flatter anyone."

He continued speaking as if he hadn't heard me.

"I'm going to tell you a story. My sister and I have hunted the woods behind our house our whole lives. On one of the few nights I went out hunting by myself, I came across a deer with its throat slit and tied upside down in a tree. I cut the deer down from the tree, but it wasn't a deer at all."

He crushed his cigarette between his fingers.

"I closed my eyes for a second, and when I opened them, I saw it wasn't a deer, but a girl. When I blinked, it transformed back into the deer. How does someone make that mistake? How does someone mistake a deer for a girl?"

I didn't know how to respond. The story he told was the first thing he'd said that wasn't a thinly veiled insult. And the intensity with which he spoke, biting the inside of his cheek, his Adam's apple petrified in his throat, left me paralyzed.

"It wasn't a mistake," he said. "I think there really was a girl there. And maybe I was the only one who saw her, if only for a moment."

He'd told that story like he'd rehearsed it. The lines too smooth, the pauses like paragraphs. He knew I'd come. He knew, and had the story waiting for me.

"What's your game?" I asked him.

He pressed closer to me. I gripped a cracked wooden post that broke underneath my fingernails, and I dropped my cigarette in the grass.

"I didn't ask you to come here," he said.

I tilted my head back to look him in the eyes, my throat tightening.

"Surprise," I whispered.

He finished his cigarette.

"Come back inside," he said.

We went back into the bar. The blue-haired girl from the lawn sat by herself, drinking from a large, blue mug. She pushed her sweater to her elbows, revealing fresh scars, dirty and purple, all up and down her arms.

"Your girlfriend?" I asked.

"My sister," Cignus said.

"Most people call me Elm," she said, and she held out her hand for me to take, "but my real name is Saint Peter."

"Saint Peter," I said, gripping her hand, "like the prophet."

"Not like," she said. "Am. I am the prophet."

Cignus pressed his hand against the small of my back. Little sparks ran up my spine, and I wish they hadn't.

"I'm taking her home," he said.

Saint Peter drove us in an ancient, rust-colored van. Cignus and I sat in the back seat, staring at each other, our backs pressed against the windows. I drew my knees up. He drew his knees up.

He unrolled the window and lit another cigarette. He tried to hide the fact he coughed blood onto his sleeve.

Saint Peter could've been driving us into the sea, I wouldn't have noticed.

"That picture in the wine bar?" he said. "'The Hunted?' I painted it after that night I found the dead girl in the woods."

"You're lying."

"Why would I waste my energy lying to you?"

"It wasn't me," I whispered to him. "The girl in the woods wasn't me."

"I know what I saw."

"I'm not dead. I'm right here."

He reached across the van and took my hand. He touched my fingers one by one.

"Are you really?" he asked.

Saint Peter stopped in front of their house. It was the same one Phaedra and I went to only a week before. Someone removed the blood paintings from the grass, and the porch stood empty and quiet.

I stepped out of the car. Before I could follow Cignus into the house, Saint Peter pulled me back.

"Be careful," she said. "You know he has a reputation."

"I can take care of myself."

"Are you sure?" she asked. "Maybe you only think that because people have been hiding the truth from you."

"Who are you?"

"Saint Peter," she said. "Do you know who you are?"

I pulled my hand away.

"I don't think about it."

I went into the house, not looking behind me to see if she followed. I passed the empty living room and the sterile kitchen. Every room appeared hollowed out, cast into grey light. The speaker was gone. The mirrors on the walls had been ripped off and scattered across the floor.

Cignus waited for me. Not at the door of his studio, but at the door of his bedroom. As I walked toward him broken glass crunched underneath me.

The house sighed as he took me into his room and shut the door. It sighed as I slipped into cool red sheets.

We were fulfilling some unspoken contract between us. A primordial agreement older than dark and stars. Once you invade someone's dreams you're a part of them forever. For the rest of their life they'll be spitting out little pieces of you.

I knelt in front of him and he pressed molly into one of my nostrils. Cocaine into the other.

"Don't kiss me," he said as my throat and mouth buzzed.

In the dark, I saw the photographs of women taped to the walls, their eyes shining in camera flash. A thousand dirty punk girls.

"Would you like to go on my wall?" he asked me.

I leaned my head back and the room tilted. I squeezed red sheets between my fists and the colors dripped onto me.

"Not yet," he said. "You'll give me a picture when you leave me."

He was rough, all angles and sandpaper. He burned away the palm of his hands with chemicals and, though the drugs made me want to kiss and kiss, his mouth was a stone.

He pushed my thighs apart with his knees. I fell halfway off the bed and grabbed fistfuls of carpet. I spit out flies.

"Lily, can you hear me?" He asked.

He spoke to me from dimensions away. I was lost in textures, burnt and soft, lost between his trembling knees.

"God, everything's so soft," I whispered.

"I used to talk to God," Cignus said. "I thought he could hear me."

I rubbed my cheek against the carpet.

"Only an expression," I murmured, my mouth being tickled by fibers I never even knew existed.

"Be careful how you use your words," he said. "Maybe I'm a devil waiting to curse you."

"You don't want to meet a real devil."

He fucked me as I lay with my head pressed into the carpet, my toes gripping the bed sheets. He fucked me because that's how you leech the magic out of someone. I may be young, but I'm not an idiot.

I could have gouged his eyes out with my jutting chest, my jutting hips. I wanted to rear up and bite his head off, but the carpet underneath me was so soft. I breathed it in even as I lay twisted, my organs bursting inside of me.

I wouldn't tell him I hadn't done drugs before, and he wouldn't believe me if I told him I was a virgin so I lay quiet even though I scarred the inside of my mouth with teeth marks and my thighs clenched and shook.

Blood stained my legs and the color faded into red sheets.

Where were you on that night, little demon, when the artist came across the deer? Did I disguise myself to hide from you? Maybe I thought I could disappear between thick muscle and fawn skin, a slit throat, mud caked on the back of my ears.

Or were you the one who killed me and dragged me up there in the first place?

I don't know how much time passed before Cignus released me and I fell off the bed, shivering. I couldn't move. He tore the red curtains off his wall and wrapped me in them.

"Want me to draw you?" he asked, while I lay inert on the floor.

"Go away."

"I need a cigarette," he said, and left me.

I'm glad you weren't here to see me grow into an adult, demon. Though I think we both knew it would always be like this. No fairytale cherry popping for girls like me, not with my firework scars and Schizophrenia curse. Knights do not rescue mad girls, because our crowns are invisible and made of dirt. I did not deserve the palatial, golden bed of the man in polished armor.

And if he offered it to me, I would have laughed and laughed.

I dragged myself across the floor, shivering, trailing red curtains like the train of a dress. I crawled underneath his desk, near the radiator.

Cignus came back into the room and found me sitting underneath his desk.

"I'm so cold," I said.

He reached out for me.

"Come here," he said, the last sweet thing he ever said to me.

He laid me on the bed and rocked me to him, to his weak heart and thin chest, until I fell asleep.

***

I awoke to a thud outside of Cignus' window, the sound of wood splintering. I sat up with a start, gasping.

Another thud, followed by a CRACK, as of a tree splitting in two. I reached for Cignus in the dark, but he was gone. I crawled off the bed and searched for my clothes on the floor.

In the backyard I found Saint Peter shooting arrows with a hunter's bow, an expensive thing, smooth draw, black liquid metal and fiberglass. It was a bow to kill bears and boars with.

She notched another arrow and drew the string.

It shot dead center into the trunk of the tree, inside a yellowing paper target.

She lowered the bow and brushed the hair from her face. Blood dripped down her wrist. On the back of her hand was a braised scar in the shape of a cross.

"You're bleeding," I said.

“So are you.”

I looked down and saw the blood smeared across my thighs. It glowed blue in the moonlight, and when I touched it I found it dried and cool.

She turned back to the tree, drew another arrow, and released.

Fourteen

WE'VE BEEN HERE before. The artist and me locked in the back room, his teeth bared and his tongue clicking. I've sat on this floor, just like this, with my knees clenched together and the red curtain draped around my shoulders. He held the back of my neck like a mother wolf as I bent and snorted cocaine from a piece of broken mirror.

The walls and the air glistened with grease; my skin was dirty, my thighs ached, and I was rotting from the inside, but my eyes were wide open.

Cignus turned toward his empty canvas. I thought I heard his bones cracking, his skin too thin to contain him. I wondered how many nights he spent here in the studio with the door locked, nothing but drugs and a red light to guide him. Enough hours and his fingers started shaking, the painting before him blurred. Maybe at the end of the night he couldn't tell the difference between the butcher shop blood, the light, his own hands.

As for me: my head was ready to pop and my eyes were stretched a mile wide.

He threw the cover off his desk and revealed a small refrigerator underneath. He stored bags of blood inside.

He ripped open a bag and spilled it into a tray, some splashing across his hands.

I blinked, and the earth shifted underneath me. Cignus no longer stood at the canvas, but back at his desk. He mixed paint and blood with molten silver. He wiped his mouth as silver tinged his lips. When he spoke, flecks of it dropped to the floor.

"I could transform you into anything I wanted," he said, and I laughed.

He pressed silver and blood into my palms. He squeezed, and the silver ran down my arms.

It spread cool through my blood. I tasted his words traveling on spit particles in the air.

"I will remake you," he said.

He squeezed harder, and the silver turned into rot. It travelled fast through my bones, sprouting like fungi on the surface. I tasted it on my tongue. If I breathed into someone's mouth, I'd kill them with the poison in me. I was transforming, yes, into something terribly wrong.

He bent down and snorted another line. He reared back up like he'd been underwater for years, then returned to his work in progress.

We've been here before. Me and the artist.

But I've said that already.

He painted with his fingers. I rolled on the floor choking. I asked for a glass of water, maybe some orange juice, anything to soothe away the drip in the back of my throat. He gave me a piece of gum to keep me from grinding my teeth together. I stuck it, chewed up, in the center of one of his canvases.

"So disrespectful," he said. "Would you stick gum on the Sistine chapel?"

"You're no Michelangelo," I said.

The rot slid through my stomach like a fat, diseased worm. It pushed at my belly button where it formed its center, like a pulsating jugular.

I grabbed the piece of broken mirror, cocaine-encrusted, jagged on the edges, and I cut a hole into the center of me.

I dropped the mirror and wrapped the red curtains around me. I crawled across the floor.

“Touch me. I’m changing colors. Touch me.”

Please, say that I’m still here. Say that I’m still human, or I might be lost.

He peeled back my red curtain cocoon. Underneath I lay naked, burning, and bleeding.

“Do you remember when we first met? What I promised you?” he asked.

“No,” I spit out.

"Lie to me again."

We fucked on the floor. I hadn’t washed myself since the last time, but he didn’t ask about the blood. Not that he could tell the difference between my blood and that from the butchers. He touched me like I was a dream. I was tearing. I was splitting apart.

I didn't make a sound.

He withdrew from me without coming. A wide swathe of blood and silver spread across his waist.

"You hurt yourself," Cignus said.

"No," I said softly, "you did."

I found the hole I cut into myself, as if for the first time. I touched the rim of the wound but couldn't feel anything at all.

"I'm scared."

"Come here," he said.

I held my arms out to him and he picked me up. I smelled the toxic rot bubbling out of the hole. My blood gurgled and spilled out silver.

"How long has it been since you've been able to admit that you were afraid?"

He carried me to his canvas.

"No," I said.

"Don't you dare turn away."

"No."

"I need this."

The blood spilling out of me was no longer silver, but yellow.

"You're scared too," I said. "Aren't you? I can feel it."

He gathered my hair in between his fists.

"Take a deep breath."

He pressed the gaping hole that used to be me into the center of his canvas.

He threw me backwards and I collapsed on the floor. He painted with his thumbs in my yellowed blood. He cursed underneath his breath. His hands drug-trembled. I crawled headfirst into the red curtains and waited to die. They'd find me with cocaine in my mouth and heated gore underneath my fingernails.

The artist shook me from unconsciousness.

"Open your eyes."

He tilted my head toward the canvas.

I saw my eyes dripping toxic silver. He framed my head with a yellow crown. Streaks of black gore rose from my forehead. Horns.

The Hunter, not the Hunted.

We've been here before.

I pressed my hands against my wound.

"I was right. You're more scared than I am," I said.

"Don't talk anymore. You'll hurt yourself," he said.

We've been here before.

He helped me into the hallway. I walked with him over broken glass and cigarette butts into the living room. It was storming outside. Someone had opened all the windows, and rain blew through the room. It pelted my naked skin, my hair, my stomach. I turned into him to escape the cold, but he stiffened and wouldn't hold me.

He pushed me onto the couch and left. When he came back with my clothes I was curled up with my face pressed down into the cushion and my skin turning blue.

"I can't breathe," I said.

"Stop panicking."

He pulled my sweater over my head and pushed my skirt up over my knees as I sat with a storm dripping in my mouth.

"You won't see me again," he said. "Because I'll be someone else entirely."

"I don't believe you," I said.

Later he'd carry me out to the car because I refused to move. He'd drive me home as I lay huddled against the car door. We'd be chased by a storm, lightning bursting, dodging traffic accidents. I'd see a burnt black hand on the side of the road, but say nothing. I wouldn't feel the pain until hours later, after I should've gone to the hospital, but I was scared of stitches, so I'd pour iodine over the wound and tape several bandages over it. Instead of sleeping I'd lay in bed, crying from the comedown, crying quietly so that Momma wouldn't hear me.

He took my hands into his own, those acid-burned hands, and he spoke.

"I'm already gone."

Fifteen

EVERY NIGHT FOR two weeks I woke to Mother's crying. I found myself wrapped in butcher paper with a red bow around my ankles and a red bow around my throat. I tore myself out of the paper, gasping, and ran downstairs.

"I'm not dead."

She sat at the kitchen table in her gazelle skull and wept.

"My baby girl, they're going to truck you away for meat."

I sat beside her at the kitchen table and lit a cigarette.

"Can the dead do this?" I asked, and I blew smoke in her face.

Still, she wept.

I'd dropped out of high school years ago. I had no car and no job. My reputation as a boy killer was fading fast and demons no longer haunted me. I had nothing but a broken hymen and bad dreams. So my mother thought I was dead. It was a mistake anyone could make, right?

"Tell me something before they take you away," my mother said.

She grabbed my wrists. Tears welled up underneath the gazelle skull.

"What's so goddamn important?" I asked.

"Do you have a boyfriend?"

She asked the same question the night I came back from Cignus' house, shaking from the cocaine, spit in my hair. I tried to sneak up the stairs but she stood at the threshold of her bedroom with butcher paper in her hands.

Dried blood encrusted my thighs and sweater. My knees shook.

"Do I look like I want a boyfriend?" I asked, and jerked my hand away.

I stubbed the cigarette out on the kitchen table, and left.

Pluto waited for me in the bedroom. I grabbed her and threw myself into bed. Her purring lulled me into sleep.

The next night, I woke up in the same way. The butcher paper wrapped around me, the color of dead scraped skin. My mother crying.

"I'm not dead."

"Just you wait for the meat truck, baby."

And the next night.

And the next.

During the day I smoked cigarettes on the back porch. I stole my mother's ID, bought some rum, and drank it with sugar and melted ice cubes. I fell asleep, hanging halfway off the couch, watching the Cosmos television series on DVD. I was useless incarnate. Momma suggested I go back to school, get my GED, get a job, maybe give Birth to a savior from a fallen star. I could do anything I wanted to.

"You're a warrior, baby," she said. "I've always told you that."

Only at night did she know the truth. I was dead meat, something to cart away.

I thought of stealing Momma's car and driving to the artist's house. I would walk past the blood portraits on the lawn, and the boys on the porch howling like wolves. I'd tear down that mirror-crusted hallway to get to him. I'd stick my hand through "The Hunter" and force him to paint another one.

I'd tell him, "I'll haunt you forever. I'll never let you go,"

I wanted him to kill me. I wanted him to blow glitter into my blood.

Anything but sitting on the couch with ice melting into my rum.

Then one night I tore the butcher paper away and found Phaedra and Cignus in my room. Cignus sat in the rocking chair with sunglasses on. He must've come from an art show, because he wore his stiff gray suit, his crisp tie.

Phaedra stood at the foot of my bed, my coat in her hands.

"Do you usually sleep like that?" she asked.

It was several moments before I managed to speak.

"Do you usually break in and watch people sleep?"

She threw my coat at me.

"We're going on an adventure," she said.

"Where have you been?" I asked.

"What does it matter?" Phaedra asked.

While I dressed, Cignus got up and paced the room. He took off his sunglasses; broken blood vessels filled his eyes.

Pluto wound around Phaedra's legs but Phaedra pushed her away.

"You still own that rat?" she asked.

"It's just a cat, P," I said. "I don't know why it creeps you out so much."

"It's not a cat," she said. "See those eyes? It's a mountain."

We snuck downstairs, past the kitchen where my mother sat at the table, sobbing. I opened the front door.

"I called the meat truck!" shouted Momma.

"Thanks Mom!" Phaedra responded.

I slammed the door behind us as we ran out.

Cignus had parked his truck in the driveway. Phaedra rolled down the window as we sped away from the neighborhood.

"Why'd you yell at my mom? You're such a bitch," I said to her.

Phaedra lit a cigarette. The wind sucked at the ends of her dark princess hair.

"You know, if you don't go to sleep, you'll go mad," Cignus said.

"I've been mad for three days," Phaedra said.

Cignus' face was bruised a ferocious purple, his neck sick and yellowing.

"Cignus. Something bad is happening to you," I said.

"It's this artist suit. I can barely breathe," Cignus said.

He grabbed his tie and tore it away. It burst into moths.

"Get out of here!" he said, coughing, and batting at the moths that filled the car.

Phaedra rolled down the window and swatted them out of the car.

"Is this a dream?" I asked.

"If it's a dream," Phaedra said, "then why don't you wake up?"

She stuck her leg out the window of the truck. She bounced it up and down so that her foot seemed to skid across the white lines in the center of the road. I closed my eyes. Opened them up again.

The road did not melt away.

Cignus pulled up to his house and parked.

"We have to hurry," Cignus said, "before the party."

We got out of the car. I bent over, heaved, and coughed up moths.

"What have you done to me?" I asked. "This has to be a dream."

Cignus grabbed me by the waist and spun me toward the backyard.

"Don't you see what's out there?" he said.

Beyond the backyard were the woods. That night, a light shone through the trees.

That crumbling house could've risen up to devour me. Everything in the dark took on an extra dimension. I felt as if the street stretched out to infinity and that I, in the middle, was shrinking.

Cignus and Phaedra dragged me into the backyard. I expected Saint Peter to be there shooting arrows, but I only found the target on the ground, torn to shreds. Propped up against the tree was the blood painting of me with mad eyes, lightning hair, and horns of yellowed ichor.

Cignus took the painting to the edge of the woods where Phaedra and he held it to the light. The light grew brighter and their faces appeared grim and bruised in the glow.

"Do you see it?" Cignus asked.

The light reflected a red line off the painting and into the woods.

It wasn't an artist that pressed my blood into a canvas and painted horns and eyes with his thumbs. It was a diviner. He hadn't created a painting for bored middle-class intellectuals to buy, but a guide to show the way.

To where? I didn't know.

"You have to follow the light," he said.

"Why me?" I asked. "And have you two been sleeping with each other?"

"It's been haunting me all my life, but it was made for you." Cignus said.

I couldn't see anything in the woods except that red light, rushing past the darkness, like a beam that could penetrate solid matter.

"Why is this so important?" I asked.

"You'll know when you get there."

"Lily, listen to me. If you go in, you might be someone else when you come out," Phaedra said.

"Don't tell her that," Cignus said.

"Somebody needs to."

"What's going to happen to me?" I asked.

"Child," he said; and still holding up the painting, he spit in the grass. "I knew you would be too scared. You're a little girl trying on a woman's body, but it'll never fit you right."

"You've been wanting me to do this from the beginning," I said. "From the moment you met me. You set me up for this."

"Now she's mad because you called her a child," Phaedra said.

"Shut up," Cignus said. "Neither of you know what you're dealing with."

"Then explain to me."

"There's no time." He said. "The blood only lasts so long, then the light disappears, forever."

"And after?"

"I'll see you at the party," he said. "I promise."

I should've run. I probably could've fallen onto the ground with my eyes closed and forced myself to wake up. Instead I looked at Cignus, covered in bruises and blood, as he held up the painting. His eyes begged me, with a look I'd never seen from him.

"You need me to do this," I said.

"Yes."

"Tell me then," I said, and my cheeks flushed, my heart beating like an insect. "Tell me you need me."

"Oh please," Phaedra said. "What are we, in grade school?"

He hesitated. His entire body shook with fatigue; his muscles must've been burning from lack of sleep. When he spoke, he spoke haltingly, slowly.

"I've always needed you," he said.

I followed the red light into the woods.

I pushed through trees draped with low vines, misted and wet. Stormwater, night water, lay in pools on the ground and in those pools lay stars. I crushed them underneath my shoes.

I looked behind, but couldn't see Phaedra or Cignus anymore, only the red light that shot out from the painting.

Someone cut the low hanging branches from the trees, recently it appeared. Their wounds were like wooden eyes. There was a human-made path cleared through the woods. The weeds and grass were hacked away, the stones cleared.

I saw no animal tracks. There were no birds in the trees, no rustling of foxes, no deer in the grass. Only the sounds of my breath and my steps.

Little blue flowers grew on the ground, like the ones I'd once seen crushed underneath a spider child.

The red light flickered in and out. Cignus was right. Soon it would be gone, and if I didn't hurry I'd be trapped, lost here.

I ran. The vines cut at my exposed face. I fell several times, scraping my knees against the hard ground. I thought I might run until my heart gave out, or until I bled out. But as I ran further, the darkness disintegrated. Warm sunlight emanated from deep within the woods.

I entered a meadow where the sun hung high in the air.

The red light disappeared.

The meadow's grass was dead and brown. The air was full of oil, so thick I tasted it at the back of my throat – a childhood smell, a reminder of cyanide and steel.

Machine oil.

In the middle of the clearing, in a patch of dirt, I found a woven basket of freshly dead wrens. Someone had tied a red ribbon around their necks.

"Who's here?" I called out.

God, that cloying smell of oil could knock me unconscious if I wasn't careful. It was what I smelled the night the demon took me to her dining table in the woods.

"Demon?" I whispered.

I crouched in front of the basket. Whoever had brought these wrens, got them from somewhere else, as there were no birds left here.

Or it had killed everything in the forest.

"Nightcatcher?" I whispered again.

Momma, momma, I need you to tell me the right way to go crazy so my heart doesn't burst. You made it look so easy.

I reached toward the basket. It tipped over, and the wrens spilled into the dirt. Their tiny mouths gaped, as if opening wide for food. I tugged at one of the red ribbons and it unraveled from the wren's neck.

"What am I supposed to do?" I called out.

Across the clearing Saint Peter emerged, her blue hair sticking to the sun, her hunter's bow drawn.

"Who brought you here?" she asked as she approached me.

I rose.

"Was it Cignus?" she said. "You're not supposed to be here."

"Is something after me?" I asked. "Again?"

"She has your scent now," she said. "We need to go."

The sun plunged down as starlight burst across the dead meadow. I heard a rustling. We both turned, and a fawn, its skin shining with moonlight, emerged from the grass.

"Oh, it's just a "

Saint Peter shot the fawn in the neck.

She grabbed my arm.

"Don't run," she said. "Just walk with me."

It seemed important not to look behind me as we walked away. Like Lot's wife, I might turn into a pillar of salt. Like Orpheus escaping the underworld, I'd lose something I could never recover.

There was something in the woods looking for us, foaming with anger, and I felt it. Anybody would've been able to feel that kind of presence. Its shadow could've broken bones.

The fawn screamed and screamed.

I took a slow, careful breath with each step to keep myself from bolting.

Keep walking. Saint Peter kept her hand on my arm. Keep walking.

That something barreled out of the woods behind us. Saint Peter tightened her grip. Its colossal shadow skimmed over the treetops, and it brought cold with it.

I heard it tear into the wounded fawn behind us, ripping into its muscle and flesh; the fawn stopped screaming. I stopped breathing.

We reached the tree line and ran.

I'd been into these woods before, years ago, trailing a dead-thing's dress behind me. Maybe the location changed, but the soil remained the same. In the years when the demon left, I thought I would be safe, but, with or without her, the shadows and their woods would follow me. One day I would awake to find little blue flowers sprouting out of my arms, my feet buried in the side of a mountain.

If I got out of here alive.

Saint Peter and I emerged from the trees into the backyard. Cignus and Phaedra were gone.

"Where did they go?" I asked Saint Peter, but she was gone as well.

The house lay empty. The street beyond the house lay empty.

I took a step forward and something broke underneath me. It was the blood painting of me, now cracked in two.

Sixteen

I WENT INTO THE artist's house, but everyone had already left. Empty bottles of beer and liquor lay strewn across the floor.

The couch and the stereo were gone. The broken mirrors on the floor were swept away. Someone even removed the light bulbs from their fixtures.

I burst into the artist's studio.

The paintings were gone. The lights were gone. The desk, the paints, the refrigerator of blood, and the stain from my spit dripping on the floor were gone and gone and gone. Nothing left but bare, peeling walls.

Saint Peter stood behind me in the doorway.

"Where is he?" I asked.

"The party is over. It's been over for a long time."

"He promised he'd be here."

"I'm sorry," she said.

For the first time I noticed how tall she was, taller than her brother. She wore a faux fur jacket and platform boots, her hair dirty and hacked away in various places. She hardly looked the part of the disciple that once chased after Jesus like a dog. The boy with ragged shoes and ragged fingertips who demanded that he be crucified upside down because he wasn't worthy to die the same way as his god.

"Where do I know you from?" I asked.

"It was a long time ago."

"One person shouldn't have to bear this much."

"And yet you do."

"Where is Cignus?"

"He has done a terrible thing, and he is hiding," Saint Peter said.

"I wasn't supposed to go into those woods. Is that what you mean?"

"If I had known he was taking you there, I would have stopped him," she said.

"I'm such an idiot," I said.

"Maybe," Saint Peter said.

I felt heaviness in my throat, a dark hole in my stomach.

"But you're looking better every day," she said. "More like your old self."

She touched my stomach. It was bleeding again from that dirty cocaine glass, spreading through my shirt, but she wasn't looking down.

"Your eyes, they're so bright. Like stars," she said.

"You don't know what you're talking about."

"What happened to the fearless girl I used to know?" she asked.

I pried her fingers away.

"Ask your brother."

She pushed me against the wall. She covered my mouth with her mouth. She thrust her bloodied tongue inside me. She ran her fingers through my hair, smearing blood against my forehead. It dripped down my eyelids, and pooled underneath the cusp of my collarbone.

I shoved her away. The mad saint reeled back, her eyes laughing.

"You don't remember when we used to kiss?" she asked. "You used to love me."

She pulled her fingers apart, blood peeling on her fingernails.

"Let me take you away," she said. "It's not safe for you here anymore."

I pushed past her and into Cignus's room. There too, everything was gone; the bed, the red curtains he wrapped me in, the desk I hid underneath.

I pried at the boards on the floor. I scratched at the nails, trying to pull them apart. There had to be a secret entrance somewhere. Or a button, disguised to look like the wood or the wallpaper. If I could find it, then Cignus would be revealed. The house would give up its secrets and this cruel game would be over. Was it my birthday? I couldn't remember. Maybe it was my birthday.

Surprise, Lily! Surprise! We were all hiding from you, but we're here now. And we brought cake.

I scratched at the floorboards until I sunk, frustrated, onto the floor, my fingers bleeding and sore.

I knew Saint Peter stood behind me, watching.

"Where is he?" I whispered.

"I'd give you the world if I could."

"Just give me this."

Cignus, it's not right to do this to a girl. You can't just fuck her and paint a picture with her blood and send her out into the woods and then never call again.

You can't leave me here.

"He promised me," I said. "He said he needed me."

"My brother promises a lot of things."

Tears dripped onto my wrists.

"You don't understand. He has to come back. I don't ever cry like this," I said.

"Let me take you home."

I couldn't pretend to resist as she pulled me off the floor. She led me outside. I shook so badly I could barely walk. She strapped me to the back of her van, and drove me home.

That's how this all ended, wasn't it? The best kind of story is a tragedy. Everyone in my life must've been cursed to die or disappear. Like Daddy. Like Charlie. Like Cignus. God knows where Phaedra went. If I stuck around long enough, soon Saint Peter would disappear. Time for me to crawl back home and suck up some of that mother's milk, spend some quality time with Momma in purgatorial madness before we both fell backwards into a Viking ship, howling toward the abyss. At least my mother and I could be at peace in our insane loneliness, rocking and howling together on deck, polishing our weapons, plucking all the hairs off our bodies in cohabited Trichotillomania.

Yet, when we pulled up to my house, I knew my mother was gone.

Seventeen

I ALWAYS KNEW when my mother was gone. Maybe it's a kind of sixth sense I developed after years of being left behind in her whirlwind, of sleeping in the house alone, night after night, while she saved the world. Maybe it came with learning to drive a car at the age of eight so I could get to school on time, or maybe it was learning to run and hide from police and social workers who'd take me away, or being forced to eat cold peanut butter and ketchup because my mother hadn't bought groceries in weeks. I used to stand outside, on the neighborhood cul-de-sac, as the other families cooked dinner, hoping to be invited in to eat. I rarely was, though I stood on the sidewalk until they cleared the tables away.

After Saint Peter dropped me off, I flung the front door open so hard it slammed against the wall.

"Where are you?" I asked.

I went upstairs to her bedroom.

I pulled apart her made bed, as if she'd be hiding underneath the unwrinkled coverlets and spread pillows. I yanked open her closet door, nearly falling as I did so. I threw her clothes to the ground, ripped her senior high school prom dress at the seams, and showered sequins across the entire closet. I went to her vanity, grabbed handfuls of her lipsticks and compacts, and threw them against the wall. I smashed her vanity mirror with my elbow.

"I've been thinking about you and me," I called out.

I shoved the closet door shut and went toward my bedroom. There, I did the same thing, pulling up the sheets and tossing the pillows onto the floor as if I'd find her hiding underneath.

"I don't think anything is going to help us. I remember the little yellow pills that Daddy forced you to take, before he left, but those didn't help. And the doctor? That didn't help either.

"I thought maybe I could escape it. That I wouldn't get sick like you. Of course, I was an idiot. I've been sick ever since Daddy left. I mean, don't you remember the spider?"

I grabbed a vase in the hallway. It was one of my mother's favorites with its flower-eyed ceramic print, a wedding gift from my schizophrenic grandma. I threw it against the wall.

"They're going to have to lock us away and shove needles full of sedatives under our eyes and, sometimes, people are just cursed. Did you hear me? Can you hear me? Sometimes they're just cursed and nothing in the world can save them."

I went back into her bedroom with lighter fluid I stashed under my bed, and threw it across the carpet. I doused her bed sheets and her clothes. I splashed it across the walls and her vanity, leaving ugly wet marks everywhere.

The pungent smell burned my throat. I pulled a lighter from my pocket.

"Can you hear me, Momma?" I said softly. "Can't you see you made me in your fucking image?"

Downstairs, a window broke.

"Momma!" I cried out, and I dropped the lighter.

I ran into the kitchen. Glass glittered on the tiles. Someone had broken the window and the curtains blew into the twilight beyond. I edged toward the window.

The only source of light in the neighborhood emanated from the open front door of Phaedra's house. It was a red door, a loud door, fitting for the mother and daughter across the way that wanted so badly to be sick. It was the only red door on the row. The only open door. The hinges creaked slowly back and forth.

Something had opened that door, had grabbed it, wrenched it open, and thrown it back until it slammed against the foundation. Something in a great hurry.

Here's another story for you:

The mad girl with the missing mother climbed through the broken window toward the red door. The wound in her stomach ripped open again with stress. When she crossed her friend's lawn, she smelled the woods spilling out of the open door, the smell of loam, dirt, and lightning-struck trees.

Maybe in a past life the girl had once been a great hunter. She'd once woven for herself a crown of ash and deer bone and conquered all who would defy her with her great hunting bow.

No longer.

Now she was a ruined girl, a girl crushed by a night sky bloated with factory smoke. She was a dirty girl who rarely bathed, and smoked too much for her own good. If she found a great hunting bow these days, she'd probably try to sell it at a pawnshop.

The mad girl wasn't prepared for what lay beyond the red door. She knew she was in the middle of a terrible, otherworldly conspiracy she could never hope to understand. The hunter could've conjured up the beasts of the forest to go into the house and destroy whatever waited for her there. The mad girl probably couldn't even bend down to tie her shoelaces without falling over, would lie in the grass screaming at her own shadow writhing beside her.

The mad girl was a stupid girl. Even without those powers, she went through the red door anyway.

She found grass, weeds, and flowers growing on the floor. Ivy hung from the walls as if it had been growing there for years. It'd started wrapping itself in lazy, suffocating circles around the couch and the coffee table, plunging itself into the piano. The mad girl picked through the overgrown weeds, nearly tripping over a dining room chair. She called out for her mother. She called for Phaedra.

The mad girl found a family photograph on the wall, one of Phaedra and her mother in white dresses and fake smiles, trying not to squint underneath hot studio lights. As she looked at it, green and white mold bloomed through the print, tearing into their smiles and their dresses. The photograph slid off the wall.

The mad girl reached the moldy and crumbling stairs. She sank into moss and was forced to crawl up the stairs, clinging to the banister. Several times one of her feet sank down into the rotting wood and, each time, she struggled to pull it out again.

Halfway up the stairs, the mad girl found Phaedra's mother trapped in the trunk of a transparent tree. It must've grown through the basement. It pushed through the broken roof.

The mother's skin burned away and her hair disintegrated. Her eyes had transformed into pills.

The mad girl pressed her hands to the transparent trunk; her fingers burned.

"Where's my friend?" the mad girl asked. "Where's my mother?"

Phaedra's mother pressed her face to the tree trunk and spoke, but the mad girl could hear nothing she said. Eventually the mother's lips and tongue fell apart.

The mad girl managed to crawl to the top of the stairs and enter her friend's room. But it wasn't the room she remembered. Where Phaedra's bed used to be, there was a hole where acid ate its way through the floorboards.

And in the center of the room, the mad girl found a carnivorous plant with snakes for heads, a quivering mass of red stalks and veins. The plant gurgled. The snakes opened and closed their mouths, snapping at her.

The mad girl cried out for her mother.

And then from the middle of the plant's mass, in a storm of pumping acid, a pale hand reached out for her. A muffled voice called to her.

"Baby girl, is that you? Don't be scared. Don't worry about a thing."

Her mother's hand scrabbled across the wooden floor searching for something to grasp, to pull herself out of the plant. But she couldn't get a grip on the rotting floorboards. They ate at her arthritic knuckles, the ones she always insisted they gave her no pain.

The girl knew if the plant ate her, it would've been like she never existed.

The plant sucked her mother's hand into its center.

When the mad girl saw her mother about to die, she became me.

"Mommy!" I screamed.

The flooring cracked underneath me. I fell backwards into the grass and rot.

Nightcatcher, did you lure my Momma up here? Did you reach out with your spindly arms and promise her a cure? Did you seduce Phaedra, that dark gothic princess, impervious to any human's allure, with these flesh-eating plants? Did you lead me here so that the three of us could be devoured together?

I crawled toward the plant. Thorns, buried within the grass, scratched at my fingers. The ivy unfurled from the walls and slashed at my face, my legs.

Momma, we were so stupid.

We should have been anywhere but here.

A snake head bit me on the collarbone. Its fangs tore into my skin and pumped me with poison. I kicked at a head that reached out to bite my leg; ropy branches grabbed my ankles. It pulled me toward the pumping center, to be devoured with my mother.

I tried to scream again, but a vine gagged my mouth. It squirted acid into my eyes and nose, and I couldn't breathe. I grabbed at the grass and the wooden flooring underneath me, trying to pull myself away from the plant, but the floor tore underneath my fingers, tore into my fingernails.

I grasped the vine in my mouth, driving my hands down into the thorns, down into its fleshy stalk, and twisted until it tore in my hands.

I pressed my cheek against the floor where I could breathe, and I called for her, my voice a hoarse whisper, my throat bleeding.

Let me die from a cocaine overdose, from a violent murder from a jealous drug kingpin. Hell, even let me die in the dark woods, my throat torn away by the thing that carried a cold shadow behind it. Tell my mother that I died fighting the giant Fenrir wolf. Let her give me a funeral for a warrior, set me ablaze, and send me sailing over a waterfall.

But don't let us die here, not with acid in our throats and snakes spit-hissing at our feet.

This is not how Vikings die.

"Help me," I whispered.

I choked on black and blood.

"Help my Momma. Please."

I kicked at the quivering center of the plant. Another branch wrapped itself around my other ankle. Fangs drove into the back of my leg. Poison tunneled through my blood, and the room started melting.

"Please."

And then after years of silence, she heard me.

The demon came floating on her black hair, enchanted hair. It crackled with energy as it filled the entire room. When the snakes saw her they let me loose from their jaws. They tried to slither away as she floated toward them. The vines withdrew themselves from her feet, but wilted and died before they could get away. More of the floorboards crumbled, and grass and flowers tumbled down into the hole where Phaedra's bed used to be.

The giant plant gurgled, almost like a scream.

The demon stretched her arms toward me.

Her hair brushed my face. She plucked out a piece of wood embedded in my cheek.

It was the first time I'd seen the demon as beautiful. Her body, untouched throughout the years, whereas I'd ruined mine, her skin like a cumulus cloud, eyes bright, cheeks flushed a deep red. Her body rose higher, lifted by her hair. She touched the ceiling with the tips of her fingers. All the while her hair transforming, growing, silver and sharp at the edges.

She threw her head back and her sharp hair sunk into the plant. It quivered and lost its color. She twisted her body and the hair twisted deeper into the plant. The ivy crumbled into ash. The snake's eyes rolled up into their heads, still trembling after they died.

I crawled toward the plant. I plunged my hands into its center and somewhere inside, among the poison and sharp, bristled hairs, my mother reached for me.

I pulled her out.

She was barely breathing and wet, her skin covered in burns, her eyes sealed shut with sticky ichor.

She couldn't speak. She stroked my shoulders, my hair. She kissed my bleeding cheek and my splintered forehead. And I clung to her like I used to. Like when I was a child and I thought she would rule the world with her stories. Like when we were Vikings.

The demon touched my shoulder. When I looked up from my mother, I found the plant torn apart. The demon's hair receded from the corners of the room. She smiled faintly.

"Come here," she mouthed.

She carried us from the house.

Eighteen

THE PARAMEDICS ARRIVED while I cradled my mother on the lawn. Her consciousness wavered, but her smile never did.

"What the hell happened?" a paramedic asked.

He tugged at his chin where a few stray hairs grew. He brushed my mother's burnt hair aside and checked her pulse. I would have mistaken him for a high school student if he hadn't shown up in an ambulance, wearing a uniform.

I pointed across the street. Could they not see the house busted open, loam spilling from the windows, the dead tree sprouting out of the roof?

"She's in shock," one of them said. "Bitch."

"What did you call me?" I said.

Or what I thought I said. I couldn't understand any of the words coming out of my mouth.

"She may be delirious. Check her vitals."

They spoke to me.

"You'll have to uncurl your fist."

"I can't," I said, shaking, but my fist relaxed.

They checked my pulse.

"A concussion maybe? We should take her to the hospital for further assessment."

When they took my mother away from me on a stretcher, I screamed.

"Do you want to go with her?" they said. "You should be in the hospital overnight for observation as well."

I knew if they took me, they would find out something was wrong with me, something worse than brain damage or a few poison scratches.

And they'd never let me leave.

"I'm not going," I said.

They strapped my mother to the stretcher. God, was that even her? I couldn't be sure anymore. Sickness and medicine turned people into lesser things. They could bring her back to me stuffed with cotton, like a plush toy, and it might take me years to notice. If I'd any strength left in my legs, I would've torn her from the stretcher. I shouldn't have called the ambulance in the first place.

I could have taken care of her myself. I would have, if I were a good daughter.

"You could be in danger. A serious concussion."

"We don't have time for this. Her mother is dying."

"If we force her to come with us she could become violent."

"No time."

They hauled her away. In the dark, her face appeared like a spider web big enough to trap the moon.

I went back into the house and shut myself in the bathroom, then covered the mirror with a towel because I couldn't bear to look at myself. I sat on the edge of the bathtub with a pair of tweezers and started picking splinters out of my skin.

She knocked on the door.

"Come in," I said quietly.

The demon slipped into the room. An insect trilled in her throat. She stood by the sink as I picked at my skin. Wooden shards and blades of grass spattered the bottom of the bathtub. I leaned over and coughed up red mud.

I peeled skin off my cheek.

The insect in the demon's throat went silent. When she breathed she made no noise, or perhaps she didn't breathe at all. I could've forgotten she was there if not for the shadow of her hair cast over the bathtub, twisting and lightning-coursed.

"I thought you were a dream," I said.

"Don't lie. You thought no such thing."

I kept swallowing but I couldn't get rid of the bitter taste in my mouth. I gripped the side of the bathtub and one of my fingernails cracked and fell onto the tiles. Taking a shower seemed impossible.

"I'll just wash the sheets tomorrow," I said.

I dropped the tweezers in the sink. My mouth felt dry, but I didn't think I could make it to the kitchen for a glass of water. Besides, I didn't want to touch anything or maybe my fingers would fall off as well as my fingernails.

The pain came later, as it always did.

The walls spun in my bedroom. The room wanted to send me flying off into orbit. I'd never be safe here again. I tried to undress, but my fingers were seizure patients and my skull was a melting bowl. I couldn't even touch the buttons on my dress.

The demon touched my neck and tilted my head down. She unbuttoned the back of my dress and I slipped out. I crawled into my bed, startling Pluto out of sleep, and stained the sheets with grime.

She lay beside me, face to face, this demon girl, with her teeth full of bugs, hair hissing, and body like a wasp's nest. When she moved, her skin rattled. She sighed, and spiders wove a crown for her head.

I pulled her close to me.

I buried my face in her cold neck. She rocked me, but I couldn't sleep.

Downstairs the phone rang.

I imagined getting a call from the hospital, and being forced to drive down there in the middle of the night. I'd cross the gray and nearly empty parking lot to the sliding doors of the waiting room. The receptionist would be sitting alone at the front desk, underneath a halogen bulb casting a pool of sick light on her head. She'd ask the name of the patient and click her tongue at me when I gave her the answer.

"Yes, I know who that is. And why didn't you bring her earlier? There's no chance of saving her now."

If I had to watch my mother shuffle down that hallway in paper slippers one more time, what would be left of me?

I leaned over the bed and started heaving, but nothing came up. The phone downstairs stopped ringing.

I reached for my phone and called Saint Peter.

"Take me out of here," I said.

I packed what I could in a small duffle bag and changed my clothes. I took off the demon's mud-stained dress and dressed her in one of my ragged sweaters and a worn skirt. An hour and a half later, Saint Peter drove up in her beaten down van. The demon carried Pluto. I took the demon's hand and together we ran down the stairs, out the door. We climbed inside the van and, with the door still open, we drove away.

Part Four: Curious Skin

Nineteen

IMAGINE THIS: SAINT PETER, with blue hair, a woman's body, and scars of inverted crosses on the back of her hands. Imagine she's standing outside a gas station, next to her van, holding her blue faux fur coat tight to her body, the wind whipping her hair. She closes her eyes - she sees God; she opens her eyes – she sees God. It's been twenty-three hours and she keeps eating psychedelic mushrooms to stay awake because there's still a thousand miles to go.

A man approaches and asks her what happened to the backs of her hands and she says, "I'm the reincarnation of Saint Peter."

"No kidding?" he says. "But that doesn't explain how you got those scars."

"Do you really want to know?" she asks.

The man nods.

"I was sailing on a ship towards the end of the universe, searching for God and the meaning of everything. And when I came to the end of the world I found a void, a great emptiness waiting for me, heaving and spitting, with God in the center of it all. But it was not God like you would imagine him, some kindly bearded old man with big bare feet sitting on a white throne next to white Jesus. This was a god of

Technicolor vomit, noise, hissing spit, and fluttering wings. And when I asked him the meaning of life, he could do nothing but screech."

This doesn't explain the scars but the man doesn't want to ask anymore, doesn't know how to ask anymore. And Saint Peter smiles and shivers and her scars break open to bleed.

She hands you the bag full of mushroom buttons and you take one. Then another. Two hours later your eyes have become gods sitting in the center of your head, and neither of you can stop laughing.

When you can finally breathe, chest aching, you say, "I think my mother will die without me," and this is profoundly hilarious in a way that nothing has ever been and nothing will ever be again, hilarious in this cosmic divine way, which starts both of you laughing again, harder than before.

St. Peter keeps driving. The road is a slit throat; the road signs are open mouths. There is no past or future. There is nothing in behind, nothing in front. There is only the road underneath the wheels. Trying to imagine where you're going would be incomprehensible, because it won't exist until you step out of the vehicle, and the universe builds it in front of you.

Yet despite all of this, when the sun sinks, you grow afraid. There's something about the darkness, the sharp white lines on the highway that reminds you what you've left behind. There is blood in-between your fingers. There are still pieces of wood in your hair. You wonder how long it'll take before they move your mother from ICU to the psych ward.

There is a dark passenger sitting in the back of the van, rubbing the film of her hands, like a poison, across the glass.

Twenty

THE ROAD DIDN'T END, and neither did the trip. I became dangerous and started to ask questions.

"Where are we going?"

"My friend wants to meet you," Saint Peter said.

"So she knows about me."

Saint Peter lit a stick of incense and stuck it in her teeth like a cigarette. Rosemary and Sandalwood filled the van. She stretched in the front seat and her shirt rode up, revealing a wound right above her belly button. It was an old wound, the edges yellowed, scars traced and retraced, as if it'd broken open and healed several times.

"Have you ever loved someone so much that you mutilated yourself?" she asked.

I touched my stomach where I'd cut it with a dirty piece of glass.

"It wasn't really like that," I said.

Something popped behind the van, like a barrier breaking. Or maybe a flat tire, but no, the sound was too loud, too thick, and the van didn't slow.

Behind us the dark waters rushed. The river where Charlie drowned was following us, sluicing down the highway. Nausea set in. It's only the drugs, I told myself. It's only the drugs.

"Where are we going?"

"Someplace you'll be safe," she said.

"You'll have to drive faster than that then," I said.

But she didn't press harder on the gas pedal, didn't speed us away from our impending death. If she looked in the rear-view mirror and saw rushing water, she didn't let me know. She only leaned her head back on the seat, a band of sweat creating a halo around her forehead.

"When I first met you, you were shining," she said.

I opened my eyes again, and could see horned faces forming out of the dark water. They strained their cheeks against the dark foam. I cowered into my chair and closed my eyes.

Maybe I should focus on something else.

"I'm sick of hearing about me," I said. "Tell me about you."

"I grew up in the Middle East, in a small fishing village. One day a man came to preach, but he had so many followers, they threatened to push him into the water. So I let him borrow my small boat to preach on so he wouldn't drown."

"And that's how you became a Saint."

"It's how I fell in love," she said. "I sold my boat and abandoned my home. My children. My wife. I threw myself at his feet and told him I'd be his slave because, without his light, I knew my organs would burst with grief."

"Then what happened?"

"I left him because I met you."

When I opened my eyes again, her head stretched across the road in a psychedelic blur. We passed a field full of shadow children dancing in a circle.

"I'm going to throw up," I said.

"We're almost there," Saint Peter said.

Don't focus on anything outside of the car, I told myself. If you focus on the blue Virgin Mary stickers on the dashboard in front of you and the torn up seats underneath you, then all of hell, with its screaming, nickering sea, might disappear.

The crosses faded from Saint Peter's arms, and in their place, bloomed acidic wounds.

"Cignus said you went to my school, but I don't remember you," I said, trying to ignore the dark water in the rearview mirror, the blurred landscape shifting into a funneled dream.

But as quickly as it came, the river disappeared.

"I was different back then," Saint Peter said.

I remembered myself back in Psychology class, right before I dropped out. I turned to the chapter on Paranoid Schizophrenia, expecting to find my mother's photograph. Instead, I found this:

- Auditory and visual hallucinations, such as hearing voices and seeing strange people
- Delusions and paranoia, such as believing everyone wants to poison them
- Difficulty forming or maintaining relationships
- Disorganized thought patterns and confusing language
- Messianic complex or believing they have superhuman powers
- *Suicidal thoughts and behavior*
- *An irrational fear of humanoid monsters that crawl out of dead trees*
- *A tendency to build Viking Ships out of junkyard scrap*
- *Propensity towards a boring death by drowning*
- *Attraction toward dangerous and selfish people - like artists*
- *Guilt for something that wasn't your fault that will follow you for the rest of your life*
- *Blahblahblah. Just die already.*

As the words mutated on the page, I tried to suppress my laughter, and started coughing. Jock Buddy kicked the back of my desk and told me he'd be fucking my ass in hell. I whipped my braid back in his face and told him I'd fuck his ass in the parking lot, but I wasn't paying attention to him. Really, I was thinking about my family's curse and how much longer it would be before it peeled back its foam lips and chased me down.

It wasn't fair. Jock Buddy would probably ditch the sneer and end up with a respectable career in marketing, and I'd be hospitalized, psychiatrized, and chased down like a rabid dog whenever I ditched my medicine.

Maybe in a past life I could've used my insanity as a shaman or a seer. But this was America, sister, where the only acceptable form of insanity is religion.

That day after psychology class I went into the bathroom. A girl stood in front of the mirrors examining a bleeding cut on her arm. She was frail and tall, with slender and knock-kneed Bambi legs. She wore thick, cat-eye glasses and hid her face underneath layers of heavy brown hair. She was a tragedy really, the kind of girl who would probably commit high school social suicide before she even had a chance to open her mouth.

"You cut too deep," I said.

"It wasn't me," she said.

"Also your mascara is running."

I dug into my purse and found a pack of makeup wipes.

"Here," I said.

She tossed her hair back. Her eyes were ghoulish, haunted. I'd seen eyes like that only once before, on a boy who couldn't sleep without tracking dirt.

"I've been looking for you," she said.

She gripped her cut arm, shaking. She didn't take the makeup wipes.

My hand began to shake as well.

"Looking for me? What did you want?" I asked.

She smeared my face with her blood.

"Nothing right now," she said, and left.

It'd been Saint Peter.

"How could I have forgotten?" I said.

That was where I recognized her from the night I found her tangled in lights in the artist's yard. Who could blame me for not remembering? The blue-haired girl in platforms, with drugs in her blood and scars heaving on her skin, hardly resembled the trembling, creep-shouldered brunette I met in a high school bathroom.

"We've been together lifetimes," Saint Peter said. "One day you'll remember."

This is how schizophrenia must work. It finds the white spaces and fills them in with rituals and astral logic. It reaches down into the dregs of the sub conscious and finds a broken girl who will look to you as her savior. What a pair we would make: the mad god, and her towering, bleeding saint. We could set up this van as a Tabernacle, and charge $20 for salvation and a t-shirt. We'd never have to get real jobs.

"Where are we going?" I asked for the third time.

"Somewhere safe," she said.

Saint Peter pulled the van over on the side of the road. We tried to bed down in the back with warm blankets, but, of course, neither of us could sleep with the universe exploding above our heads, the horse-headed nebula opening its mouth to scream, the earth but a moist eye. St. Peter lay on the floor of the van with her pupils big enough for horses to run through, sweating all over. She stripped off her clothes and huddled inside a blanket.

The demon rested her head on me and her black hair spread out across my lap like a fan.

"She is a dark and pretty thing," Saint Peter said, her chest heaving, each breath hissing hard through her teeth. "You should be proud to have her."

Whether she spoke to the demon, or me, I didn't know.

She unzipped the hunter's bow from a suede bag. She opened a can of bowstring wax, but instead of applying it to her bow, she drew patterns in it with her fingernails. She hummed underneath her breath - gospel hymns - ones that I'd never heard before.

If someone asked me then why I invited the demon into my bed, or why I brought her with me as I ran from my childhood home, I wouldn't have been able to say. She'd been chasing me my entire life, a night terror, the kind of monster, you can only hope, will terrify your children into obedience. But as I looked across the van at her, playing with Pluto by taunting her with the spiders dangling from her wrists, I only wanted to cling to her.

Right before sunrise, the demon, Pluto, and I went outside underneath the pale spatter of stars. We walked to the field off the highway. We were coming down from the high of the mushrooms. I grew sleepy and slow, my jaw aching. My skin seemed too heavy to carry anymore.

I almost expected the demon to burst into flames in the sunlight. But, when the sun hit her, she didn't ignite. She closed her eyes and inhaled the light. Wisps of dandelions blew into her hair.

It could've been an almost romantic moment, but then I thought of my mother, alone in a hospital bed. I thought of plastic tubes snaking around her arms and tugging at her veins, while nurses drugged her with enough tranquilizers to make sure she'd never walk straight again.

"I'm a terrible person," I said.

"Me too," the demon said, "but I wasn't a person for long."

"I'm letting my mother die."

"You could always go back," she said.

A crow landed on the demon's arm, trying to eat a centipede crawling in her hair. She grabbed the crow and twisted its head off. She ate it, tore its wings off and pressed them to her mouth. Its body fell into the grass. Pluto jumped out of my arms and started to play with its headless body, biting it, circling it.

"Look," she said. "I could be an angel."

She rubbed the bloodied wings against her lips, her cheek. Underneath their black feathers, she smiled at me.

"You're a monster," I said.

"You thought you were the only one?" she asked.

I should leave her. I could push her down into the grass and jump into the van and tell Saint Peter to drive drive drive.

She tried to touch my face with the black feathers. I stepped backwards.

"Keep those away from me."

Her smile faded. She dropped the feathers. They floated to the grass. My hands curled into fists. I'd raised them, ready to strike the demon.

I stared at them, taut with energy, as if they didn't belong to me. She didn't move to avoid an incoming blow, didn't flinch.

"I've waited for you," she said.

Slowly, still tense, I uncurled my fists.

She drew one of my shaking hands to her lips and gently kissed the knuckles. Her lips were smooth and dry.

"I came when you called me," she said. "I took care of you."

My stomach bottomed out when she looked at me. When she pressed her body against mine, my heart ached. She arched her back and I ran my fingers down her spine, each vertebra, one by one. I gathered her skirt in my hands and pushed it up against her thighs, squeezing until my knuckles turned white.

"Didn't I take care of you?" she asked.

I kissed her mouth. Kissed her again and again, breathing hard.

I always thought she was made of spiders and chitin, rotten water, but I touched only cool skin.

***

The demon and I went back to the van and Saint Peter climbed into the driver's seat. We arrived in the city in the middle of the night. It was not what I expected.

When You're Asleep, You Never Know Where Your Hands Will Be:

A Play

CHARACTERS

MAD GIRL: a schizophrenic loser, late teens

THE SAINT: a self-harming art model, late teens

DEMON: a shadow whose reality or unreality is disputed, late teens

THE WITCH: drug addict, possible reincarnation of Hecate, early twenties

PLUTO: a black cat, middle-aged

Act I

Scene One

[The stage is the living room of a dark, dilapidated house, owned by a diesel punk witch. The only light is the candle underneath THE WITCH'S face. THE WITCH sits on a burgundy couch. The couch is her throne. A pack of dogs lies sleeping at her feet. There are machines, like industrial tubing, embedded in her forehead. There are machines hooked into the crumbling wall behind her.]

[Enter Stage Left: SAINT and MAD GIRL, who is carrying PLUTO]

MAD GIRL. (To the Saint) You told me we were going somewhere safe.

THE SAINT. Yes, but nobody can keep you safe forever.

MAD GIRL. I'm going to throw up. Get me out of here.

THE WITCH. You don't even know where you are.

[THE WITCH blows the candles out. They are cast in darkness. There's a soft grinding noise coming through the walls. MAD GIRL cries out softly. There's a scratching sound like MAD GIRL is trying to tear the skin off her face]

THE WITCH. You shouldn't be acting that way. You're an old goddess, sister.

THE SAINT. She's dehydrated. She's malnourished. She hasn't been awake for years.

THE WITCH. Why would you ever fall asleep?

THE SAINT. (Whispering) Please, be kind to her.

[MAD GIRL begins to weep. THE SAINT presses MAD GIRL's face into her chest to muffle her crying. MAD GIRL's body convulses. PLUTO jumps out of MAD GIRL's arms]

THE WITCH. I'm getting sick of kindness.

THE SAINT. She's not ready to accept this.

THE WITCH. Well how long is it going to take? I'm getting bored. I have neural pathways you couldn't dream of, and you want me to just sit here and be nice?

THE SAINT. The plan was ruined.

THE WITCH. (Speaking to the invisible audience) I'm building a chaosphere out of used parts. I could destroy the universe, if I wanted to, but I haven't found another I like yet.

[A soft blue light starts glowing from above, growing slowly in intensity, illuminating the entire living room. The sleepy dogs at THE WITCH's feet stir. They're more like monsters than dogs, great black mastiffs with glossy fur. Their eyes are baby blue. Their claws are like glass. PLUTO lies among them. THE WITCH shifts on her throne, and, out of her lap spill eyeballs and little blue flowers]

MAD GIRL. (Whispering to THE SAINT) I want to go somewhere safe.

THE WITCH. (Overhearing) You'll never find a place like that. Now be quiet, and pay attention. I don't want to have to show you this again.

[The blue light gets brighter. The light reveals they're standing in front of dark blue curtains. The curtains part to reveal a small, dark, empty stage]

THE WITCH. (To MAD GIRL) Where did everything go? You can't come into my house and change whatever you want. Tell me what you've done!

MAD GIRL. This is the wrong play.

SAINT PETER. (Whispering to MAD GIRL) It's only the actors who are wrong.

[MAD GIRL tugs at the SAINT's jacket and at her hair. She's never known fear like this.]

[THE WITCH stands up abruptly from her throne. Her dogs begin barking and eating eyeballs off the floor. She's looking at the stage behind the stage. We cannot see her face]

THE WITCH. I did not cast you for this role.

[A soft blue spotlight casts down on the empty stage. DEMON appears to materialize on the stage from the blue light. MAD GIRL hardly recognizes her. DEMON is wearing gaudy bright red lipstick and a shimmering flapper dress. Her black hair has been tied in a topknot. The dogs keep barking.]

THE WITCH. Who let you in here?

[THE WITCH motions for her ghouls to head toward the stage. The ghouls writhe across the floor toward her, but when the demon holds her hand out, the ghouls stop.]

DEMON. I'm going to sing a lullaby.

[A microphone materializes on stage. The demon creeps toward it. Her motions are nearly too quick for the human eye, almost stopgap. She seems to walk through dimensions, flickering in and out of existence. She touches the microphone like a sex organ.]

DEMON. (Her voice reverberates throughout the stage. Only MAD GIRL exists for her in this moment.)

You know how lonely I get, honey,
waiting for you to come home.
I get so lonely, I lie down and listen to flowers grow.
We could be stars together.
You could shine and I would explode.
I'll build storm clouds for you
to dream on.
Cities for you
to rule in.
Oh, but even though I get so lonely,
I'll only wait for you, honey,
Wait until you come home and see
What a garden I've grown for you
All of these beautiful flowers
All of these beautiful trees.

THE WITCH. Love is the worst kind of pain.
THE SAINT. Then you've never been in pain.

[THE DEMON is still singing. Her hair is coming undone. Her lipstick is smeared down her chin, as if melting]

DEMON. (Continuing to sing)
You know how lonely I get, honey,
waiting for you to come home.
I get so lonely I lie down and—

[The microphone stops working, cutting the demon off.]

THE WITCH. I'm done with children's games.
MAD GIRL. She wasn't finished. Let her finish.
THE WITCH. This isn't how the ritual works.
THE SAINT. You're a new goddess? Then do something different.
THE WITCH. (To THE SAINT) I've never heard you be so disrespectful. Something must be wrong. I'll forgive you this once.
MAD GIRL. (Pulling at her hair, in mental pain) How does the song go again? I can't remember.

[THE WITCH crosses the room toward MAD GIRL and THE SAINT, trailing behind her a gown eaten away by dust, sewn together with bones. The tubing attaching her head to the wall stretches out as she moves. The dogs follow after her, sniffing at the feet. MAD GIRL pulls away from THE SAINT's arm. She is shaking all over. THE WITCH touches MAD GIRL's chin.]

THE WITCH. Listen carefully to me.

[MAD GIRL appears barely coherent. Her head is lolling against her shoulder. The dogs sniff at her arms and legs. Her clothes appear to be disintegrating. THE WITCH embraces her, but the motion is aggressive, like grabbing a disobedient toddler.]

THE WITCH. Are you listening to me? I'm going to give you a potion to wake you up.

MAD GIRL. (Delirious, trying to pull away) I am awake. I'm only in the wrong play.

[Fog rolls onto the stage. The grinding noise coming through the walls get louder. DEMON has stopped singing. Her hair is completely undone. The microphone is gone. The blue light fades, and DEMON steps down toward MAD GIRL. THE WITCH releases MAD GIRL, who goes spinning into the DEMON's arms]

DEMON (To MAD GIRL). I could sew you a robe of stars.

MAD GIRL. I'm not my mother.

DEMON. You have her mouth.

MAD GIRL. Don't say that ever again.
DEMON. You have her head.
MAD GIRL. I won't be her. I won't.
DEMON. Whatever you are, you'll never be the same again.

[The grinding noise through the wall grows even louder.]

MAD GIRL. What the fuck is that noise?

[DEMON kisses MAD GIRL on the mouth, leaving a smear of lipstick]

THE WITCH. A new kind of medicine.

Scene Two

[They are all standing on the overgrown lawn of THE WITCH's dark, dilapidated house. The lighting is dim, to suggest nighttime. THE WITCH is summoning ghouls to build a giant machine in the middle of the lawn. Ghouls crawl out of her skin. They fall from her wrists like, and, on the ground they writhe into human shapes. When they're fully formed, they pick up scraps of metal and bend them, weld them together with their teeth.]

MAD GIRL. Why can't anyone hear me screaming?

THE SAINT. This is a dark city and a lonely city.

MAD GIRL. I'm going crazy. You were supposed to help me.

[Laughter comes from every direction, including the audience]

THE SAINT. I am helping you.

MAD GIRL. You can't even stand up straight.

THE SAINT. (Laughing.) You know I'm a fuck up. I did too much cocaine.

THE WITCH. Have some more. Mad girl, you too. You look sober.

MAD GIRL. No more drugs, okay? No more drugs. That was the worst acid I've ever had. I was fighting lions in the Coloseum for a thousand years.

THE WITCH. I am the queen here. You do as I say.

[The dogs bound out of the front door of the dilapidated house, which is really an empty frame, rolled onto the stage. There are now ten or twelve dogs instead of six. They've grown bigger. Their eyes are no longer blue, but silver. Some of them carry deerskin pelts in their mouths. Others wear the ribcages and horns of deer. They surround MAD GIRL.]

THE WITCH. Hold out your hand.

MAD GIRL. What is happening to me?

THE WITCH. Haven't you ever been to a higher state of consciousness?

MAD GIRL. If that's what this feels like, I don't want to be.

[One of the dogs spits slobbery pills into MAD GIRL's hand.]

MAD GIRL. Gross.

THE WITCH. Can't you see I'm trying to help you? Take them.

MAD GIRL. No way.

THE WITCH. I've sunk Viking ships on hydra-headed pieces of ice. I've conquered distant galaxies with ships made from the ether of ghosts. I've taken the Internet to parallel universes and used it to enslave kings with its knowledge. Do as I say, and take those fucking pills.

MAD GIRL. (Backing away). I don't care. I won't.

[The DEMON appears behind MAD GIRL. She moves. It's sensual and slow. She wraps her arms around MAD GIRL, mirroring her body, and presses her ear into her mouth.]

DEMON. All you have to do is hold your arms out, and I'll take your hands.

[MAD GIRL, reluctantly, swallows the whole handful of pills. Her eyes widen and her entire body goes slack. She falls onto the grass in slow motion. The ghouls step over MAD GIRL's inert body as they continue to work on the machine. None of the other characters on stage move or speak, as if they're frozen in time. This continues for several uncomfortable, long minutes.]

THE WITCH. (Her voice startling and unfamiliar after the silence) She's hopeless. She's not going to wake up.

THE SAINT. You don't know her like I do.

[DEMON bends down to MAD GIRL, her hair trailing over MAD GIRL's eyes, her mouth. MAD GIRL has gone unresponsive. She is in a distant universe. We can assume she is having the worst trip of her life.]

DEMON. (Speaking to the inert MAD GIRL) You can push through fear to the other side. It's like piercing a membrane.

THE WITCH. If Mad Girl could only get past this petty idea of consequence and causality, she'd transcend her worthless human consciousness.

DEMON. (Looking up at THE WITCH) That doesn't sound right.

THE SAINT. (To THE WITCH) What are you talking about?

THE WITCH. Never mind, I forget. Most things are still made out of meat.

[The machine groans. Its mechanical arms move up and down, as if being pulled by levers from the inside. It is painted a dark black, like the ghouls themselves. MAD GIRL writhes in the grass, choking.]

THE WITCH. (Looking down at MAD GIRL.) I will admit. She is strong, and brave. But old goddesses can be so stupid sometimes.

THE SAINT. (Pointing upwards) Look up.

[THE WITCH, THE SAINT, and DEMON look up into the sky. Baby spiders like black wisps, floating on almost-invisible, thin spider webs, are floating above them on currents of air.]

THE SAINT. Where are they going?

THE WITCH. Toward the city. Like all things made of meat. They go there to die.

DEMON. Never kill a spider. If you do, they'll never show you the way again.

[THE SAINT and DEMON continue to stare at the spiders floating past. The dogs surround them, barking and slobbering. They bite the air, trying to eat the spiders that float too low.]

[THE SAINT kneels beside MAD GIRL and shakes her. MAD GIRL is unresponsive. Oil drips from the mouth of the machine and flows around them, killing the grass. They now appear to be standing on an island, surrounded by oil. The rushing sound of the river pierces the walls of the stage. DEMON looks around, searching for the source of the sound. Some of the baby spiders, flying past, snarl into her hair.]

DEMON. She's getting close.

THE WITCH. It's too soon. She'll destroy us, and we'll have to do this all over again.

THE SAINT. My brother. I could kill him for what he did.

DEMON. Her anger is like a bullet train. Her anger is like the Gulf War. Her anger is as vast and meaningless as dark matter.

THE SAINT. We're going to die if Lily doesn't wake up.

WITCH. Listen to me. Listen.

[The grinding of the machine stops. The rushing of the river stops. The ghouls fade away.]

WITCH. She's never going to wake up.

Act II

Scene One

[The stage is a Viking long ship on a foam-white sea. It's nighttime, and the stars ignite like firecrackers. MAD GIRL writhes in pain on the narrow, wooden deck of the ship, with PLUTO, licking at her face. Ghouls row the oars, faceless and silent. THE SAINT adjusts the sails.]

[A scream echoes off in the distance, somewhere far off across the fog-covered water. MAD GIRL lurches up, gasping.]

MAD GIRL. I'm confused. When will this play be over?

THE SAINT. (Still working the sails.) Your brain, in its fragile state, is unable to comprehend the situation. You've stopped processing reality in the normal way.

MAD GIRL. You mean I took too many drugs. This isn't real.

THE SAINT. Reality has nothing to do with this. Focus on the real issue.

[MAD GIRL gets to her feet and runs to the side of the ship. She vomits white into the foam-white sea.]

MAD GIRL. (Wiping vomit from her mouth, trying to keep her footing on the rocking ship) And what is the real issue?

THE SAINT. Something is after you.

[An enormous, black tentacle rises out of the foam-white water. It's darker than the dark sky; its suckers are like luminescent, radioactive spots. It slaps the water, causing huge waves in the water. MAD GIRL falls backwards on the wood as the ships rocks back and forth.]

MAD GIRL. (Frantic) Did you see that? There's a monster out there!

THE SAINT. (Still working the sails, not really paying attention) It's the wrong one.

MAD GIRL. But what do I do?

THE SAINT. We keep sailing.

MAD GIRL. But it's going to kill us. We need to get rid of it.

THE SAINT. (Bending down to pick up something from the deck) Well, this is yours anyways.

[THE SAINT tosses MAD GIRL the hunter's bow and a quiver of arrows. MAD GIRL catches both. She loops the quiver around one shoulder. She holds the bow, run her fingers up and down the wood. She points the bow out into the water, tests the string, as if she is familiar with this weapon. As if she's used it before.]

MAD GIRL. I have a disease.
THE SAINT. They've told you many lies.
MAD GIRL. This is The Witch's fault.
THE SAINT. No. There are many people to blame, but not her.

[The giant tentacle rises up above the water once more, and then slaps the water. The Viking long ship goes into a tailspin. MAD GIRL, PLUTO, and THE SAINT struggle to keep from being thrown overboard. The shadows do not move, and are not moved by the spinning of the ship.]

MAD GIRL. Someone is calling me from the ocean.

[MAD GIRL braces her feet against the side of the ship. The dragon-headed mast begins to tip toward the waters, about to sink. MAD GIRL notches an arrow in her bow. She takes aim at the tentacles rising out of the waters]

THE SAINT. You've killed this monster before.

MAD GIRL. Then, why is it still here?

[The tentacles grab the sails and rip them apart. Sparks, lights, electricity, barrel down from the sky. The shadows have stopped rowing. The oars fall into the ocean. The shadows remain motionless]

THE SAINT. There will always be monsters to kill.

MAD GIRL. Just tell me how to fix this. I have a thousand degree fever.

THE SAINT. Everything is telling you. Look where we are. I'm trying my best because I've never met anyone with a heart like yours.

[As the ship sinks, MAD GIRL struggles to hold on. She slings the quiver of arrows over her shoulder and clutches the bow to her chest. Her deerskin blows in the wind, but her antlers remain fixed, as if fused to her skull.]

MAD GIRL. When will this be over?

THE SAINT. Not now. Maybe not ever. But I'll always be here with you.

[Blood drips down the arms and chest of THE SAINT. The torn white sails clothe her like a shroud and lift her into the air.]

THE SAINT. You have to try to remember.
MAD GIRL. It's destroying everything. Won't you help me?
[MAD GIRL shoots another arrow into the tentacle. One of its glowing suckers bursts, showering her with hot metal, incinerating half her face.]
THE SAINT. It's like bursting through a membrane.

[MAD GIRL falls off the Viking long ship and into the water. She falls and falls through the ocean. The hunter's bow falls with her. The dead Kraken falls with her. It's spitting sparks, convulsing, and its flesh is necrotizing and turning gray. Because this is psychosis, MAD GIRL doesn't need to breathe.]

[MAD GIRL stretches her arms outwards, down into the water. Two pale arms reach up and grasp them. They touch. Their fingers intertwine.]

DEMON. (Her voice echoing through the water) I'm with you. If I whisper to you from the bottom of the earth, all the seas will boil.

MAD GIRL. Hold me.
DEMON. I am holding you. Wake up.

Scene Two

[DEMON stands on the stage behind the stage. There is no microphone. A blue spotlight illuminates DEMON, but everything else is dark. She looks almost human in her makeup and jazz outfit. She's holding PLUTO in her arms, petting her head. Everyone else is gone.]

DEMON. Lily.

DEMON. (After a pause) Lily. Halloween only comes once a year.

[From offstage, a saxophone plays softly]

DEMON. Lily, every deer grows antlers. Can't you feel your body beginning to take on a new shape? Can you feel that pain shooting through your head? Your skull is becoming a crown. You don't know it yet, because your bone is covered in velvet like blood. When you're ready, the velvet will shed away, and the bones will die, but you will be left with a most beautiful treasure. And I'll be there with you, to lead you to our palace beyond the garden. Beyond the woods.

DEMON. Remember the night you crawled into our tree to hide from her? I was hiding that night too, you know. She was angry then, but she's angrier now. Do you remember her name? I'm sure you do.

[The saxophone stops playing]

DEMON. Come. Halloween is almost here.

[PLUTO jumps from her arms and runs off the stage.]

DEMON. I'll only say this once.

Part Five:

A Letter to the Girl That Ate My Skin

MY DEAREST DEMON:

I'm sure you remember Halloween night when I became an apocalyptic angel with torn netting wings and a toy pistol at my hip. Saint Peter wore a bloodied crown of thorns, and told me she dressed as herself. The Witch, who went by the name of Genie those days, sat on the couch in blue velvet, with a basket of candy to give to children that never visited.

As for you, well, you were never into costumes, baby.

At midnight we snorted cocaine together on the white edge of the bathtub while boys pounded on the door. When Saint Peter unlocked the door I ran out and the boys stroked my hair, my cheek.

"Is that pistol real?" they asked. "Do you have any drugs?"

"Kiss me, I'm Salvador Dali," I said.

I think what I meant to say was, "I am drugs," but I don't think they were listening to me anyway.

I went into the kitchen, where more boys took turns drinking shots of cold vodka. I took shot after shot.

"I feel invincible," I said as I crouched on the ground over my broken shot glass.

Later, you came to me through the bathroom window, as I lay on the floor, shivering and nauseous. In the next room, Saint Peter, Genie, and the boys laughed. Vomit rimmed the toilet rimmed the hem of my dress.

"Why are you on the floor? Weren't you going to be a scientist?" you asked.

My dearest demon, I can tell that you've never had a girlfriend before.

And you speak as if you've never used your voice, like an Ophelia, crippled, with her hands pulled back, whispering lisps. Maybe until that day when I first crawled inside your tree, you never spoke at all.

From the window, you held your hand out to me. I stood shaking and you led me outside onto the lawn, underneath the rustling stars. In your arms I became a girl of exposed nerves, without skin or blood.

You whirled me around until I was dizzy and at the edge of the lawn, on the glittering concrete, vomited again. I wiped at the back of my mouth, heaving, ribs splayed out. In my delirium, I bent down and kissed your feet.

I think I'm beginning to understand.

You don't believe anything this dirty world says, so you can tread right over it, as if it's a layer of thick scum that skins the water.

I kissed your ankles and your knees. I am not afraid anymore of your spiders and the cold spots on your shoulders.

It appeared you were floating. You had a string in your teeth and when you tugged, the trees collapsed.

At that point, I couldn't tell if your skin was a sort of hallucinogenic drug, or if I was just going crazy again.

You slipped your tongue inside my mouth, and when you pulled it out, the colors of the earth inverted. The sky deepened into a rich darkly green, and the grass, turned into velvet. You took me into the broiling meadow where the blue flowers were Technicolor and sweating purple.

Beyond the meadow lay a chasm.

"I'm not ready to go down there," I said.

"You've been down there before," you responded.

"One day you're going to murder me," I said.

"Never."

"Eat my bones."

"Never."

"Take me into hell."

You purred and rubbed your head against my legs. Your insect noise pulsed through my bones. I writhed in the grass in my torn angel wings. I could taste the earth through my fingers, and it tasted sweet.

Demon, you are drugs and you are my Salvador Dali. You are the monster under my bed and the girl my mother would've wanted me to marry.

You took the toy pistol from my hip and pressed it to my heart. Bang. Bang.

I would not go down into the chasm, even though my outstretched fingers touched the edge, even though it called to me in my father's voice.

"Treat me like a real girl," I said. "Take me somewhere nice first."

You could've pushed me over the edge, but instead, you led me to a cool grove and fed me water that trickled down your wrists until I stopped dry heaving.

For a while after that, we didn't wander into the forest anymore. You took me to the roof and taught me how to make my body float with my mind. We traveled to the city and walked on the side of skyscrapers, your hair a guide around my ankles and wrists. On a boat in the middle of a lake we drank port wine and dined on leeks, foie gras, and tabs of acid.

We stepped on the water and skimmed across it as if it were glass. The water cooled and calmed. When the moon stretched across the lake, we saw sunken boats, little gold coins, and a dead boy twenty years old with his skull a nest.

We took a road trip with Saint Peter in the night, all the while huffing nitrous oxide and smoking joints. You trilled behind me, touching my shoulders, running your fingers through my hair. Saint Peter said we'd keep driving until we touched God. We'd stick our fingers right into his pearlescent center.

We made it to the edge of the city before running out of gas and money.

Demon, many would disapprove of our relationship. This became apparent that night, on the side of the road, the nitrous oxide evaporating in my blood, when you sat in my lap and a black van swerved past as the driver yelled, "faggots!" And how later, when we stopped at a diner and the waitress asked your order, you let a tarantula loose into her blouse.

I've cradled in my lap Charlie's insomniac shuddering head, and I've been fucked half dead by the artist, shrouded in blood and flies, but nobody's ever held me like you. You are warm underneath bed sheets, my baby cocoon, and even though our bed is covered in insects, I would invite no one else. When you tilt my head back with your skinny fingers and whisper "Hush, hush, close your eyes," you give me dreams in which I am a goddess.

After the money ran out, I turned into a grifter and a thief. Maybe you were content to eat locusts and stick your hands into honeycombs, but I never got used to the textures. I could've just gone back home and gone to college on Momma's money, like most young punks. Though, have you noticed you can actually see the sky here? The air doesn't taste sour and smoky. I can run from one side of the street to the other without collapsing because there's not six inches of black factory tar lodged in my lungs. It's clear and clean here. The sky is not chasing me with threats of cancer and emphysema; there is no spillover of carnivorous plants feeding off the toxins of the earth, no Momma to wheedle away from the mask that would transform her into an Exorcist.

I could breathe.

I started going with Saint Peter to bars, to steal wallets from young men while we kissed them. She hooked me up with a friend of a friend, and I dealt weed out of our rickety small bedroom to college kids, bored scientists, and wives with bad backs. I lifted toothpaste and razors from drug stores, socks and panties from high-end clothing stores, with my aluminum foil lined bag to block the security detectors. Nobody ever taught me how to manage my money, oh the tragedy, so I wasted what little I earned. I bought a plush blue coat I found in a vintage store. A bone necklace for my sweetheart. A sushi dinner with escolar and a bottle of imported Japanese sake. A night at a dance club chasing down ecstasy dealers and girls with cocaine noses in the bathroom.

You don't need to save money when, at any moment, you feel as if you will die. It's like your heart is tied to a string around your fist, an invisible clock ready to be smashed.

Do you remember when we convinced the faux-French "Francois" into taking us home for dinner? At least he wasn't lying about being rich, though it's kind of hard to fake a good suit and well-bred posture. I remembered, after he fed us Chinese leftovers and a two hundred dollar bottle of wine (he made sure we knew how much it cost), you reached over and loosened his tie.

"I swear I've seen you before," the Francois said, as you leaned over and gave him a mouth of bugs.

"Hey Francois," I said, mad drunk on his wine. "Aren't you going to fall in love with us?"

When I went to set the wine glass down on the table, it fell to the floor and shattered. I didn't care, I was already rolling across the table, my back crushing the violet vase and bending the silverware. Francois, what golden eyes you have, I've never noticed how your swallow gets stuck in your throat. Never invite a mad girl and her demon into your house; they'll ruin the good carpet.

Now just drape my skin over your arm, hiss, I'm trailing piss and honey, hiss. I could unzip for you. I'll be your red and warbling muscle-bound monster, and you'll be my toy.

Demon, this language has been inside of me since I can remember. It's been eating its way through my organs, poison rot and festering crystal. It felt so natural to touch his lips where the spider clung, and open my mouth to hissssssssss.

To ke-ke-ke-ke-ke-ke.

Francois, with the golden eyes, coughed up the spider. He breathed the word "monster," and it struck me as hilarious. They've called me child murderer, baby girl killer, but never "monster." And never a "monster" with such sober shock. I loomed over him, bigger, monstrous, ready to roar. Yes, I'll be your monster, Francois the rich and Frenchless. Look at the acid scars on my throat and arms. Look at the scars on my thighs as I hike up my skirt. You wouldn't believe the stories I could tell you.

We fled his house dressed in vintage dresses, with diamond and pearl necklaces strung around our throats. We ran off laughing into the darkness. When you outran me, your hair reached back to tease my throat. I discarded my heavy lace dress in the middle of the street, to catch up to you.

Only at the end of the street, at the DEAD END sign next to the bridge, did I stop to ask.

"What am I doing here?"

You pulled a string of black pearls out of your throat.

"How did I get here?"

I could've been a scientist, at least that's what I tell myself. In truth, they'd never let a dirty skinned lesion-filled little brat like me into their hallowed halls. And why should they? I couldn't even find Cignus in the sky.

Police sirens wailed. Francois must've called them after we ran off with his grandmother's trinkets.

I grabbed you by the arm and we dove off the bridge into the tunnels.

In the tunnel, the sound of dripping pipes in our ears, you were still pulling pearls out of your throat and wrapping them around your wrists. Overhead the police cars pulled over. Flashlights shone across the dried-up creek.

I took your hand again, and we delved deeper into the network of tunnels.

I'm such a silly girl. "What am I doing? How did I get here?" I should've known by then that you never answer those questions. The stars would swallow and spit me up first.

Soon we were laughing again, tugging on the black pearls around each other's necks, kissing and stumbling in the sewer water. We went further down into the tunnels, chasing each other, busting cobwebs. Our laughs echoed for miles, but if the police ever decided to hike up their britches and delve down here, they'd never find us.

I came across a full-length mirror, a wooden chair, a pallet, smokes, and half a bottle of Jameson. People must live down here. Scavengers, more tired than the two of us, huddled underneath faucets and pipes in a place where the police wouldn't disturb them.

Maybe they'd go blind down here, Demon, but not us. Our eyes are shining. They've been waiting for the dark.

"Why are we here?" you asked, mocking, tongue pushed between your teeth.

I gripped you by the throat, black pearls crushing between my knuckles.

"You're mine, isn't that what you said?"

You gently tapped my fingers around your throat.

"Yours," you whispered.

I fell into the chair, and it slid across the tunnel floor. I was alive, squirming, and hot. The demon knelt in front of me and her hands slid up my knees.

I was full of nighttime. If I wanted to, I could bite through my skin, fashion for myself a new body.

And yet the drugs had worn off long ago, hadn't they?

I knotted my fists in your hair.

"I'm going to eat you alive," I said.

You pushed up my skirt, the wooden chair splintering against my bare skin.

The dark concealed my blushing cheeks. Your eyes rolled up into your head as you inhaled me. You scratched my knees, whispering in spider language.

Whispering, "Love," whispering, "Fuck."

You were cool wherever I touched you, but my skin boiled.

Look at me now, Mom, I wanted to say.

See how I've tamed the creature that once tormented me. She's my pet now, spider girl with the pink tongue. See how she shivers when I wrap my legs around her small waist. See how she pants. See how her face screams with lightning when I ask her, "Do you want it, do you want it, want me, want me." When I knot her hair in my fingers and pull her closer.

See me say:

"Drink, baby, drink. Don't you look away. I know I once pushed you away, cursed you, called you a bad thing. I would've killed you if I got my hands around your throat, but now, that's over. I want you to drink."

And when you pressed your mouth between my legs, when I felt your teeth, I transformed into an animal, legs digested, head twitching, my organs spilling out before me. I wanted to speak your name, but I didn't know your name, I'd never know your name. So it was "Demon, Demon, Demon, Demon," my tongue melting in my mouth, my toes smoking in my shoes.

Maybe the ghosts of people who lived down here lurked in corners of the tunnel, trying to find where they left their Jameson, wanting a place to sleep. And here were two girls, fucking in their chair, in front of their mirror.

But it didn't really matter, because, God, your tongue was so cool.

I came hard, black spots dancing in my eyes.

You said to me, "My horned goddess, they're beautiful."

I looked into the mirror.

There was a girl there, with velvet-tipped horns growing straight out of her head. I reached up and touched them, soft on the edges, glass-white. They were horns, and the girl was I.

I leaned back in the chair and my horns scraped against the concrete wall.

"My family will be so proud," I said. "Their daughter, horned goddess, Queen of the deer. I'll never get a sweater over my head again."

I touched the horns again, just to make sure they were still there. They must've been growing for years. It'd taken the inverted night, the chase, demon sex in this tunnel, for me to see them.

"Beautiful," the demon whispered.

I touched my chin, my mouth, my hands trembling, and you crawled into my lap and kissed me everywhere my fingertips fell.

A fantasy that I have sometimes:

In the middle of the night we toss in our dirty bed. Someone's burned us bad, and we're sick with the stench of cheap drugs. I grasp your fingers, sweating.

Then we sink.

We hold each other as we sink through the floor and miles of strata, until we arrive at a grand hall. It's the land of the gods. When we rise we shake off those bad drugs and sweat. We realize why we struggle and shake, why we've become losers and deadbeats and grifters and junkies. That world above didn't belong to us. We were curious fools; we wanted clean air when we could've been breathing jewels.

But now we can go home.

My throne is waiting for me, and as I walk toward it, my blood turns into wet rubies.

When I sit down, I see my reflection in the mirror at the end of the hall. My horns are fully-grown and quivering with gold. My body is coated in silver and my fingernails drip with sweet drugs, the sweetest you've ever tasted. They're drugs with no bad hangover and no cheap burn. No comedown, no overdose. One taste and you'll never dare to leave.

With a finger, I beckon you to me. You walk with a pack of dogs quelling in your hair. You are my consort, my queen. My demon and my slave. I spread my legs and you kneel.

Your eyes are festering.

You eat my silver skin. It's a slow and fine feast. First you shred the skin of my feet away from my bone, into tiny strips to dissolve on your tongue. My legs and knees are next. You glow as you swallow pieces. When you suck my fingernails the drugs melt your skin into pale silk.

In the tunnels below the city, we didn't encounter any monsters or homeless knife boxers. Not even a shuddering, lone policeman, praying his flashlight battery wouldn't die. I pulled down my skirt and we left the way we'd come, through the entrance underneath the bridge. We emerged underneath the night sky. I no longer heard the sirens. I felt crystals expanding in my blood.

You peeled your dress off and threw your pearls in the weeds. You were naked before me with the moon trapped in your stomach. You ran and I caught you in my arms.

I whispered, "We'll never have this again."

"We already have," you said, but I was mourning you already.

You bounded into the empty creek. I threw away my stolen jewelry and chased after you. I'd find you and I'd catch you. You wanted me to catch you, up in the trees with your hair whispering, your arms snarled in the branches. I'd find you pale and naked, squeezing the sky between your knees. You'd pretend to be stuck up there, kicking your feet, your playful smile poisonous enough to kill snakes. I'd press my head to the tree trunk and offer my horns for your descent.

And in that hall of gods, I will whisper:

"Momma was wrong when she told me I'd eat them alive.

"Here my baby, eat this feast I've made of me."

Part Six:

Machine Like a Baby's Fist

Twenty-One

I LURCHED AWAKE IN a cold bath, naked and numb, unable to even scream. I pulled myself out of the tub and onto the tiles. For several long seconds I felt I couldn't breathe, my hair wrapped like a fist in my mouth. I crawled across the floor and ripped a towel off the rack to cover myself.

Saint Peter and Genie sat at the kitchen table, drinking tea in the dark. I knew it had been dark for a long time.

Saint Peter ran toward me. She smoothed my wet hair, touched my face, felt my heart.

"Oh god. Lily."

"Why was I in the tub?"

"Do you remember last night?" she asked.

"I don't remember anything. I'm freezing."

"You wouldn't wake up. No matter what we did."

"You just left me in there?" I asked. "My head feels like a goddamn cathedral bell. Everything hurts."

"You should go to bed," Saint Peter said.

But I couldn't sleep, because, maybe next time, I would wake up in the center of a frozen lake, or in a black tar pit. I popped the last of my aspirin. The water heater didn't work, so I took a cold shower. My razor was too dull for me to shave and the tiny bar of soap disintegrated between my fingers.

I thought of how many people must die each year from slipping in the shower. Probably thousands.

I couldn't find a brush, but at least the hair dryer still worked. I ran my fingers through my hair, trying to untangle the knots. My head kept throbbing despite the aspirin.

I threw on ragged, dirty clothes. I couldn't remember the last time I'd done laundry. We ran out of detergent a long time ago. I just took a shower, but I already smelled like sweat and grass. I curled my feet against the cold tiles, and they cracked. I stretched, and the bones in my back cracked. Nausea hit me. I ran to the toilet to vomit, but there was nothing in my stomach. I gagged and gagged.

I emerged from the bathroom again to find the sun had risen. It seemed like it'd been months since sunlight filtered through the house.

Saint Peter threw her cardigan over my shoulders because I couldn't stop clenching my teeth with cold. I sat at the table, cross-legged, tucking my blue feet underneath me. Genie stood at the kitchen countertop. The black dogs lay around her feet.

"Why does my head hurt so bad?" I asked.

"You really don't remember what happened?" Saint Peter said.

Something moved in my periphery.

Three dirty-faced, tall boys stood in the entryway. I hadn't even heard the front door open, or footsteps sound through the house. Their eyes darted around the room, refusing to make eye contact. Their fingers twitched with involuntary spasms. I couldn't distinguish one from the other and I recognized none of them.

"You said you had a fourth," one said after a long pause.

"Oh," I said. "Oh. You're talking to me."

I darted out of the kitchen and grabbed the weed stashed in my bedroom. When I came back, Genie had turned away from the stove. The dogs ran toward the boys and sniffed their hands and legs.

"Would you like some tea?" she asked.

I was sure they'd never walked into a punk house, at six in the morning, to be greeted by a red headed witch, dressed in a crushed velvet cloak, holding a silver tea tray, with a pack of black dogs quelling at their feet. And all the while, her outstretched arms bleeding sigils, her smile not quite a smile, the kettle going off with a scream.

The dogs started barking.

The boys didn't demand that I weigh the baggie on a scale, or try to haggle the price. They threw the money on the kitchen table and ran.

We laughed about the way their eyes scanned the room, like they were expecting police to burst out of the walls, and how they shied away from the dogs as if they were foaming at the mouth. The Witch poured us more tea in silver cups. She served us biscuits, fresh from the oven. Saint Peter fed crumbs to the dogs underneath the table.

As I ate, my headache faded. The sunlight coming through the windows warmed my face.

"Can you imagine," Saint Peter said, tugging on her blue hair with blood underneath her fingernails, "anyone scared of us?"

The dogs nudged Saint Peter's knees.

"You're spoiling them," Genie said.

She rummaged through the freezer. It was normally empty, but as if through witch magic, it now overflowed with frozen food.

"Who wants hash browns?" she asked.

"I'm starving. It feels like it's been years," I said.

We didn't eat very often. We couldn't afford to eat and support drug habits at the same time. I justified it to myself, even on the nights when I cried in bed after a comedown, serotonin in my brain depleted after a night of partying on cocaine and MDMA. As long as I wasn't shooting up heroin and meth, I'd be okay, I thought. I'm not a real drug addict. And it was for a good cause. Maybe the river, with its boiling, rushing current of dead children, and Charlie's pale, veiled face, could be suppressed with the right type of crystalline alkaloid.

Maybe vicodin and xanax bought on the street could make my dreams, like smears of paint, indecipherable from one another. Charlie, jumping into the water, would become a black wave. Cignus, flies buzzing across his face, my mother wrapping me in butcher paper. It would all smear into shades of green and blue.

Not quite sweet dreams. But close enough.

"Do you know what I miss?" Saint Peter said. "Greek food."

"Weren't you a Greek fisherman?"

" A saint for much longer" she said. "I don't even remember how to gut a fish."

The Witch cooked the frozen hash browns, humming to herself. Someone had placed a small, potted houseplant in the center of the kitchen table, with yellow daffodils, and for once a plant wasn't coiling to strike me like a snake.

"I wish we had TV," I said. "I always watched Carl Sagan when I was hung-over."

"We don't have TV, but we have Wi-Fi," The Witch said.

Only an hour ago I'd woken up in a bathtub full of ice, hadn't I?

"I'd kill for a gyro," Saint Peter said, "or some dolmades."

"If you walk into a Greek restaurant looking like this, they might believe you."

I reached across the table and took her wrists in my hands.

Her wounds were green and scaly. I saw acid burns from plants and puncture wounds from snakebites, venom tattooed underneath her skin.

I couldn't distinguish my arms from hers.

"Strange." I said.

"What's strange?" she asked.

I let go.

"I just. I don't think I've been sleeping enough."

The demon crept from her nesting place on the ceiling, clutching Pluto to her chest. She sat at the table. Genie prepared her a plate of biscuits and a cup of tea, but the demon didn't touch it. Her teeth were full of shining bug shells. She played with a Daddy Long Legs that ran across her palms, darting in and out of her fingers. I held my hand out, and the Daddy Long Legs crawled onto my fingers, across the back of my hand.

"I used to be so scared of these," I said.

The Daddy Long Legs, its legs like bent wires, walked back to the demon's arm, then climbed into her hair.

I took a sip of tea. At first it tasted sweet, but masked a bitterness underneath.

"What's in this, anyway?" I asked.

"Sagewort," The Witch said, not turning away from the stove.

"Oh."

My insides spasmed.

"Do you know another word for sagewort?" The demon asked.

I didn't answer because the ripples in my cup of tea turned red and my stomach felt ready to fall out.

"Wormwood," the demon said.

I looked down in my lap. A bloodstain bloomed across my shirt. I pulled it up, my hands shaking, and found one of The Witch's sigils, etched into my stomach, where my wound used to be.

"That's weird." I said, the first thing I could think to say.

I felt fine only a moment ago.

"She's having a miscarriage," Saint Peter said.

"Let's lay her down," Genie said.

"No," I said. "Keep her away from me. She poisoned my tea."

Pluto jumped into my lap. The dogs surrounded me, slobbering and heaving. Their noses touched my bare legs. I thought they'd tear my skin apart. I pushed their heads away.

"I can't be having a miscarriage," I said.

Genie threw aside her velvet cloak, and underneath she wore a suit of rusted chainmail. Only then did I notice her red hair, knotted and dirty, as if it hadn't been washed for years, and her fingernails, caked in black dirt. Her eyes quivered with astral fire that cast a shadow across the entire room. I couldn't feel the sunshine anymore.

The skin of her fingers peeled back and ghouls sprouted out of her bones.

"Why did you poison me?" I murmured.

The demon caught me before I hit my head on the floor. Pluto skittered away. The demon and Saint Peter dragged me to the couch in the living room.

"Get me out of here," I said, squeezing my stomach between my fists, my face breaking out in a sweat. "I'm not pregnant."

"Well, not anymore," Genie said.

"Why are you hurting me?"

I closed my eyes and reached out for the demon. Her hands were far away, so far away. The living room stretched into a coliseum. I thought I'd never touch her again, but her spindly, cool fingers reached across the impossible distance and grasped my wrists.

"We were so happy. I found you in a tree," I said.

My stomach spasmed again.

"Breathe," Saint Peter said.

"Fuck. I took the last of my aspirin."

Saint Peter placed a wet towel against my forehead and a dry towel underneath my legs.

"I found you in the tree. Wasn't that only yesterday?" I asked.

"You don't remember what happened yesterday, do you?" the demon asked.

"No. But tell me we were happy once."

"Yes," she said. "We were."

I pulled the wet towel over my eyes and mouth. I twisted onto my stomach, but it didn't ease the pain. I pressed my hand between my legs, but I couldn't stop the flow. The blood spilling from me could've lifted the couch up and carried me away.

"The blood vessels in the velvet provide nutrients to the deer's horns," the demon said.

"I swear you've said this before."

"I've rehearsed it."

"I'm dying," I said. "And we were having such a nice breakfast."

The couch rocked underneath me. Like a boat. Like a Viking ship.

They surrounded me - Saint Peter, The Witch, Pluto, the dogs, the demon. They seemed to grow multiple limbs, sprout proboscis from their heads. They touched me with hands and snouts and teeth, touches that zapped my brain and burned my skin. The dogs howled. Pluto's wail was almost human.

"Why are you trying to kill me?" I asked, yet I didn't recognize my voice.

"We're trying to show you something," The Witch said.

"Good god, what could possibly be so important?" I asked.

"We were wrong," Saint Peter said.

"About what?"

"We can't protect you from her."

"Who's after me?"

It was a name I couldn't quite remember.

Something bit me. A fawn. A white-speckled, knobby-legged fawn. I pushed its head away.

"I imagine you're experiencing an unusual rush of images right now," The Witch said. "Along with disorientation. Paranoia."

"No shit."

"Are you afraid?" she asked.

"Let go of my arm."

"It's like pushing through a membrane."

The fawn would tear at my flesh until it peeled from my bones. Everyone would see my muscles and fat were strings of carcinogenic waste. My dying organs would spill out onto the carpet like bags of prepackaged, rotting meat.

"Let go!" I said. "You poisoned me!"

My bones were rotting. I shouldn't have let myself forget. I tried to cut the disease out of my stomach, but I couldn't. And it'd been swimming in my blood ever since, nesting in my medulla, growing, pulsing with gray colored pain, transforming into a disease I could never recover from. Miscarriage? Least of my problems. From inside, my body's cells grew spiny quills to attack me. From outside, a hungry river, a black chasm, and poisonous woods chased me.

And something else. Someone else. I couldn't pretend anymore that she wasn't coming after me. At six years old I hid from her by crawling into a rotting tree. She tormented my mother with poison. She'd caught my scent in the woods the night Cignus sent me in with the light emanating from The Huntress.

"Through your fear you can control anything," The Witch said. "You could change the rotation of the earth."

"Then why can't I remember her name?"

But she couldn't speak anymore. The ghouls cut holes from the inside of Genie's skin and spilled out of her shredded hands and waist. She ran her fingers down my throat, her mouth agape, and ectoplasm oozing from her lips.

My stomach burst. I screamed.

I wanted to come to the city and break the curse that had followed me since my conception. I wanted to forget about my mother, forget about my father, and forget about the river that followed me like a hungry mouth, like a raving ghost who mistook me for its murderer. It wasn't supposed to happen like this.

I pushed past everyone. I ran toward the front door, barely making it halfway across the room before I vomited the tea. I kept going. I wrenched the door open and tripped over metal tubing on the porch. I shoved over a ghoul bending iron into the shape of fangs.

Run. Run past the machine in the lawn getting bigger and bigger. Run, even though you're bleeding out and falling apart, and at any moment could run right out of your skin.

Yet, where the neighborhood used to be, I found only a black pit that sucked away all sunlight. I ran across an endless lawn, across endless space.

Of course the darkness followed me, and of course, it had a woman's name and a woman's body. Should've listened to your mother. Should've never taken that pomegranate seed. I could've been eating hash browns right now, but I fucked that one up.

The grass burst into black pills beneath me. Yes, I remembered these pills, the ones that Momma used to put in her purse. She dry swallowed them by the handful, until the day when she thought she didn't need them anymore, and caused both of our lives to collapse.

How she used to laugh, "Yes, I'm insane."

She never told me, "One day, you'll be insane too, baby."

I fell into the pills. I kept falling.

Saint Peter found me unconscious, in a ditch, half a mile from the house, blood in my mouth and blood between my legs. I woke up to the wail of an ambulance. Blurry, uniformed figures plunged their hands down through grass, through black pills, and reached for me. I grabbed at weeds and pulled them up from the roots.

"I don't need to go to the hospital," I said to them. "Fucking assholes."

They placed me on a stretcher. They held me down when I tried to get away.

"Don't move. We need to make sure you won't hurt your spine."

I wanted to tell them to stop repeating themselves because their voices echoed in my skull, rubbing on the inside of my brain like sandpaper. When they checked my pulse, I couldn't feel their fingers, like all sensitivity had burned away.

"Have you taken any illegal substances?"

"You want the list?" I asked.

"We need to know what you've put in your body."

"They put something in my tea," I said. "I'm having a miscarriage. I have a disease. It's rotting everything."

After fourteen hours in the ICU, the doctors placed me in the psychiatric ward.

Twenty-Two

NURSES STRIPPED ME of my bloodied clothes. They tore away my shoes and my socks and my dead cell phone. They took my blood pressure like gutting a fish. They scraped at the wound on my stomach like tearing into a pulpy fruit.

"It's infected," they said.

"Have you been treated for STDs?" they said.

"She's dehydrated."

"Do you have any insurance?"

When I couldn't answer their questions, the veins in their necks seemed to balloon to suffocate me. Their pursed lips were butcher tools. Their faces were like cold cuts, their hands like broken toys.

"Just another druggy."

"What did you say to me?" I said, my speech slurred, my legs trying to keep from collapsing.

"Give her a sedative."

"If you prove to be a threat, we'll put you in solitary confinement."

"Need to tell the doctor. Aggressive. Noncompliant."

"Put her in the furnace with the rest of the useless girls."

"I'm still a person," I said.

I didn't remember the needle plunging into my arm, only warmth traveling up to my shoulder, then the sudden inability to move my limbs. My head lolled back. I couldn't swallow the spit in my mouth.

They dressed me in hospital gowns and took away my bloodied clothes, pinching them between their forefingers like rancid garbage.

My legs stopped working. The nurses dragged me down the hallway. They seemed to resent me for this, even though they were the ones who caused my rag doll condition in the first place.

"Do you remember your name?" They asked me.

"Beelzebub," I tried to say to spite them, but I couldn't speak.

I always knew I'd end up here, in paper slippers and a tongue that refused to work. Just like Atreus would have always cooked the son of Thyestes. Just like Oedipus would have always fucked his mother and gouged his eyes out. Just like Gilgamesh would have always had his flower of immortality, stolen by a serpent lurking in the well.

Just like my mother.

Every hallway led to this hallway.

I wondered if my mother's ghost passed through me, crackling neurons, touching me with her schizophrenic cells. If she could see me now, shuffling down this so-familiar hallway, would she make me hot chocolate, shake her braided hair, and laugh like she used to? Would she tell me, "We slew the great wolf. Warriors don't cry, baby"?

The nurses laid me down on a bed underneath a prison window.

"Keep the lights on," I said.

They turned the lights off.

I expected the psych ward to explode with noises of women weeping, men screaming. There would be ex-Christ figures, robots, and ghosts. Girls with the voices of babies, boys who babbled in ancient Egyptian. Like in the movies. Yes, I belonged here. I screamed more than anyone I knew. Bring on the noise.

But nobody screamed or cried. There were no ghosts or robots that spoke in incoherent languages. Nobody rushed down the hallway, naked and giggling, a team of doctors with syringes chasing after him.

The only sound in the ward came from the shuffling of the nurses' shoes as they patrolled the corridors. The silence was worse than anything else I imagined.

Every fifteen minutes a nurse shone a bright flashlight into the room to make sure I hadn't killed myself. Even with the heavy sedatives, I couldn't sleep. If they couldn't see my eyes from the hallway, the nurse would stomp across the room, huffing, and stand there until I rolled over and showed the whites of my eyes.

"Why in god's name?" I asked.

"You're on suicide watch."

"Where were you twenty years ago? That's when we needed the miscarriage."

She huffed again and stomped out of the room. She'd been spit on so many times by punk girls like me.

The nurses talked in the hallway. They thought we couldn't hear them.

"I don't get paid enough money for this."

"My son's going to become a diabetic if he keeps eating so much chocolate."

"If only I were prettier. If only I hadn't gotten pregnant."

"I would've been a model. Seen the world."

"She's vomiting blood again. Big faker."

"Take all the anorexics in the world. Put them in concentration camps. That'll cure them."

They woke me at 7 A.M for a cafeteria breakfast that I couldn't eat. Doctors sat among the patients, writing notes on thick pads.

Across the table from me sat a girl named Dark Catherine. She couldn't eat either. She rearranged her sandwich in the shape of her dead boyfriend. There were cuts up and down her wrists, across her throat, her cheeks. Cuts like she'd marked the days off with her skin.

"Dark Catherine? Really?" I said.

"You think that's funny? Well I'm not giving anyone false ideas," she said, "about who I am."

"You could be anyone you wanted," I said.

"If you really believed that, you wouldn't be here," she said.

She walked her plastic fork across the table. She walked it in between her palm spread out on the table. All of the doctors taking notes glanced up at her at once, but their pens didn't stop moving. One of the doctors brushed aside her hair, and I saw on the underside of her wrist three scarred, sharp points.

"You're like everyone else," she said. "They can diagnose everyone's problems except their own."

She laid her head down on the cafeteria table as she walked the fork toward me. She danced it around my food tray, my hands.

"I'm sorry."

"I'm sorry," she said, mocking me, "What are you sorry for? You're just a stupid girl."

Later there were pills. Pills in a tiny paper cup. I didn't need to ask their names. I knew. Risperdal, Haldol, Xanax. The nurse didn't wait to see if I swallowed. Someone called her name from the other side of the building and she ran down the hallway, swearing.

I swallowed anyway. I stumbled to group therapy sick and dizzy.

Group therapy consisted entirely of women, some in their street clothes, some in paper gowns like mine. They sat in chairs with their bodies curled inwards, some looking down at their shoes, at others. The therapist sat at the center of the circle, cross-legged in a high backed chair. She wore a sleeveless blouse revealing the bluebirds tattooed up and down her arms.

There were no more chairs left. I sat against the wall.

"Tell everyone your name," the therapist said.

"They let you be a therapist? With all those tattoos?" I said.

"Your name, sweetheart."

"I had a teacher once who told me nobody would hire you if you got a tattoo."

"That's right," she said. "We've all been told a lot of hurtful, untrue things in our lives."

Nothing seemed real against white halls, white walls. Nothing seemed real in paper gowns, sitting in a circle, around inked birds flocking onto pale, Ph.D. trained arms.

"My name is Lily," I said. "You're the most beautiful therapist I've ever seen."

Afterwards I tried to listen to the stories the women told, but their words were like chopped records, the consonants cut away.

After the meeting was over and the women filed out of the room, I tried to get up, but I couldn't move. Vertigo kept me from understanding how my legs worked. The therapist leaned down next to me.

She smelled of the woods.

"I can't move," I said. "They gave me my mother's drugs."

"Sweetheart," she said.

Sweetheart became a slow, thin line that stretched across the room until it was no longer a word, but white noise.

"I need to get out of here," I said. "This place is making me crazier."

"Oh sweetheart."

Sweeettthhheeeaaaaarrrttt.

"You're too dangerous," she said.

I spent another night on the thin mattress underneath the barred window. They'd relegated to checking on me every half hour instead of every fifteen minutes. There were no comfortable positions to lie down in anymore. I tossed and turned, my spine a churning sea. I called for more pills. Nobody came. I bit down on my foam pillow and screamed.

I saw the harsh glow of the flashlight as it came through my door, but no stomping or huffing accompanied the light. The presence behind the flashlight was thin, and quiet. Their feet made no sound as they crossed the linoleum floor.

The flashlight travelled up and down my body. I buried my face into my pillow.

"You're not a nurse," I whispered into my pillow.

"You called for pills," she said. "Take your medicine."

If I didn't look, she would go away. That had always been my problem. I looked, and the spider children stirred in the leaves. I looked, and the earth ruptured out from underneath me. I looked, and Charlie jumped one last glorious jump into the dark river, arms outstretched like wax wings.

The flashlight hovered on my face, the light passing through my eyelids. The insides of my eyes burst with red and yellow spots.

"Take your medicine."

I opened my eyes, blinking into the harsh light. The flashlight did not waver. It appeared to be suspended in mid-air, without a hand to guide it.

A palm extended toward me from the light. A tiny, childlike palm. Empty.

"You were stupid," she said, "to leave your friends."

She dropped the flashlight. I lunged out of bed and tried to grab her. My hands grasped emptiness. The flashlight still spun on the floor from when she'd let go of it. I picked it up and fumbled for the switch to turn it off.

A nurse saw me from the hallway.

"What are you doing?"

I still couldn't find the off switch.

"Someone was in my room," I said.

She huffed. Stomped. She grabbed the flashlight out of my hands and turned it off. The room plunged into darkness; her face resembled a child's crayon smear.

I couldn't understand why everyone here was a bad caricature.

"I need to get out of here," I said. "Someone is after me."

Then I started laughing. Because I was a bad caricature as well.

She gave me more sedatives.

She said, "This will be noted on your chart."

"I've never met a chart that mattered."

I laid down, because this was all a bad dream. It had to be. My entire life, a bad dream.

***

I finally met with my Consultant Psychiatrist, four days after being admitted into the ward. We sat in the cafeteria after lunch. I knew they'd increased my dose of pills, without telling me, after the incident with the stranger in my room. At this dose, I could barely sit on the bench. I could barely eat. If I closed my eyes, vertigo could make me believe I sat on the ceiling.

"I'm sorry I couldn't visit with you until now, Lily," he said. "We've had some trouble getting information on you."

I wiped at my mouth. Drool.

Of course.

"You were found on the bad side of town. Unconscious, in a ditch. It appeared you'd tried to kill yourself by stabbing yourself in the stomach and uterus."

"The bad side of town?" I said. "Maybe to a rich doctor."

"The night nurses heard you talking to people who don't exist. Expressing paranoid thoughts."

"I know. I'm a paranoid schizophrenic. I guessed it. Do I win the prize?" I said.

Yes, there were names for people like me, but only one that mattered. Hopeless.

"These conditions. They're very manageable with the right medications. And we don't lock people up anymore. Not for things like this."

"Then let me out of here."

"It doesn't quite work like that, either," he said.

"I don't have a family," I said. "My mother is crazy. I have no money. Just let me go."

"Trying to kill yourself is a serious thing."

"You'd want to kill yourself too, if you were me."

And then I swore he said:

"You're dangerous, sweetheart."

Sweeettthhheeeaaaaarrrttt.

Twenty-Three

THIS COULD BE THE rest of my life. The rest of a long, boring, terrifying life. Take the pills. Soft pills, red pills, blue pills. Pills to make you blind. Pills to make your eyes fall out of your head. A buffet of pills. Go to therapy. Listen to women, as sad and scared as you, talk about kids they left behind, talk about how they might be cured by picking up crocheting or learning astrology. Watch, as their hands turn wrinkled and pale from lack of sunlight. Ignore the scraping and shuddering at the barred window. Tell the lady therapist with the bird tattoos that she looks beautiful everyday. Know that, you could never get a tattoo yourself, because they'd probably start tearing into your skin and trying to eat you.

I lay on my bed, spinning, when the demon came and brushed her fingers against my face.

"Oh god, thank you," I said. "It's been so boring here."

Her face was ragged and red. Dead insects fell out of her hair.

"Nightcatcher," she said.

The bars of the window bent. The river rushed toward me, angry and boiling. If it could have a face, it would have the face of an old woman, a boil on her nose, her teeth made of galloping horses.

No. No. No. The drugs aren't working.

Something's after me. Stop forgetting. It's something that's been searching for me for a long time, possibly forever, running circles around the earth. Around the entire galaxy, huffing dark matter to fuel its mad hunt. It would distort space and time in my head to slow me down. It needed to devour me, strip by strip, not only my body but also my mind. Own me. Own everything of me, my past, my present, my nightmarescape, my skin, and the hunter's poise. To force me to lay out everything that belonged to me so it could hold it up to the light and admire it. To preserve me in glass and resin, my bones crystallized and waiting for its touch.

Nightcatcher. The name I'd forgotten.

I heard my mother screaming. Poison in the sunlight. Poison on the bleach-soaked apples. Nightcatcher.

"Someone came to me." I said, "A few nights ago."

"And you're still alive?"

The wind outside the window howled loud enough to give me a nosebleed. The bars of the window crumbled.

We ran out into the hall. There were no nurses on duty, of course. And even if every patient on the ward screamed at once, I wouldn't be able to hear them over the noise of the wind and the river. If the earth turned up the volume a little louder, my fingers in the demon's grasp might disintegrate.

The linoleum ruptured. A carnivorous plant shoved its head through the crumbling tiles and dirt.

Acid dripped onto my hands and burned my skin away. Again.

Because of my medication, I saw it happening from far away, through a thick veil of unreality. I would've kept staring at my hand, watching the skin bubble like a research project, if Saint Peter hadn't called for me.

She stood at the end of the hallway, the hunter's bow in her hands. She knocked an arrow back as a plant burst from the ceiling above her head, moving out of the way before it could snare her blue hair in its fibrous mouth.

The entrance behind her blew open.

The violent air sliced my arms and legs. We couldn't go out there. Anything could be out there. And everything WILL be out there. The machine and its temporal lobe shattering noise. The heat of the river that could crush my lungs like a collapsing cave. Monsters that climbed into plants and made them angry, angry, angry.

Yet the tiles behind us were crumbling away. Steam rose out of the rubble like the sweat of hot-blooded plants.

We ran into the parking lot. The Witch pulled up in Saint Peter's van. The demon threw open the passenger side and we piled in. The Witch peeled off.

She was laughing, honest to god, laughing.

She jerked the van to cut across the middle of the parking lot. My cheek slammed against the window.

"What's so fucking funny?" I said, pressing my hands against my cheek, which was already beginning to bruise.

"She visited you," The Witch said, "but she couldn't kill you. Not yet. Oh god, she was so angry."

"Why?"

"Because I'm magic, babyheart."

We raced down an empty highway in the middle of the night. The old tires squealed with the effort. The engine smoked, and its burning, acrid smell filled the entire van.

It still couldn't overpower the smell of machine oil.

I knew there were all sorts of things behind us in the dark. Squirming things, wet angry things. Ghosts who could rearrange themselves into the shapes of my guilt. Those stupid fucking plants.

And The Nightcatcher herself, child's hands, rage that could stretch planets.

There wouldn't be a hospital to go back to. There wouldn't be a reprieve, ever again.

The demon panted into my throat. She gripped me by the wrists.

Then The Witch stopped laughing.

"There's something in the road," she said.

It happened in less than two seconds.

"There's something in the road. Somethingsomething. In thethetheroadtheroad."

She slammed on the brakes, and the van flipped.

One last chance, I thought to myself. If I remembered how to open my eyes I'd wake up, back in the hospital.

The demon's tiny body slammed against my sternum. My stomach dropped as we turned over and over in the van. I should've worn a seatbelt. Saint Peter reached for me and fell over my head. All the windows of the van shattered. A set of house keys, left on the bottom of the van for months, pierced my shoulder like a knife.

Then the van stopped rolling. I fumbled for an exit. The crumbled glass, still left on the edges of the window, sliced into my fingers.

"Oh god," Saint Peter said.

A carnivorous plant reached through the van and pulled me across the highway. I tried to resist, make my body go limp, but it only pulled me harder. My elbows and knees scraped against the asphalt, leaving behind skin and blood.

It dragged me into the forest, away from the highway.

I grabbed its head and squeezed. It secreted acid. The skin on my hands was already peeling away. The acid followed the lines of my veins, through my wrists, my elbows.

A girl leaned against a tree and lit a cigarette. She wore mud-caked pumps, her exposed legs scaly and green.

"Do you like her?" she asked of the carnivorous plant, in a familiar, smoky-dipped voice.

I clenched my arms, gritting my teeth, heaving with pain.

"Phaedra?" I asked, "Phaedra, why couldn't you have gotten a cat like everyone else?"

"I did. As I recall your girlfriend ate its eyes."

Twenty-Four

THE PLANT'S HEAD released me, and I fell backwards.

My head hit the ground. I struggled to get up, but Phaedra kicked me over with her heel.

"Stay down, loser," she said. "I have things to tell you and you're going to listen for once."

That cold little bitch, she loved every moment of this. She always wanted to be a noir femme fatale. She probably had wet dreams of this moment, when she could act the Miss Poison Ivy, have me prostrate on the ground, while she lazily smoked a cigarette.

"Well you better hurry up and tell me," I said. "I'm a busy girl."

"You're a lazy, drug-addicted coward," she said.

"And you're a sociopath. I thought that's why we were such great friends."

She pressed her muddy pump into my throat.

"Did you ever think about anyone besides yourself? You could've stopped for one moment and looked behind your shoulder. Instead you left us all. Me, Cignus, your mother."

"I thought you could take care of yourself."

Her pump crushed my throat and I couldn't speak without pain. Dirt and grit touched the back of my throat. The cold air pushed its way into my split knuckles.

"Tell me what you're going to tell me, bitch," I said.

She released my throat, and I started coughing.

"Shut up and look," she said.

She held her wrists out. There were holes in her skin, pierced through the bone. Her entire body was covered in holes and drained of blood.

She slipped her still-lit cigarette through the hole in her wrist and pushed it out the other side.

Through the holes in her body, the river poured, boiling and red. I dragged myself away from her, across the dirt.

The river seeped through my shoes and scalded me. I cried out and grabbed a tree limb to try and pull myself out of the water. Phaedra shuddered, like she was trying to laugh but couldn't quite remember how.

"She's behind you," Phaedra said.

I looked into the dark, out into the place where the river flowed, beneath the trees and dense clouds. The river rushed to her, parted around her, this creature blackened and bristling. She smiled at me with a glowing mouth, and then she fled.

"Phaedra!" I called, but she was gone.

The river was gone.

I ran back to the highway. Saint Peter and the demon were climbing out of the wrecked van. Saint Peter, miraculously, still clutched the hunter's bow and the quiver of arrows.

"Where's Genie?" I asked.

"Still in the van. We don't have a phone," Saint Peter said, limping toward me. "We can't call an ambulance."

She bled in places stigmata couldn't reach. The demon bled from her forehead, her skin a network of shredded glass. Her wormwood eyes were so bright and big; they could've caused traffic accidents.

I went around the van to the driver's seat. The Witch lay upside down, unconscious or dead, her neck at an unnatural angle against the steering wheel. Her legs were crushed behind her back.

"Can we move her?" I said.

"What if her neck's broken? We could kill her."

She coughed up blood, but didn't wake.

I went back to Saint Peter.

"Give me the bow," I said.

She stared past me, as if she'd heard me calling from the other side of the woods. She had a concussion, probably. And I didn't even know if there was a hospital within the nearest fifty miles. Not after the one we just left collapsed in on itself.

"It's mine, isn't it?" I said, and outstretched my hand. "Give it to me."

Saint Peter handed me the hunter's bow. It felt warm and familiar in my hands.

"Where are you going?" Saint Peter asked.

"I'm going after the thing that did this," I said. "Stay with Genie. Flag down a vehicle if you can."

"I'm going with you."

"I said stay here. So fuck you and stay here."

I looked at the demon, who stood beside me, shining and broken.

"Come with me."

Twenty-Five

I CHASED AFTER The Nightcatcher, and the demon followed. I slung the bow and quiver of arrows across my back as we ran across the highway into the woods. The distant city threw its light across the trees. The shadows of skyscrapers tattooed my arms.

The trees opened up like a mouth. Come here. Let me eat you. They were monster-headed, their foliage like claws.

The puddles underneath us were full of stars and the stars were riddled with holes.

The city light reflected like glitter in the demon's cheeks and her skin shone night silk. She touched my hand and squeezed. I squeezed back.

The bowstring dug into my aching cuts.

"Why did she take Phaedra?" I asked. "Why would anyone?"

"Maybe she wanted to be taken."

The demon clung fast to me. I'd become used to her smell, its cool crispness, almost blankness, like the smell of ice. I thought I could even become used to the spiders that sat engorged on her fingernails, or the larvae that occasionally dripped down my shirt.

"She's not here anymore," the demon said. "Let's go home. I'll make you warm."

And I might have turned back, except I smelled The Nightcatcher's molting fur hanging off the tree branches. She'd run through here and left her scent behind. If we didn't walk fast enough, it would contaminate our blood.

"She's not here," the demon said.

I wanted to believe the demon, I really did. I wanted to think that the shape at the end of the path was only a scarecrow swaying in the breeze, and that the way the moon shone down, only gave an illusion of that sleek textured fur. I wanted to believe that the thing didn't move when I took a step and tilted its head to regard me.

It skittered away into the trees.

Nightcatcher, was it you who tried to destroy my mother? Was it you who called to her that night I found her being devoured alive?

The trees rustled.

The demon crouched and scratched at the dirt. Her living hair caught my throat and black widows scurried across my fingers. I unslung the bow from my back.

I'd used this bow before. It fit the shape of my hands, as if worn down through the years. Saint Peter had kept it safe for me, until the time I asked for it back. There was a memory buried within me, a distant, darkened memory of a ship rocking underneath me and a great creature rising out of great waters.

I knew how to notch the arrow and aim.

I knew I needed to breathe to slow the world down, or I'd miss my shot.

Inhale. Exhale.

The trees rustled behind the demon. I turned, and there she was.

Learn to breathe. Heh heh heh heh. Slow it down. Slower. Learn to breathe, even though the air is turning to poison and your lungs are filling with smoke.

The Nightcatcher had poisoned my entire life, but it could end here. I could reverse this. My mother and I might be schizophrenic, but if The Nightcatcher was real, I could go home tonight with her head in my travel bag and tell my mother there was nothing left to fear. There'd never be another night where The Nightcatcher crept into our home and forced her to swallow bleach.

I aimed the bow at her. I pulled the drawstring back and dropped my shoulders.

"Don't," the demon said.

I breathed in.

"Don't."

I breathed out.

Her head emerged from the trees. She reached down, not with two hands but eight. Her eyes were baby blue.

I shot her and she tumbled into the dirt.

I stood still for a moment, panting. I thought she must've feigned injury, waiting for me to come close. But then I saw the arrow, embedded into her skin, and her blackened blood splashed against the leaves.

As I walked toward The Nightcatcher, she twitched and genuflected. I pulled the drawstring back, ready for the killing blow.

But when she lifted her head up, I saw it wasn't The Nightcatcher at all.

It was the baby-faced spider, her mouth opening and closing as she gasped for air, blowing black bubbles from her ruined lungs. It was the same little Arachne that Momma once took me down into the woods to watch die.

I lowered the bow and I slumped into the grass. My hands couldn't clench the bow anymore, and it fell from my fingers.

The spider child gurgled.

"I told you," the demon said.

I tore at the grass and when I looked down, my hands were full of blue flowers.

Baby Arachne reached for me. The fine hairs of her limb brushed against the back of my hand. As gently as I could, I took that limb in my hand and kissed its furry tip.

"I'm so sorry," I said.

Baby Arachne sighed and, just as it happened years ago, she slipped away.

I turned to the demon.

"You've got a little something," the demon said, and touched her lips.

I rubbed my mouth with the back of my hands and it was black.

***

That night, the demon and I dug a grave for baby Arachne with our bare hands. Dirt pushed its way through my split knuckles, but I didn't dare stop digging. Maybe The Witch was dead, and Saint Peter had fallen asleep on the side of the road with a concussion, but I didn't dare. I kept swallowing, but I couldn't swallow the grit in my teeth and on my tongue.

Let my blood mix into the dirt, let the baby Arachne's black ichor stain every bed sheet I ever climb onto. I pulled the arrow out of her side, and it came out with a sick little puckered noise.

It was I who pushed the dirt over her head. It was I who covered her mound with flowers.

I bit down on my bleeding knuckles. I pushed my head into the soft mound. The demon held me.

Twenty-Six

WHILE THE DEMON AND I were in the woods, Saint Peter managed to flag down a car and get her and Genie to a hospital. The van was totaled and towed to a scrap yard.

The demon and I headed back alone. I didn't know how many miles we were from home, or if there was even a home left at all. I couldn't trust myself anymore. Once I had a brain, not riddled in holes, a body, not on the verge of falling apart, a time where I could crawl into my bed and not have to wonder if I'd wake up in the middle of an underground ocean.

The demon tripped and fell into the gravel on the side of the highway. She struggled to get up, and then fell again. The locusts in her hair cried for me. Her hair looked like road kill in the night. I carried her on my back until I collapsed. Then she carried me.

Nobody pulled over to ask if we needed help.

We arrived at the house just before dawn. I threw the bow and arrows onto the floor of our bedroom. Pluto jumped onto the bed, mewling. The dogs gathered at our feet. Despite how exhausted we were we couldn't sleep for hours. We stayed up and washed our faces in the kitchen sink. We brushed the dirt and grass out of each other's hair. The dogs licked our wounded legs, but we were too tired to push them away. We collapsed into bed and stared at the ceiling, shivering, drowning, twitching.

I don't know when I fell asleep, but in my dreams, The Nightcatcher chased me through the woods. She shot fish hooks attached to wires out of her hands. The hooks tore into my back. As I ran, the wires snarled in the trees, snaring me, entrapping me, tighter and tighter the more I ran. The hooks broke the bones in my back. I crawled across the ground, into a grotto.

A doe lay on the ground, heaving in labor. I cut her open and the pink, foam-mouthed fawn tumbled dead into the grass. I crawled into the doe's uterus and closed the skin around me to hide.

The Nightcatcher tied the doe with wires and suspended her from the trees. She kissed the doe's cold, clover-stained mouth and I felt the kiss on my mouth. The Nightcatcher left. I rocked inside the doe, upside down, cradled in her warmth. I rocked in and out of the dream.

The artist cut the doe down. I crashed to the ground. He pried her open and found me inside.

"Where have you been?" I asked, and spit my broken teeth into his face.

He spit them back.

I awoke to Saint Peter standing by the window. She'd become so thin, her skin like a shredded canvas. She leaned her head against the window and sighed heavily, like her ribcage shrunk too small for her to breathe properly.

I sat up and pulled the blankets around me. The demon slept beside me, Pluto in her arms.

"Are you okay?" I whispered. "They didn't keep you at the hospital?"

The moonlight was like splinters in her eyes.

"I've missed you so much," she said.

"I've been here the entire time."

Her brown roots were growing in and her blue hair faded nearly to white. Her sweater hung off her shoulders in threads, her skirt torn with holes.

"You don't understand," Saint Peter said.

But I did understand. Her clothes were falling apart and I was making her fall apart. I stopped eating, and she displayed the evidence on her body, a mirror of my mistakes. Once she carried her stigmata as crosses, but she replaced them with snake bites and burn marks. For me.

"You're going to destroy yourself," I said.

"Do you know what they call people like me?" she asked.

She crawled across the bed and pressed her face against my knee.

"Ecstatics," she said when I couldn't respond, didn't know how to respond, "because nothing feels better than hurting for the one you adore."

"I don't deserve this from you," I said.

"Stigmata comes from the Greek word stigma. It means brand. Like you would brand a slave."

She breathed against my leg.

"I don't own you," I said.

"We used to touch like this," she whispered. "We used to sleep in a bed covered in yellow flowers."

"Please," I said. "I can't watch you do this to yourself."

She lifted up her head, her hair like a dirty crown. Once she walked on water and preached on top of a mountain in all languages of the earth. Now she was with me, in the depths of a dark city, in a dirty punk house, stepping over needles and waking up hung-over every morning. Hey, let me total your van and slap your skin with poison fangs. Hey, we're out of coffee, why don't you let me drink your blood.

Maybe if the stories were true, her other god didn't treat her any better - after all, he left her to die as a martyr, crucified upside down.

She reached for my face and I grabbed her hand to stop her. Red marks spread on the inside of her arm where the bowstring had slapped against mine.

"I'm not good at taking care of myself," I said. "I'm going to kill you if you stay."

"You have before," she said.

"Please"

"I didn't mind."

Saint Peter gripped the inside of my thigh. She lifted up my dress. The demon and Pluto continued sleeping.

"I can't," I said in a frantic whisper.

It was as if speaking any louder would shatter all three of us.

"You're different this time."

God, look what I'd done to her - thinned her down, burned her, branded her, scarred her, scratched her, punctured her. And I'd been too wrapped up in my own problems to notice. Here, let me leave you to die while I lose my goddamn mind. Off to the hospital for a little vacation - all the while she's puncturing herself with my damage. What do you want me to say? Hey baby, get a little closer, there's still a little cocaine left on that stomach wound?

"You used to hold me as I slept," Saint Peter said, "You kissed me here. And here. We ate mushrooms in the great forest. We travelled to places I can't even dream about anymore."

"And how did that work for us? If any of this is true, and I'm not just losing my goddamn mind, why are we here and not there? I can't imagine getting any lower than this. We screwed up somewhere."

Though maybe next time, instead of being humans, we'd be reincarnated as two fighting beetles, or vermin cupped inside a heroin addict's hoodie.

"You need to leave me," I said.

"Don't say that."

"Look at you," I said. "No, don't even. Look at me, and see what you're doing to yourself."

"It's because of her," Saint Peter said. "That's why it's different this time."

Silence.

"Yes," I said.

"You don't even see me, because of her."

"I see you."

"It's too late. We used to be best friends. More than that."

"You need to leave," I said again.

"I need to keep you safe," she said.

"By letting me destroy you?"

"I died for you. I've protected your woods for years."

"You said it yourself, you can't protect me any longer."

"I won't leave you."

I grabbed her arms and wrenched them from my dress. I forced her to look at them. Her thin, poison filled, scarred arms.

The demon still didn't wake.

"Please," I said.

"I can't."

In the dark, she was not only sick but sick forever, her tears preserved in the cold light. Her skin cracked wherever I touched her. Her blood was the color of dust in her veins.

"Do you think I'm your goddess? I'm begging you to leave. I'm begging. Look at me."

The demon shifted and stirred in her sleep, but she still didn't wake.

"The Nightcatcher only wants me," I said.

"I only want you," she said.

I bit down on my tongue and blood spilled from her mouth.

"Oh Jesus fuck. Please. Don't do this to yourself."

Her fraying skirt touched my lips. I wrapped my hands around her small, cold thighs as she pressed further into me.

I whispered into her ear.

"I won't do this to you."

She gripped my dress tight enough to break her fingers. She wasn't even looking at me as she tried to kiss me, breathing hard, her knees pushing in between my legs.

I grabbed her face.

"Look at me. Come back to me."

For a flickering moment, she looked at me. She loosened her grip on my dress.

"Things are different," I whispered. "I'm going to kill The Nightcatcher."

We probably could've stayed on that bed for the rest of the night with our hips and legs locked together. But, after a few minutes, Saint Peter's limbs lost all their energy. She relinquished her grip on me and slumped backwards on the bed.

The moonlight gnawed at her protruding spine.

"Okay," she said.

I called a taxi while she covered her face in the sheets. I grabbed her bag and began to pack her things. Without speaking, she rose and helped me. Her clothes were strewn throughout the house, along with everything else, her candles, little ritual books, and psilocybin mushrooms in a bag underneath her bed.

We must've stayed in that house longer than I realized.

I tried to give the hunter's bow to her, but she shook her head and wouldn't take it.

When we were finished packing, I gave her what little money I had left. We stood by the window, both of us unable to speak.

Already the wounds on her arms were fading. The snake venom lost its bright coloring. The scars of bite marks, once ferocious and red, were now pale pink. When she noticed them disappearing, she pressed her hand over her mouth and her body shook with silent sobbing.

Outside the taxi honked.

With tears running down her lips, Saint Peter kissed the sleeping demon and the sleeping cat. She picked up her bag and turned toward the door to leave, but I caught her by the hips. I drew her into me. I kissed her on the mouth, kissed her hard until her lips parted. My tongue touched her bloodied teeth. I gripped her bony shoulder blades and held her tight.

I whispered to her.

"I promise I will find you again. After all this is over. I will find you, and I will let you rest."

I gave her my last cigarette and lit it for her. She inhaled like she couldn't remember how. I followed her to the front door. I stood on the porch, in the cold, as she ran toward the waiting taxi. She loaded her bag into the trunk, her knees barely able to support her. She slipped on the gravel in her platform boots and grabbed the open door to keep from falling. She hiked her torn skirt to climb into the back seat. Before she closed the door, spots of blood welled up on her forehead.

Her own crown of thorns.

Twenty-Seven

THE WITCH CAME BACK from the hospital in a wheelchair. Her kneecaps were crushed and her eyes crossed. There were bandages around her throat and bandages up to her elbows. Her exposed skin was bruised like an explosion, fire dark and orange.

"Are you okay?" I said, the stupidest thing I could say.

The dogs ran out the door and surrounded her, whining, licking. I wheeled her into the house and they followed, tails tucked, heads down.

"I have bones that will never heal again," she said, "but that's not important. You need to dye your hair. Now."

Fatigue kept me from asking why.

"With what?"

"There's dye and bleach underneath the sink. In the bathroom."

I went into the bathroom, found the dye and the bleach. I bleached my hair, washed it out. I sat in the bathtub and massaged the dye in the hair. Washed it out.

I emerged from the bathroom, a redhead.

The police knocked on the door. They were looking for two ragged girls who broke into a house on the west side and stole dresses and jewelry, one blonde-haired and one black-haired. Skinny girls who hadn't eaten in days, ruffians with drugs in their blood. Seen coming into this house.

"We'll let you know if we see anyone like that," I said.

I tugged on my freshly colored hair. I hugged myself in my too-thick sweater, hoping it would hide my thinness.

The police left.

"They'll be back with a search warrant," Genie said, "If you have drugs, take them or hide them."

"Broke into his house? That fake French motherfucker wanted to show off his cheap jewelry so we'd fuck him, now he's too embarrassed to admit it," I said.

"He smelled like old perfume," the demon said. "Like his dead mother."

At least Saint Peter wasn't here to deal with this. She didn't have to see Genie come back from the hospital in a wheelchair, her legs bent back.

She didn't have to see me try to cook dinner for the first time by myself, burned the pasta, and burned the sauce. She didn't have to watch me as I tried to cut vegetables with my ruined hands. My fingers wouldn't obey me, I sliced my thumb, screamed, and the dogs cowered.

I threw a stainless steel pot against the wall and the dogs fled.

She didn't have to see my misdirected anger at the demon. Exhausted and sick, we fought. I screamed at her, "Bitch. Demoncunt. I'll never fuck you again. I blame you for all of this."

Afterwards, I curled up in her lap. "I'm sorry, demon. I'm sorry."

She chewed on the ends of her hair and stroked my back.

I caught a reflection of my new hair in the mirror, and remembered something my mother once said.

"When you grow older, you'll dye your hair a bright red, because it's the closest you'll ever feel to being on fire."

Prophecies. I hated fucking prophecies.

The Witch sat in the middle of the living room in her wheelchair, covered in tattered blankets, the dogs circling around her. Her hair was tied against the wheels. With one hand she carved new sigils into her wrists, overlaying scars. With the other, she shoved blue flowers into her mouth.

More ghouls escaped out of the cuts in her hands. They escaped from her mouth in thin, wriggling strands. Sick though she was, crushed and broken, the ghouls kept coming. They were bigger than I remembered, more visceral than before. Not only the shapes of people, but of rats and dogs and cats.

"You'll die." I said.

She looked up at me with eyes like rusted fencing.

"So?"

I ran to the demon, through the corrugating shadows, sobbing and ruined, into her arms.

A walk would make everything better. Get out of the house for a while, stretch our legs, and remember that we're not trapped underneath sigils and dream symbols, in witchcraft and poison. The demon and I checked for police patrolling the streets then sneaked out together into the cool air.

Winter came, and we hadn't noticed. Our thin and tattered jackets were not enough to keep us warm, so we walked together, huddled, clutching, and shivering. Thanksgiving probably passed while I smoked in my room to the grind of the machines and my stomach growled for 4 a.m. munchies. Christmas would be here soon. It would be my first Christmas away from home. My mother, even wracked with Schizophrenia, still managed to get me a gift every year, even if it was a knife to chase away ghosts, or a book of matches, or a pink dress like one I would've worn as a child; she tried.

The demon and I walked into a glowing meadow where the moon hung like a silver crescent in the sky.

"It's so bright," I said.

The demon's hands tensed and when I kissed her she froze.

Then I realized. We'd walked this way a hundred times before and never seen this meadow, glowing and bright.

"Something's wrong," I said, "wrong with the moon."

I bent down and plucked a flower. In my hands, the flower turned to smoke.

She tried to pull me away.

The trees collapsed around us. The crescent moon fell out of the sky and crashed at my feet, a dirty, yellow paper cutout that could've fit in the palm of my hand.

The walls of the meadow slid in, the metallic night sky crashed on top of my head, and I fell to the ground. I slipped from the demon's grasp as the walls threaded together, trapping me in darkness.

The dirt underneath me turned to water, and the river flowed into my mouth, nose, and eyes. I swam. I had to or I'd drown.

I searched for a way out. The water sucked my shoes under. I coughed. I called out for the demon. I tried to tread water but the current was too strong.

And, after days of staying awake, I was tired. So tired.

She tugged at my fingers in the water. She pushed sand into my mouth. All my wounds tore open and my blood glowed as it leaked out in the darkness.

On the verge of drowning, I gripped the dirty embankment and managed to crawl away from the river. The water howled as it moved. Water for wolves. I crawled through the mud, my blood a glowstream tracing patterns across my fingers, illuminating the dirt.

She sat on my back and pulled my hair.

"Stop," she said.

And I collapsed.

"Look up at me," she said.

She twisted my hair around her wrists and forced my head up. Her fingers smelled of thick machine oil. I couldn't see her, but I felt her, thin and dripping like a wet rat, human-shaped, plastic for bones. But she was strong. Stronger than me.

"I said look up at me."

I coughed up mud.

She climbed off my back and hauled me out of the dirt by my hair, forcing me on my toes.

The hush place my mother spoke about, was real. The hush place that followed her from the kitchen windowsill to the stomach of a carnivorous plant was here. It seeped through my skin, sunk its teeth into my blood, and wailed as it rushed past. It made the air cold here, so cold that I couldn't move my fingers, my jaw. My bones would rust in that cold, and no matter how far I swam in the water and mud, I wouldn't be able to find my way out.

"Did you know there's blood in your teeth? You look like you're eating lights," she said.

She released my hair. I stumbled backwards, trying to keep from falling into the mud.

"I wanted the other one."

"The demon?" I said.

"I'm going to let you go now," she said.

"Why do you want my demon?"

Silence. I couldn't feel The Nightcatcher next to me anymore, and I thought that maybe the river swept her away. I took a step forward. Another. The mud gurgled underneath me. No matter how much I strained to see, there was only the sewn-in darkness, my blood like little fireflies.

She appeared beside me, the air screaming around her, as she cloaked me in her hair, and whispered into my ear.

"Everyone needs a pet."

The river sunk into the ground; she left me alone in the empty meadow, the mud still caked onto my clothes, the moon paper cutout at my feet.

I picked up the moon, folded it, and put it in my shirt pocket. I found the trail leading out and walked back home.

Waiting for me on the porch steps was the demon, head in her hands. I tried to call for her but my throat was scabbed and sore. I fell in the lawn on my way toward her.

The ringing in my ears sounded like the river screaming as it rushed over me. The machine on the lawn, nearly finished, loomed over me. Not just any machine, but a beast, a bad science fiction killing machine. Its head was a ragged claw, its nose a gunmetal proboscis, plus two protruding, rusted limbs, studded with nails. Why had I never noticed until then? All those months the shadows worked on the machine, and I never noticed its deathskin, its slobbering mechanical arms, its glass-rimmed mouth. I'd been too busy trying to scrape together money for drugs, and chasing the demon across planes of ecstasy, to see the terrible thing The Witch was building.

The demon knelt beside me. She bloodied her hands on my shirt and spoke. I tried to tell her it was too loud, I couldn't hear her. I vomited in the grass. I gasped and gasped. We had to get away. The Nightcatcher hadn't just been waiting outside the house, she'd been clawing her way into The Witch's head and into the shadows carved from her arms long before we even came here.

I called for the demon. I called for Saint Peter, long gone.

The demon carried me into the house.

She's coming for you, I tried to say. She's coming for you. We have to call Saint Peter. Saint Peter will know what to do. Where's my hunting bow? Get the bow. We have to go after her. She's coming for you. Get help. I don't know what she's going to do with you, but nothing good can happen in the hush place. Look at me, I'm bleeding everywhere. You're getting the sheets dirty. Let me go. Stop holding me down. Stop kissing me. She's out there. The machine's going to kill us all.

The police are looking for us. They're at the door. Can't you hear them knocking on the door? Aren't you listening to me?

The noise is so loud it's going to liquefy my brain. Cut off my hair already. I won't be a Viking warrior. Not again. My tongue has turned into foam. The tongue is always the first thing to go, but you already knew that. You're suffocating me. Get my hunting bow. She's here with us right now. We have to dismantle the machine. My tongue. It's turning into foam. Help me or I'll never speak again.

The demon pinned me on the bed.

"Listen to me! Why aren't you listening to me?" I asked.

She whispered.

"The police aren't here. She isn't here yet. We still have time. A little while."

I was too hot. I tried to throw the blankets off.

"You're shivering," she said.

"Why do these wounds never heal?" I asked. "No matter how much time has passed, they never heal."

"Just rest," she said.

The river rushed out of the demon's eyes. No matter where I ran, no matter what sort of tranquilizers the hospital gave me, the river would always be with me. The water filled the bedroom, lifting the bed to the ceiling.

On the other side of the door The Witch screamed. The demon rocked me in her arms and whispered.

"Just rest. We still have time."

Yet, I know my demon. I know when she's lying. I know when she's afraid.

Twenty-Eight

THE DEMON NURSED and bandaged me.

"I've been preparing your palace all my life," she said, trying to soothe me.

It would be a palace on top of a mountain at the edge of the world. The palace would have a roof of glass so that we could see the stars and the moon. She'd build me a telescope so I could find the planets, and cradle them to me like pillows. In the winter, snow would fall over our palace, trapping us inside. She'd wrap me in furs, bring me spiced wine, call me "baby" and "goddess" and suck my clit until the snows melted.

I scratched at my bandages. She pulled my hand away.

I thought I would sweat out of my skin.

She cradled my head in her arms for hours. She forced me to drink water, even when I insisted it burned me. When I cried she whispered,

"Pay no attention to the river."

Later the demon took me into the bathroom and I took a shower, lying down in the tub. She peeled off my wet bandages; the water turned the color of tongues.

"Why does The Nightcatcher want you?" I asked the demon.

She rested herself against the wall, her eyes fluttering and heavy from lack of sleep.

"I don't know," she said.

She traced the patterns on the wall with her nail and cut into the wallpaper. Above her head, a glossy spider spun her web. Her spiders had insinuated themselves into every corner of the house, transforming the ceiling into a silk cityscape.

She told me once the spiders were psychic, the patterns of their webs changed, depending on the emotions around them.

They spun webs ragged and disjointed, webs that went nowhere, webs that hung down like sad faces.

"I'm a pest to The Nightcatcher. An insect," the demon said. "She shouldn't want me."

The demon wrapped me in a towel. I lay in bed with the towel still wrapped around me, my hair knotted around my fists.

The demon opened her hands and spilled dead birds onto the bed. Little wrens, with mouths gaping, ribbons tied around their necks.

I never got around to telling her, "Stop leaving dead things in my bed. Those aren't the kind of gifts you give to people." I couldn't, because it was the best way she knew to show me she loved me.

"I wasn't always a demon, you know," she said.

She lay beside me. She was smaller than I ever remembered. She could have curled up inside the sleeves of my dress.

"Once, I was a girl," she said. "I lived in a town full of sunshine, in a time when my father still loved my mother. It was a place where the fields glowed in the summer with fireflies big as our heads. I was going to be a scientist. Just like you, Lily. I wanted to find the Wormwood star my mother talked about. It's from the book of Revelation. They said it wasn't a real star, but I knew better.

"I fell in love with a boy, because he made me feel good when he kissed me. He took me to Christmas dinner with his family and bought me spring dresses and pressed flowers in between the pages of my books. He transformed me into a strawberry girl, sunshine girl. He took me to the highest point in the city, like he was the devil and said, 'This could all be yours' as he knelt in front of me with a ring in his hands. I said, 'I don't want it all, I want you, my love, I want you.' And I threw my arms around him and knew I'd never have to be lonely again."

"Have you ever felt that way?" she asked me. "Like you met the one person who would make sure you were never lonely again?"

Yes, I wanted to say. Yes.

"We were married. That was the only time I ever remember feeling beautiful. We lived in the countryside and had two children, two little girls with wispy blond hair and dark eyes. I thought I was happy.

"Except every time I looked in the mirror, I didn't see a girl. I saw a demon. I'd seen her my whole life, hiding behind my skin. She followed me everywhere I went. I started to scratch off my skin. I scratched and scratched, even when my husband said I wouldn't ever be able to go back to the way things were. Even when my children clung to me and begged me to stop. I couldn't. I couldn't stop. I scratched until I tore the skin of the girl away."

This is the end, I thought. She's telling me this because she knows this is the end.

"Do you know what happened after that?" the demon asked.

"Tell me."

"They didn't love me anymore," she said softly.

I couldn't stop shivering. We had to get away. There were too many poisons and slinking things out in the dark. The Nightcatcher would steal my demon away. The machine would descend upon the house, pry open the roof, and devour us. The earth would collapse. We were running out of time, I needed to grab the demon by the collar and run.

Instead, we curled into each other, too tired to move, and collapsed amidst the bodies of dead wrens.

She sighed in my ear, scattering spiders, and we slept.

***

When I awoke, the demon was gone.

I dressed and went searching for her. I searched from the living room to the kitchen, to the attic. She was not there. I went outside to the backyard where the trees were burnt husks and the grass was wild-haired and black. I went to the porch and to the empty driveway where Saint Peter once parked her van. She was not there.

My veins throbbed like war weapons. My blood spilled out of every cut. The Nightcatcher couldn't just take the demon away from me. She belonged here. She belonged with me.

The Nightcatcher thought she was scary? She should wait. I'd become a raging beast, rabies from osmosis. I'd tear the sky down and strangle her with it.

The Witch sat in the living room in the dark. She rolled her wheelchair back and forth across the floorboards. The wheels creaked, slowly, encrusted in her dried blood.

"I've lost her," I said.

"She's waiting for you."

Ghouls wriggled out of her mouth. They snuck out through her eyes.

"Where?" I asked.

Her skin sloughed off the muscle. Through the bandages, she smiled. Pressure built up underneath her cheeks. She pointed toward the door.

"There's not much time left."

The black dogs at her feet howled.

On the lawn ghouls slipped inside of the machine, into its gears, its angry eyes, and its rusted arms.

The dogs rushed past me to the machine. They surrounded it, barking, foam on their black muzzles.

The machine roared to life.

I ran down the street. A taxi waited at the end of the cul-de-sac.

The Witch, queen of psychedelic drugs and black-hearted machines, had called me a taxi.

I climbed into the back and the cabdriver turned to talk to me, then paused when he saw me shivering in my tattered, thin jacket, my legs locked and arms crossed.

"Do you have any money?"

"A little." I said, lying. "Take me downtown."

"Downtown is a big place."

"Take me anywhere. I don't care."

He took off. The night sky churned purple foam, a color as angry as I was. The skyscrapers were burnt metal.

The Witch said, “Go find here,” but I didn’t know where.

The taxi crossed the bridge toward the city; the ocean underneath us was corrupted like computer static.

“I’ve seen a lot of kids like you.” He said. “You should go back to someone who loves you.”

"I didn’t ask for a therapist,” I said.

“You don’t have any money, do you?” he asked.

He stopped at the next corner.

“Just get out,” he said.

I opened the door. He took his foot off the brake and the taxi rolled forward. I stumbled onto the curb as he sped off.

I picked a direction and started walking. She couldn't expect me to find her like this. I wasn't a demon. I didn't have ice in my blood, or a golden chip in my head, pointing the way. The streets were strained and dark and empty because of the cold. It was ferociously cold, colder than I remembered, the kind of cold that children die in.

The blood drained from my face and fingers. I could barely walk.

I ran into Francois with a blonde haired girl on his arm. She was small and blue-mouthed, and wearing a black pearl necklace bigger than her throat. He'd thrown his coat around her shoulders and pulled her close to his chest.

"Francois!" I called.

I laughed, stumbled, and grabbed a light pole to keep myself from falling. It didn't matter I was on a sacred mission, I couldn't help myself.

"Do I know you?" he asked.

"You never called me back. You were going to teach me your French tongue."

I stuck my tongue out at him. He pulled the girl away from me, shielding her ears with his hands. He must've shed the Francois persona; being a Frenchman could only take you so far when you didn't know French.

As I laughed, choking, clinging to the light pole so I wouldn't fall over, baby spiders flew past me, riding the air currents.

"What are those?" the girl said. "What's wrong with this city?"

I followed the spiders because it seemed like the kind of sign to follow. Invisible webbing stuck to my eyelashes, my mouth.

The current split them into two paths, one heading toward an alley, the other toward a bridge. A few spiders flew into my hair, and then leapt off and swirled above my head. I followed them into the alley.

It was a dead end.

I stood next to a pile of fetid trash as the spiders blew past me and into the air. I looked behind me to the street. Francois and the girl were there. Francois was talking to someone on the phone.

"Yeah," he said. "She's here."

"Who are you talking to?"

"You better come and get her. I'll make sure she doesn't go anywhere."

"Fucking fuck," I said.

I curled my fists and was about to head toward him, when the demon found me.

Her hair, my baby's hair, dark and hot with magic, came to me from above. It was living hair, stained with black ichor - wild things growing there. It grasped me by the wrists as her insects spoke softly to me.

"Come here."

The girl in Francois' arms saw the hair winding itself around me, and she burst into tears.

The demon's hair pressed itself into my eyes, nose, and mouth. It tied itself around my waist as if winding me up for a dance, then pulled me upwards.

She led me up the alley, down the street, and through a collapsed window. I cut my feet on delicate glass and junkie's needles. I bled across platform ladders, dirty boards, and toppled bars.

I walked through heaving, whiskey-soaked skins that used to be human. I went down an elevator shaft, her hair lifting me so that I walked on the walls. My feet left behind bloodied prints.

She took me down a flight of staircases. My hands burned against the railing as she hurtled me from one wall to the next.

She opened a door and I flew down the long, gray hallway. I flew into an abandoned hotel basement. She released me on the floor and her hair retracted.

I found her kneeling beside a rusted, reignited boiler.

The demon did not belong here underground, in this heated box of metal with her skin cooking. She wore my boots, thick woolen socks, and one of my sweaters. She wrapped herself in layers of scarves and chunky gloves.

"I thought I'd lost you," I said.

She folded her arms and turned her face to the fire.

"You will," the demon said. "I just wanted us to have a little while longer together."

Her hair drew me close. I buried my head in her soft sweater and felt her jagged bones underneath. In all the layers of my clothing, she no longer smelled like herself.

"I won't let her take you."

"There are things greater than both of us. She's one of them."

"I'll kill her," I said.

"You have to stop fighting. You can't fight her."

"I should have known. It was you The Nightcatcher wanted all along." I said.

"We couldn't have known."

I wouldn't admit to myself I couldn't save her. Kill The Nightcatcher? I couldn't even kill the thing inside me that I hated.

"Why did we have to come here?" I asked. "Maybe I could've saved my mother. I should've never set fire to our tree. Maybe it was a gateway out of this hell."

"You'll drive yourself mad," she said, "with what could have been."

She clung to me like a child and I rocked her. How small she was, how well we fit together. For all I knew she'd been in the crib with me when we were infants, our clumsy feet reaching out for each other, past bedtime, both of us eating spiders like children sometimes do.

"You can't go," I whispered. "You're all I want. Please."

She stroked my hair. She pressed my forehead to her own, and, though she was sweating, her skin chilled me to the touch.

In her eyes, the Wormwood star collapsed. When I tried to look away she tugged on my hair.

"Don't," she said. "Not now."

I cupped my hands underneath her chin. The demon's mouth parted.

Pay attention, this is what it feels like to lose your shadow.

Ke-ke-ke-ke-ke.

She slipped her webbed tongue into my mouth and her insect noise vibrated inside my head. Burning. Pulsing. She kissed me again and again. Until the fire in the boiler dimmed and a chill crept over her.

The smell of machine oil.

"You need to go," she said.

"No."

Her hair hissed and wrapped around my wrists and ankles. I coughed up black hair, billowing hair, as she pushed me toward the exit. Needles and spiders scraped against my skin. I braced myself against the doorframe with my arms and legs.

"You can't make me leave."

"She'll kill you," the demon said.

There was a sound like a bullet train. No, the sound of a stampede. The sound of a great rushing wave. It was the sound of hell. Forget the wailing and of teeth, hell was a rushing noise that intensified until it replaced the blood in my head.

The demon's hair released me. It was as if someone reached through the wall behind her and grabbed her by the back of the neck. Her eyes were wide and empty, her throat exposed. She swallowed. And although I thought the crushing noise would kill me, I heard her as if she spoke beside me.

"Lily," she whispered. "I'm afraid."

I will fight this. I will fight The Nightcatcher. I am weak and ready to fall apart, but if you come for my demon, I will destroy you. I will plunge my fists into your face, if you even have a face at all. I will tear you apart with my teeth, even if your skin is made of metal.

I ran to her. The floor stretched between us, the basement walls collapsed like they were set props, made of paper; there was a great darkness like deep space beyond them.

The demon had been dragged across the floor, toward the darkness beyond the wall. Oil oozed underneath her. The oil grew a face that chewed gashes in her cheeks and tore her clothing apart.

She reached for me.

It seemed as if I'd run for miles across the boiler room before I gripped her arms. I tried to pull her away, out of the oil sucking her hair into its mouth.

I screamed.

They can't take you from me, demon.

Demon.

"I won't let you go," I said. "I promise."

You're all I have left.

Maybe my curse was that everyone I ever cared about would look at me with those eyes - eyes that, if they had mouths, would gasp. Eyes calling for help, windows to the soul, shutting me out forever. They said, "You could have saved me Lily."

"You could have saved me by staying away."

The Nightcatcher dangled a fake paper moon in the darkness like a fucking smile.

The Nightcatcher pulled her across the floor toward an infinite nothingness where there was nothing to fight, nothing to kill. I stumbled as I tried to hold onto the demon. My arms ached. Everything in me strained. If there's any blood left in me, take it from me. Quick, tie my hair to your hair. If I can't pull you out then I will go in with you.

But the darkness was her darkness and I wouldn't be able to follow. It would sew me in a bubble, separate our fingers, split my nails apart. Out there, I could be destroyed in any way The Nightcatcher pleased. I imagined her laughing, but there was the only the terrible sound of rushing, boiling, gushing, incoherent noise.

She'd collapse the earth on us to get the demon.

The darkness swallowed my demon in pieces. It could've taken her all at once, but it taunted me. It wound up her legs. I wouldn't let her go. It wound up her waist. I wouldn't let her go. This was a bad horror movie, baby. Let's wake back up in our tree. I promise, this time I won't run when you show me the glittering insects in your lap.

I won't let you go let you go let you go.

Her face transformed into a rigid mask, her mouth half open and her eyes burning red. Her face didn't even belong to her anymore.

Nobody could endure that much fear and keep their face.

The darkness, like a molten case, crawled up her spine. I tried to tear it off her. It burned my fingers. I tried to pull her back from the invisible grasp by the hair, but her hair was a dead thing without magic, and it wouldn't respond to my touch.

As The Nightcatcher dragged her further across the floor, the demon left behind dead spiders, smeared beetles, mottled feathers spattered in dried blood.

She was slipping through my fingers.

I couldn't hold on.

I fell to my knees, skinning them on the concrete floor. And I started to beg.

"Please," I said, "I'll give you anything. I'll be your slave. Please. Anything, just don't take her away from me."

But there was no response except the howling noise.

Please.

I never got to tell you.

Anything at all.

The demon opened her mouth to speak.

But she couldn't speak. The darkness spilled down her throat like the silt bottom of a river. Even as it burned away my muscle and exposed the bone of my ruined hand, I didn't let go.

See Nightcatcher, I won't let go. See.

The Nightcatcher grabbed the exposed bones of my hand and squeezed until they snapped.

I let go.

She pulled the demon away.

I tried to run after her, but the concrete walls slid back into place. The boiling noise rushed away. I slammed my hands against the wall once, before collapsing.

I was left alone, on my knees, panting, surrounded by the shells of dead insects. I wanted to scream, give her back, give her back, but I couldn't even speak.

And I knew they wouldn't have been able to hear me.

What was that throbbing? Was she back? Wait, no, it's only the blood rushing through my ears. If adrenaline had a noise, it would be white noise, searching for a way to burst out of my throat.

I crawled up the stairs I'd floated down. I walked through the empty hallways of the hotel above the boiler room, dragging my feet, squeezing my hand to feel if the bones were broken.

I felt them shifting, fragmented, but no pain.

I hoped to catch a glimpse of the demon upstairs. A sound. A strand of hair. Some reminder. One last chance for me to save her.

But she was not there.

I walked out of the hotel. I stood still for a long time on the street, shivering and shaking, my hands drained of blood.

Nothing we'd done to keep The Nightcatcher away had worked - running away from home, the sigils, the rituals, the hunter's bow.

My demon was gone.

I walked away from the hotel. I turned the corner.

In the middle of an empty street, in broken shadow and glass, waited the machine.

Twenty-Nine

WHEN THE MACHINE SAW me, it opened its mouth, a rusted jaw on springs, a black Hades of a mouth, and it roared.

I ran and it chased me.

It was so cold, I couldn't feel my legs. There was a great emptiness underneath me. I called for help. I called and called, but nobody came. The machine screamed behind me, the sound of its gears like a locust swarm; I kept running. This lone street wasn't the only thing I found abandoned; it was the entire city. Neither a person nor a car passed me. The streetlights exploded. The skyscrapers shut off their lights, covering the city in greasy pools of shadow. This wasn't a city anymore, but a facsimile of a city, a stage-set after hours. A fog overtook the streets, obscuring any sense of direction I might have had.

The machine called my name. In its rusted tongue, my name sounded like a bleeding pet.

Lily.

I ran down alleyways, thick with fog. My heart pounded my rib cage until it ached and cried out. My body wanted to curl up and tremble on the ground. I'd had too many sleepless days, too many bleeding days. There was only so much blood that could be bled, only so many veins that could be ripped apart, before they couldn't be put back together again.

"I don't have her anymore!" I called out, but it didn't want the demon. It wanted.

Lily.

I lost my way. Every skyscraper and storefront I ran past loomed dark, blacked out, the fog obscuring every window, every street sign. The machine always stayed right behind me. If I turned to look, I would see a nightmare - maybe my mother's face in the center of its crooked machinery, her eyes gouged out, on leaden spikes. Or the dark river, boiling red, in its metal stomach.

I couldn't look behind me. I couldn't slow down. I'd seen its mouth open, and knew it wanted to swallow me.

Lily.

A thing that said my name like that would know all the right ways to hurt me.

I found the ocean sitting in cold lightning. It would've fried my skin if it touched me. I ran down the middle of the city bridge, usually congested with traffic, now abandoned. My shoes fell apart. I ran onto glass and rocks, and through dirty water.

When the machine rolled onto the bridge, the bridge swayed. It swung me from side to side. My back hit the railing, and I had to grab on or be thrown over. The machine breathed heat through its rusted gears.

The bridge swung again, pushing me off the railing. It would outlast me. It was a machine, and I was a broken girl with half her guts spilling out of her chest. The entire city shut down for it to chase me. There was no demon to save me. No Saint Peter. No witch.

When the machine screamed, my organs twisted. Its infinite hunger shrieked through my blood. It was Lily-shaped hunger. Maybe The Witch thought she'd been building this machine to protect me, but The Nightcatcher slipped inside her head. It fed her the hatred of me. She never knew she was building an insidious mechanism to destroy me.

I imagined that inside its stomach was a rotting pool, a prison for me. The machine would carry me around inside its stomach forever, roaming the world as I dissolved. Just like one of Phaedra's carnivorous plants, once you were swallowed, there was no way to get out. "Crawl into me," the machine whispered, crane-head, breaking sockets; "Aren't I seductive enough for you? Crawl in."

It wasn't only the machine bearing down on me, but the entire city. I felt the skyscrapers close behind, windows snapping like teeth. They'd fall on top of me and tear me apart.

They'd speak:

"Without your demon, you really are so very weak.

"The first thing to go will be your feet. Sore feet, blackened on the bottom, stuck with glass. They'll disappear right out from underneath you.

"Then your hair. That red hair boys want to snort like Adderall. It'll come off in patches as you run, because the wind touches you like an acid."

I made it across the bridge.

It groaned and its cables snapped. I ran toward the sea, through a maze of buildings. I reached the warehouse district, gray buildings, shuttered windows, lonely metal cranes.

Momma would never know what happened to me. She'd never know.

I couldn't run much longer.

I'm sorry, I'm sorry, I'm sorry. For everything I couldn't do.

I ran through an open garage door of a warehouse. I saw the garage button on the wall, and slammed my palm down on it. The garage door began to close. The machine screamed.

I turned away from the closing door. In the dark, I struck a railing and my body vaulted over it.

I hit the bottom of the warehouse's empty concrete floor with a crack. The garage door closed. I lay still, my arms clenched, waiting for the machine to crash through the building.

But there was only silence.

Thirty

MY PANICKED BREATH drifted through the empty building. It'd been abandoned and all of its stock cleared away.

No one would come for me.

I didn't want to move and discover I'd broken my spine. For a long time I waited for the machine that didn't come, choking on dust.

I thought something moved in my periphery, shifting near the wall.

"Hello?" I called out.

I started coughing again.

I rolled onto my back. Pain, pinching and hot, shot through my body. But, I managed to stand and stretch. I hadn't broken my back. Maybe a pinched nerve, some bleeding, but that wasn't anything new. I stretched until my joints popped.

Maybe the machine was gone.

I made my way along the wall in the darkness, feeling with my fingers until I grasped the stair railing. I climbed the concrete steps to the second floor. I skirted along the wall until I moved past the garage, and found a window, its metallic blinds pulled down.

I reached out for the blinds. Hesitated. My fingers shook.

I touched the blinds then slowly, carefully, peeled them back from the dusty window.

The machine sat outside, silent, head extended. Waiting.

I reeled back from the window. I sat on the concrete floor, or else I would've fallen.

The cold came. Fear-cold that couldn't be taken away, because I had no demon to comfort me. It started in my fingers and toes. It worked its way to my chest. I could've been sitting underneath a glacier.

I pressed my hair against my eyes and mouth.

Already my tongue felt dry. I had no food or water. I had no phone. No way to contact anyone. There was no way to get out of the building without the machine knowing and coming after me. Grabbing me. Crushing me. Eating me.

This was the end of the story, then. The hunter goddess never gets to her palace in the forest. She never prepares a feast for her demon and gets to whisper, "eat of these blood and jewels, eat of me." She never gets to lead a trembling fawn to water and snap its neck for the wolves to devour.

Instead she forces her saint away and her demon dies in the boiling water of the Hush Place. Carnivorous plants eat her childhood friends. Her friends waited for her to come and save them from The Nightcatcher, but instead, she collapsed and died on the floor of a warehouse, hiding from an overgrown robot.

Didn't you remember you had schizophrenia, idiot?

You don't get to have a happy ending.

"Help," I whispered, my voice small. "Help me."

I slept and dreamed the kind of dreams where I didn't even remember being human. Time warped around me, and the warehouse ceiling exploded, propelling me beyond the grasp of gravity. These were the kind of dreams, I imagined, that you'd have when you knew you're going to die.

In my dreams I searched for my demon. I'd forgotten myself, but I remembered her. I'd see her silhouette rushing past a window, her dark hair clogging up a still-wet shower drain, but I could never catch up to her.

When I woke, I crawled to the window.

In the wet and gray daylight, the machine still waited.

I huddled at the bottom of the window, hoping for warmth from the sunlight, but there was none in that overcast sky. My blood labored, sluggish, veins clenched. Lack of food had me shaking from low blood sugar. I sucked on the lapels of my jacket, trying to get some moisture, but it didn't seem to help. I'd never been thirstier.

Night came again, colder than before. I slipped in and out of sleep. I felt my heart slowing. If the machine came crashing through the walls, I wouldn't be able to run. I could only hold my arms out, like a child, and let it devour me.

"Help," I tried to whisper once more, but only rasped.

A dirty, dim sound.

Something scurried through the walls. Demon? Nightcatcher? No, something smaller, coming out of the walls.

Spiders. Tiny baby spiders. They ran across my arms and my legs as I lay on the floor.

There were thousands of them scurrying past me, trailing behind them little strands of webbing that dragged across my skin. I resisted my first impulse to pull my hands away and scream. The machine would hear me.

I closed my eyes and shuddered.

Be somewhere else. Be somewhere else.

No, try to remember that moment in the sunlight when the Daddy Long Legs crawled from the demon's fingers to yours, and you laughed.

"I used to be so afraid of spiders."

I sighed and turned my hands upwards. They rushed over the palms of my hands.

Where were they going? Surely they knew a way out, a warm place I could hide. I grabbed the railing, pulled myself up, and followed them down the steps.

Fatigue strained my limbs. I'd gone days without eating before, but never days without water, without drugs, without sunlight. My bones curled from a cold that might never go away.

I reached the bottom of the steps.

I followed them to a wall, and the wall turned around.

It was not a wall, but an enormous creature, bigger than the walls could contain. She grew out of the architecture, broken wiring in her legs.

She had the face of an older woman, pale skin, elegantly aged - the lips slack, eyes blue. Light radiated from her eyes. The Spider Mother.

Her babies slipped underneath her.

She was not looking at them, she was looking at me.

I felt delirious. I couldn't swallow. I knelt and pressed my head to the floor.

"I'm sorry I killed Arachne. I'm so sorry. My mother was wrong. I am not a goddess. Please forgive me."

She paused for a long time.

"Was that one of my children?" she asked.

"I know it was."

In that moment, it seemed normal for a giant spider with a woman's face to be growing in the walls. She had a gentle grandmother's face. At least, how I imagined my grandmother would have been. I used to fantasize about running to her house when my mother became The Exorcist. My grandmother would live in a small cottage in the middle of a sweeping garden. She would always be waiting for me on the front porch when I arrived. My mother's cloak was made of stars, but my grandmother's was made from sunlight. She'd pull me into her sweeping embrace and bury me in her warmth. She'd tell me that I didn't need to be afraid of stories and mythologies. She'd say, "Look how the flowers have grown." She'd teach me the names of all the constellations in the sky, and Wormwood would not be among them.

But, the truth: she was a schizophrenic just like my mother. I heard she died a savior of the world, choking on her own spit. She thought she could bend metal with her mind and stop global warming, but she couldn't even crawl out of bed.

The Spider Mother bent down and spoke

"Tell me about my daughter," she said. "I have so many children. I never get to see them grow."

The hair on her legs stirred like a meadow of black grass. I could have crawled on top of her and been lost for days.

"I only ever saw her die," I said.

She pressed her face closer to me, and breathed cool air onto my face.

"Then you know more than me," she said.

"She had a soft face, and huge blue eyes," I said, swallowing. "She reached out for me, and I held her limb. She was only a baby. She was so soft."

I rested my face against the crag of her chin. She sighed, and the warehouse trembled.

"She was so kind," I said. "Even when I killed her, she didn't hate me. I don't think she knew how."

"Then she is my child," the Spider Mother said.

"You're not angry with me? For what I did?"

"A few survive," she said. "But most don't."

And as the spiders continued to run past me, they left bits of webbing behind, between my fingers. I realized that they were not only rushing toward the Spider Mother, but outward as well.

"Where are they going?" I asked. "How long have you been down here?"

A small smile spread across her face. Everything she did was slow, as if her thoughts rippled from the mountains of her legs to get to her brain.

"I have been here so long that my body has grown into the wall. Behind me there is a web, and beyond that, is a doorway. Through the web

I wove strands that extend past the universe. Some of my children go through the doorway, some go other ways."

"What's behind the doorway?"

"I don't know."

"Then why would they go there?"

"Because they don't know what's waiting for them outside either."

"Well, I do." I said. "I know what's out there."

Her response, minutes away, shuddered through her legs like an electrical storm. She hasn't had to speak to a human in so long, I thought; she's almost forgotten that we cannot communicate in vibrations.

Then, she spoke.

"Do you?"

A baby spider crawled into my palm. Her body was small, but I could still see the sweeping eyelashes on her baby face, with tiny, molded cheeks. Her face was indistinguishable from the face of Arachne.

She kissed me on the thumb before darting behind her mother, and into the doorway beyond.

I looked into the Spider Mother's huge pools of eyes. And as I did so, they ignited with light that seemed to emanate from the core of her being. I saw myself reflected in her eyes.

My horns had never left me. I touched them. Yes, they were real. They were heavy and knobby, like horns a thousand years old.

I was always the girl that the demon saw, even before I could see for myself.

"You could crawl behind me," the Spider Mother said. "You could leave and find what's beyond the doorway."

"Thank you," I said. "You are kind."

I climbed to my feet. As I climbed the stairs, I felt only the weight of my horns.

I opened the garage door.

It was nighttime, the stars wreathing the head of the machine, the air still. I waited for the machine to scream, but it remained silent and inert as I approached. Its head stretched across the ground, its mouth wide open with its teeth of wire and blades exposed.

I climbed inside.

Thirty-One

INSIDE THE MACHINE I found a glowing meadow.

I came across my mother, feeding dead wrens to a giant red pitcher plant. She stood on dead and poisoned ground, a basket of dead wrens, ribbons tied at their necks, poised at her hips. She picked up the wrens one at a time, and fed them to the plant. At the bottom of the pitcher plant, through its sheer skin, I saw the wren's shadows as they slid down to be digested.

"I've been here before."

My mother turned toward me, the gazelle skull tied around her head.

"You shouldn't feed that thing. It belongs to The Nightcatcher. I smell it." I said.

"Don't worry about that," she said.

"Do other people have to deal with things like this?"

"No. But you're a warrior, baby."

I stepped away from the shadow of the tree line. Sunlight suffused my skin. The red cuts on my arms and legs glittered.

"Do I look like I'm up to fight anything?" I said. "I can barely stand."

She fed another wren to the pitcher plant. It reached for her arm, and its juices dripped onto her skin. My mother's skin turned a darker shade of red.

"Do you recognize where you are?" she asked.

"No. I wish people would just be straight with me."

"Look around you," my mother said. "Look at these trees, how they bend for you. Look at the grass, how it strains for you."

"The grass is dead."

"You could make it grow again. If you wanted to."

"If you hadn't gone crazy none of this would've happened."

"Shh, baby. It doesn't matter."

"Don't talk to me like that," I said. "I'm not a kid anymore."

I laughed, clutching the horns on my head.

"I just climbed into the mouth of a machine to find an ancient woods. I find you here, feeding dead birds to a giant living plant, and we're still arguing like we've always argued."

She reached the bottom of the basket, and grabbed the last wren.

"It's different this time," my mother said. "Look around."

I saw, for the first time, where I was.

"On the night you were born all your grandfather's horses died."

We were surrounded by woods that shimmered in the darkness, the light collapsing at the edges of the meadow. The trees were like dark jewels, glimmering in the places not covered in moss and ivy.

"I've been here before," I said.

"You have been here many more times than you think. Can you remember?" she asked.

The last time I'd seen my mother, she'd been melting into an ambulance stretcher. I stopped thinking of her as human. She was The Exorcist, eyes bugging out, arms whirring, bleach and bleeding gums.

Here, her eyes were calm underneath the mask.

"I'll remember when I'm ready," I said.

My mother held the last wren out to me.

"I won't feed that plant," I said. "I'm going to kill it one day."

"Maybe when you come back, you'll find you don't want to anymore."

My mother placed the wren back into the basket. She untied the gazelle skull. Underneath she was the way I remembered her as a child. She was Saga, goddess of storytelling, her blonde hair a crown of light. The mother I remembered who could tell prophecies I believed to be true. Yes, the mother who made stories real. Her robe spun outward and burst with stars.

"She has my demon," I said.
She held the skull towards me.
"It's time to come home."

Thirty-Two

I RETURNED TO The Witch's house. When the machine upended itself from the lawn, it destroyed the roof and crushed the porch. Glass and scrap metal lay strewn about the grass and, as I approached the door, it swung off its hinges and fell.

I found Pluto hiding underneath the collapsed porch. I held my hand out to her and she came to me. She rubbed her chin against my arm, her whiskers tickling my skin. She mewed, a wounded noise, a noise I'd only heard her make on the night she lost her eyes. She had aged over the years, her black fur mottled with gray. I tucked the gazelle skull in the crook of one arm. I picked up Pluto with the other arm, holding her tight against my sweater. Together we entered the house.

The living room was like a murder scene; the couch split in two, the baseboards upended. I didn't see any signs of The Witch, or where she might have gone.

I searched for blood, bits of hair, an arm sticking out from underneath the table. Nothing.

I went into what was left of my room. The dresser drawer lay smashed on the floor; the drugs I'd never sold were torn from their hiding places and scattered. The hunter's bow and the quiver of arrows lay underneath a collapsed board. I moved the board, then picked them up and carried them across my shoulder.

Rays of light, cast through the broken ceiling, revealed something on the bed that I hadn't seen in a long time.

The dead-thing dress.

It was the same one that the demon brought to me; the one I'd worn on my 16th birthday, I was sure of it. The one I'd destroyed. It was untouched by glass or debris, as if someone had tiptoed through the ruins and left it here for me to find.

I brushed my hands against the hem of silvery-throated insects.

I found my bag in the debris, the same one I'd packed so hurriedly to run here. I shook the debris off the bag, folded the dress, and placed it inside. Pluto kept making circles around the room, sniffing, scratching. Occasionally, she'd mewl as if in distress.

"What are you looking for?" I asked her.

I tried to pick her up, but she bolted into the hallway. I chased after her.

"Pluto? What's wrong?"

I followed her into the ruined kitchen where the refrigerator had fallen and smashed the kitchen table, leaving spilled food rotting on the floor.

Pluto jumped onto the ledge above the sink and looked out the window into the backyard. She cocked her head to one side, watching. Waiting. She let out another mewl of distress. Blood and bird feathers ringed her mouth. I never fed her anything but wet cat food, but with no one to take care of her, she must've been forced to hunt.

"Pluto."

Finally she turned to look at me, and her wormwood eyes were losing their glow. I'd never seen such sadness in an animal before.

"You're waiting for her, aren't you?"

I picked her up. She was so thin I could feel each individual rib. I didn't know how long she'd been here, waiting for the demon to come back. I couldn't keep track of time anymore. Days were a facsimile of real time.

I was afraid to look at a clock; maybe the arrows would start moving backwards.

I kissed Pluto on the back of her neck.

"We'll find her. I promise."

***

It might've taken me a week to get to The Witch's house in the dark city, but it took me much longer to get back home. I trekked homeward through endless, rolling hills that groaned in the night and shone like heated lamps in the day. The gravel beat my shoes into bloodied scraps. The string of the bow carved a red line across my back. Pluto mewled in my arms, crying for her, with her mottled nose pressed into the crook of my arm.

When I couldn't walk anymore, I hitchhiked with truckers, bad mothers, and businesspeople that wanted to tell a story.

And the story would go something like this:

On the top of a hill I saw a girl holding a ragged, black cat. And on her back, she carried a duffle bag and a composite bow the color of a black polished mirror, like nothing I've ever seen before. When I stopped on the side of the road she walked toward me. Up close, I saw how sick and thin she was, as if ready to collapse underneath the weight of everything she carried.

Yet still she walked.

I opened the passenger seat of my car and, without a word she climbed inside and shut the door. I drove back onto the highway. She pressed her forehead against the air conditioning vent, breathing in small, little gasps. I pulled into a drive-through for food.

"What do you want to eat?" was the first thing I said to her.

She chewed on her knuckles and smiled, but she didn't answer me. Even the devil couldn't grin like that.

I ordered her a cheeseburger and a milkshake. She gave half of the cheeseburger to her cat, and ate the rest, obviously starving. She drank the milkshake so fast I thought she'd vomit. I kept driving. The sun was going down and I had to turn the AC off. I know it was because the sun was going down that the air got cold, but I couldn't help but think it was because of her.

She still hadn't spoken.

In the dark, her red hair didn't lose its color. The rest of her was dull and beaten. Her skin was sunburnt and covered in scars. God knows where she got them. She had a slash on her throat leaking pus, infected scratches. Her clothes were held together with pins and her ribs protruded from slits in her shirt. But her hair was healthy and strong. Alive.

I should've driven her to a hospital. I should've asked her where her parents lived and turned my car around. But my hands felt stuck to the wheel. My neck felt bolted to the chair. I've never felt so out of control before. I'm serious; you should've seen this bow. It had the curve of the moon inside it. In the shadow of the night her face could've been anything, a lion's head, a flower's center.

But I knew she was grinning.

"Stop," she said, so quiet I almost didn't hear her.

I never noticed how dark it was out there, beyond the headlights of my car.

"Stop," she said again. "I'll get out here."

I wanted to tell her there was nothing out there, that she needed medical attention, that a girl her age shouldn't be carrying around a weapon that could take the head off a bear.

But I stopped the car.

She opened the car door. I knew she would go out there, into the dark, beyond the headlights, and nobody would be able to save her.

"You're very sick," I said.

She climbed out of the car with her cat and her belongings. Her hand lingered on the door handle, and her fingers quivered. I couldn't see her mouth, and it was if she spoke from her veined eyes.

"I know I'm sick," she said, "but isn't it kind of fun to be damaged?"

Part Seven:

Like Bursting Through a Membrane

Thirty-Three

IN THE TIME I'D been gone, my childhood home transformed into a charnel house. My mother broke all the windows from the inside and placed rodent skulls on the ledges. Roof shingles, smoked black, fell into the driveway.

The other homes in the neighborhood had long been abandoned, FOR SALE signs staked into every lawn. Phaedra's house suffocated underneath crushing ivy, as if it'd been neglected for years. Not a single light remained on the street.

Inside the lights flickered on.

When I went inside and saw her, I knew the mother who came to me in the woods, was not the same mother who lived here. This was someone older. Someone who hadn't felt sunlight in a long time.

She sat in the living room, in swaddling clothes, strips of blankets and knitted quilts she'd ripped apart and stitched together, the infant terrible, the mother cannibal. Joseph, Mary and savior. Kali and Jezebel and stripper-whore. She was all images of woman, superimposed on each other. She was the one who hung all my childhood memories on a tree and wore my failures on her head like a barbed crown.

She untangled herself from the snarl of blankets and rose toward me. How similar we were. In a few years, I'd look just like her, with the dark tangled hair and the eyes of a bird, with her wasp skeleton and honey skin.

"You haven't been taking care of yourself," I said.

"Neither have you," she said. "But your horns are growing in nicely."

She embraced me.

"Come upstairs."

I brought my bag to my bedroom. The room was as I remembered it. There was the mirror the demon once used to show me how I'd grown into a woman, the macramé lamp I used to read under long after bedtime, the bed with its dusty pink coverlet. I walked through the room, running my fingers across everything.

"You're not mad at me?" I asked my mother.

"I couldn't be," she said. "It's time for you to get ready."

I lay all of my things on the bed: the gazelle skull, my dead-thing dress, and the hunter's bow.

I undressed. Momma laced me into the dead-thing dress and the spiders clutched my throat. She tied the skull mask into place, a black ribbon at the back of my head. The bone pressed heavy into my face.

Oh Mother, how strong you could have been; the storyteller and the goddess, instead of the divorcee who let her head fall into the sea. You could have burned your fingers in hell and come out laughing. You could have spit flame into the faces of the nurses who shoved you into paper slippers. Instead, you scrubbed your teeth with bleach, bled into the sink, and ran from window to window chasing The Nightcatcher who poisoned your brain.

Or maybe you knew she'd come for me all along and you had no choice but to wait.

"The hush place," I said, picking up my hunter's bow, "that's where she is."

Momma led me downstairs and out of the house into the dark. The door snicked closed behind us.

We walked through the fields toward the river, the same fields that Charlie and I once walked in summer heat. The dead-thing dress clacked and tugged my skin.

***

The Nightcatcher tread behind us with bare feet and wherever she crushed the grass, it never grew again.

"I may not part with her," she said to me. "I may not give her up for anything.

I felt stifled and hot underneath the mask. My horns bled.

"I want a new pet, and she's so sweet. She was born to be sweet," The Nightcatcher said.

I kept walking, hands balled into fists, my face burning.

"I could make her serve me forever," she said, "make her kneel. I'd be good to her. She'd learn to love it."

I snarled. It was a sound I'd never heard come from me before, a wet and throaty animal sound.

"She's mine!" I said,

I stopped. When I looked behind me, The Nightcatcher was gone and half a dozen deer stood a few feet away from me. More were coming out of the fog, tiptoeing gently, like hobbled women.

"Look, darling," Momma said. "Those deer have your eyes."

I held my hand out to the deer. I opened my mouth to speak to them.

Ke-ke-ke-ke-ke.

The deer tiptoed forward and a small fawn reached out to nuzzle my hand. Her nose blue velvet, her eyes, demon eyes. Through the corner of her mouth I saw the glint of fangs.

My shoes fell apart in the grass, and my feet cracked apart. From the skin of my pale feet emerged newborn hooves, three pronged and black.

(Once I was a girl.)

And I felt my horns spiraling from my head.

(But I scratched and scratched.)

My face melting into the mask of bone.

(Scratched and scratched.)

My spine tearing my back, lapping at the back of my head.

Until I was a girl no more.

Not a transformation, but a revealing.

The deer followed us to the river where Charlie once jumped, and never resurfaced.

"I had so many questions for you," I said to Momma as I stood at the edge of the bridge overlooking the water, "but I can't remember now. And I'm not sure they ever mattered."

My mother, with the bird nest in her hair, smiled, and her fingers stiffened around her throat.

I looked into the water below. Turgid waters. Water with teeth. I hesitated, took a step back, and heard the rustle of the deer stepping backwards with me.

"It's not too late," she said. "You could still turn around."

"Mother," I said.

I turned back to the waters kicking up froth. I gripped the hunter's bow in both hands and stepped onto the side of the bridge.

"Mommy, I love her."
I jumped down.

Thirty-Four

I HIT THE WATER and plunged downwards. I held tight to the hunter's bow. My lungs burned. The water grew murkier and murkier until starlight couldn't reach me.

I fell into a cave below the river. I gasped, inhaling a rush of oxygen. It was a cave where the walls whispered, quivering like a womb.

The hush place. It was a network of ancient tunnels. The town must've been built on top of them.

The Nightcatcher must've used these tunnels to appear wherever she wanted; at my mother's window to torment her with poison, to whisper like a river in my ear when I couldn't sleep, to crawl into a meadow to set a trap for my demon and me.

I got to my feet.

The ceiling rose a hundred feet above me, made of suspended, boiling water. No going back. Yet, there were so many tunnels leading in every direction; I didn't know which way to start walking.

I stood still for several moments, trying to slow my breathing and to make sure I hadn't actually died on the way down. There had to be some clue, some marking, some whispering, godlike voice, to lead me in the right direction. If only I could find, on the floor, a single spider. One of the demon's spiders. I'd recognize them anywhere.

But there were no spiders.

Then a child's silhouette stood up in the darkness. I couldn't see his face or any of his features masked in the shadows, but I knew he hadn't slept in years. I recognized his frail shaking, the twitch gap-stop of his motions. He dripped water as he approached me.

I crouched down so we were eye to eye and I saw his bloated, waterlogged face. Red liquid smeared his chin. Blood, I thought at first.

But no, it was the juice of pomegranate seeds.

He held his hand out to me, also smeared in red. I slung the hunter's bow over my back.

***

Charlie led me through the tunnels.

The air, moist and hot, made it difficult to breathe. It felt like being buried underneath a volcano. Sometimes bright light streaked the tunnels and I could see the walls scratched and marked with the same symbols The Witch drew on the walls and carved on her skin.

Protection symbols, maybe.

Or maybe something transcribed to The Witch in sleeping hours, or written down in a gold-embossed tome of spells to soften the lie. The words became sigils so that the writer would forget, but the sigils never forgot.

Charlie and I walked like two dreamers, like children, almost too nervous to hold hands. He stumbled, sleep-drunk, and on his bare shoulders I saw the scars of whip marks he'd once inflicted on himself.

Did he look at the walls and see his own broken future?

Or did he see my history etched there, the golden-haired huntress with the deer lying down to sleep in my lap, the hunter's bow played like a violin? Did he see the girl with a shadow that breathed on the back of her neck, and a mother who ground herbs into a poultice that, if eaten, could scratch the surface of the universe away?

I saw Wormwood.

Wormwood, the walls said. Your origin and your epitaph. The ambrosia flower that could make you into a goddess, or the living dead. Wormwood. It's sweet on the back of the tongue.

We came to a long hallway where moss grew on stone tiles underneath us. I noticed child footprints, sunk into the moss, crushed and faded brown, as if he'd walked here many times before. Without looking, Charlie stepped into the imprints.

"Do you know how long you've been down here?" I asked.

"I've been waiting for you a long time," he said. "But now you're here, and it's like I never waited at all."

I followed in his footsteps. My hooves were smaller than his child's feet.

"Did you get the cigarette?" I asked, and I laughed, because it seemed such a trivial question.

"Yes," he said. "When you threw it down to me, I saw your face reflected in the water. You were so far away. I wanted to reach out and tell you not to worry about me. But she reached out for you instead."

She.

"I burned her," he said in his quiet, shredded voice, "with your cigarette. The entire river boiled. She cried out and sank back down into the darkness, and she could not grab you."

"Did she hurt you?" I whispered.

"She couldn't," Charlie said. "I'm not the one she wants to hurt."

"I wish I could have found your teddy bear for you."

"I don't miss him. I have lost more than that."

"I'm sorry I didn't jump into the water after you."

He turned to me. Shadows coiled around his arms. He wiped at his mouth with his free hand, but the pomegranate stain wouldn't go away.

He grasped my hands.

"I will never forgive you," he said. "Because I have nothing to forgive you for."

"I was scared. I should have jumped in after you," I said.

"Then you wouldn't be here with me now. In this moment. And I wouldn't give up this moment for anything else."

He kept leading me forward, and as he did, she spoke to me through the walls.

"Lily.

"I've got a little something for you. Can you guess what it is?

"It's got two arms and two legs, and can walk backwards on its hands. It eats cat's eyes and dead birds.

"It's a rotten thing. I wouldn't touch it, you'll get diseases.

"If it gives me one wrong look I'll break every bone in its is face."

If walls could've smiled, they would've smiled with black-winged teeth, with her mocking, sharp tongue. My jaw and brain rattled. The walls pressed closer.

"How much further?" I asked Charlie.

"This way."

The fog rolled in at our feet, and rolled back.

We entered a brass atrium. Tunnels branched off in several directions, spiraling outward. Built into the center of the room was a dry, brass fountain. I leaned over the edge. At the bottom of the fountain lay old coins, covered in dust. Greek, maybe. Or older.

The coins transformed into broken pieces of glass that reflected my skull mask. My cracked, red eyes were veined with fear and lack of sleep.

It was the face of The Exorcist.

"You look like your mother," he said.

I reached up to tear the skull off my face, but I stopped. Something to do with the reflection of myself, repeated over and over in fractals at the bottom of the fountain. Something to do with the way my eyes, swimming in red, could still smile.

"No," I said, "I'm stronger than her."

We left the atrium.

We walked through hallways so old and hot that the walls turned to glass.

We walked through haunted tunnels that whispered my name. And, oh my dear, they'd been waiting so long to call my name.

The tips of my fingers cracked and bled. The backs of my hands burst with crystals. My teeth bulged until my mouth swelled with pain.

I couldn't tell where the gazelle skull ended and my skin began, if there still was a difference at all.

I came across a cracked part of the glass wall. Maybe the demon dragged her nails across it while thrown over The Nightcatcher's shoulder. She must've carried my demon down here. I could imagine her hair, like an ocean, filling the corridor behind her in frantic waves, her legs kicking.

My aching hooves could barely sustain the weight of my body. I wanted to lay down in the middle of the dark tunnels, and rest until my feet stopped throbbing.

But I had to keep going. Nothing good ever happened in the middle of a metamorphosis. Think of all the caterpillars that died mid-ecdysis, their slick and slimy wings trapped in their own cocoon, until they died.

Think of the demon, and push forward.

We passed more claw-marked walls, the sigils that demanded my presence. Through the water-grave ceiling and the walls, The Nightcatcher continued to taunt me.

"Lily.

"Lily, your girlfriend is a bitch in heat. I've got her on her knees; she's fucking my fingers."

If Charlie could hear her through the walls, he didn't say.

"Go right. We're almost there," Charlie said.

We turned a corner into another hallway and, at the end of the hallway, a golden door floated in the black, miles away.

Beneath me blew a desert. I stepped on bones that surfaced up out of the sand.

Inside me, my organs were turning rotten, like the fleshy pulp inside too-ripe fruit.

The skin on my legs split.

I had to focus on the door at the end of the hallway. Focus on the door. You won't be buried in sand with Charlie, waiting for another girl-hero to trip over your head. You've got dirty blood but that blood is stronger than this. Just get to the door.

"Lily."

The Nightcatcher again.

"Lily."

No, it was Charlie, speaking in a voice like a child's rattle.

"I want you to know what's going to happen when you walk through that door."

I took another step. Another. Charlie coughed a dirty river on the back of my hands. The next time he spoke it sounded as if his lungs were filling with water.

"She's going to destroy you. She's going to eat you alive, strip by strip of flesh. She'll break your bones for fun and sit on your face as you scream. She'll call out her monsters to pull what's left of you apart and reassemble you into what she wants."

We were nearly at the door. Something alive stirred underneath my hooves. A snake, maybe, slithering through the walls. Jagged bones cut into the tender parts of my legs and snagged on the lace of my dead-thing dress. Yet I was nearly there. The golden door grew closer, with an entire mythology carved into its panels. A huntress and a deer, a woman on a Viking's ship, a laughing pantheon of gods.

"Maybe she'll make you forget everything," Charlie said, "but if she doesn't, I want you to remember this."

"I'll try," I said, "as best as I can."

"Remember that, if I were born of the underworld, you were born of flowers. You are the blood the forest feeds upon and it is you who gave the woods their dark magic. Time doesn't exist and, in another world, I never left you. I've transformed your wounds into a scepter for a queen. The Nightcatcher may think that she's had her victory - but your veins are buried in the map of the earth and she can never have you. She thinks she can own the universe because she's enslaved gods and eaten stars, but she couldn't even kill me, living here in her tunnels, because you protected me with your love.

"Lily. I've seen the way out."

I approached the golden door.

My fingers split apart. The bones inside curled. The gold glittered, faintly incandescent, making the icons carved into it, move back and forth.

Charlie withdrew his fingers and slipped backwards, into the darkness.

"Why can't you go with me?" I asked.

"You know why."

Then the door opened.

I went inside where she waited for me.

Thirty-Five

THE NIGHTCATCHER SAT on a throne of crystal, underneath a domed ceiling that swirled with birthing galaxies, stars dipped in god's blood. The great destroyer, the terrible queen, surrounded by velvet curtains and glass lamps. Oh mighty one. Oh eater of gods. When Zeus tried to rape you, you grew teeth between your legs. Cronus couldn't swallow you. Artemis couldn't best you. Kali tried to choke you to death with her noose, wrapped in tiger's skin, but you didn't need to breathe.

The gods were there in her throne room, her slaves and pets, naked except for golden chains around their wrists.

They'd been preparing a feast before her throne on an enormous table. Aphrodite, eyes downcast as she carried silverware, her once lush golden hair, shaved away. I saw Loki setting the chairs, great trickster, the blood leached from his fingers and acid stains on his cheeks from the world serpent Jörmungandr. Ishtar, goddess of love and war, lay at The Nightcatcher's feet, licking wine off the nightcatcher's fingers. Thor set out steaming soups and enormous silver trays of vegetables and samosas. She'd cut his nose off. Severed his right arm.

I'd expected The Nightcatcher to be an enormous beast, a ragged, dusty, and spitting thing. Only an ugly creature that leaked milk and spit could've taken my demon away from me.

But the creature that sat on the crystal throne owned a cherub's face and a child's curveless body. She wore a silver cloak, and a headdress of amethyst and bone, with tasseled fringes that hung across her cheekbones. She resembled a devil preserved in porcelain, dressed in clothes woven from an old sky never torn with pollution. Her eyes were wild bright poison. Her nails were cat's claws, gorged red. She lounged against the throne, her feet propped against the armrest.

I drew the hunter's bow.

"Where is she?" I asked.

She snapped her fingers.

"Stay," she said.

I drew an arrow and shot at The Nightcatcher's throat.

She reached up to deflect the blow, but the arrow severed her wrist from her arm, and pinned her hand against the wall behind her.

A salad plate slipped from Aphrodite's fingers and broke on the floor.

As if from a great distance, I saw the blood spurting from The Nightcatcher's wax doll hand, staining her crystal throne and spraying against her silken finery. Yes, she could bleed.

Then, I was running across the room, stepping onto a chair, rolling across the feasting table. It didn't matter I was weak, broken, and ready to break, or that my new horns weighed more than my body. I could be a monster, Francois taught me that, I could be The Nightcatcher's monster. I'll break a thousand salad plates, crush a thousand pieces of dessert silverware, break the wrists of a hundred god's reaching out to try and stop me, to get to her.

I rolled to my feet and, before I stood, I drew another arrow. I ran to the end of the table, pulled the bow taut, and stared down the feathered tip at The Nightcatcher's poison eye, ready to release.

My stomach burst and blood spread across my dead-thing dress.

The child queen laughed. The stars shattered. The table underneath me rattled. The cups rolled. Nameless gods, with faces made of sand, eyes like desert suns, bandaged her amputated arm. They pulled the arrow from her shoulder and her blood sprayed out, hissing with steam. They licked at the wound with soldering tongues.

She spoke in a voice made of dirt and boiling water.

"You'll never see her again."

"Why do you think I missed your throat?" I asked.

"Because you're a poor shot," she said. "Because you're a disgusting, disease-riddled slut with bad manners."

"No," I said, "so that after I took my demon back, I could make you beg for your life."

I buried my next arrow in her shoulder.

The force of it would've knocked a bear back, but she only jerked a little in her chair. Her nails dug into the arms of her crystal throne. Her eyes rolled back in her head.

I drew another arrow.

"I'm the disgusting, disease-riddled slut that you want," I said.

A dark stain spread down from her shoulder. The smell of her blood was like sandalwood. Even with a severed hand and an arrow in her body, she retained her composure.

"Why would I want you?" she asked, as if the arrow striking her, hadn't even made her lose a breath.

"You want me. You took my demon because you want me. You, with all your gods and playthings. And you barreled across the universe to find me."

The Nightcatcher laughed again and I stumbled, trying to keep my footing, as the table rattled once more.

"You're a very sick girl," The Nightcatcher said.

"Don't try to trick me," I said. "My whole life they've told me I'm a child murderer, bitch, punk. I'm worth nothing. I'm an insect. They did it to my mother, and they did it to me.

"Because they knew how strong we could become, and they were afraid. So they tread on us. Spit on us. In return we tried to destroy ourselves. That way we'd never rise up and conquer them. We couldn't even conquer ourselves.

"But that all changed when I met my demon. My shadow."

I held my breath. I waited for the stars to hurl down and incinerate me. Stop this child's game, Nightcatcher. Why do the gods not rise up to defend you? Why do you not transform into a smoking hydra to devour my head?

But she only sighed.

"Your demon is dead." The Nightcatcher said. "Didn't anyone tell you?"

Pain spread through my chest. It was the kind of pain that unravels from its center, like a spider web.

"That's not true," I said.

"I killed her."

"Then I'll kill you."

She looked me up and down, like a freshman girl in high school, someone thinner than you, prettier than you. Every cruel girl could say with her eyes, "Why are you wearing that? Why don't you lose some weight?" And you couldn't help but wonder, for a moment, if her eyes transformed you into someone you didn't recognize. All it took was up, down, and sneer.

And I looked down.

The bow was gone. All that was left were my shaking hands and emaciated arms, a hospital bracelet around one of my wrists. A hospital gown fluttered at my ankles. There were paper slippers on my feet. I stood not on a great feasting table, but on a thin, yellowed hospital mattress.

"You're a very, very sick girl."

I knew this would happen to me, having watched my mother go insane and my father fall apart. When my mother shuffled down that hallway from the psychiatric ward in her paper slippers, I shattered into pieces on the waiting room floor. I'm broken if you're broken, Mommy, because you fed me rotting milk.

I want to be the fawn that jumped back into its mother's womb, send you to lay down in a grove as I float and heal in your amniotic sac. We could forget together. I will heal you and you will heal me.

But I know we can't. Time is reversible, but consequence is not.

Lily.

The Nightcatcher didn't even have to speak to say my name.

Why did your mother name you Lily?

"My demon can't be dead," I whispered.

"You thought you were a great hunter? That you carried the black bow that slew a kraken? You had nothing but a child's toy. Sick little girl. Dirty punk girl. You'll die with rat poison injected into your veins."

The throne room was disappearing, replaced by the whitewashed walls of the hospital. The gods were fading into nurses, their faces quivering, pained with red, and aged by childbirth. They grew nametags on white button-downs. Alice. Bertha. Name: I could kill every girl in this goddamn hospital.

The goddess I thought used to be Aphrodite shrunk down into Agnes, and held out a paper cup full of pills.

"Of course she's dead," The Nightcatcher said, even her and her throne fading into the wall. "She wasn't even real."

Agnes rattled the pills in their paper cup. I whimpered and took it from her.

"No," I said. "No, I can't be here."

"You've never been anywhere else."

The Nightcatcher's voice became softer and softer. It shimmered like a wavering thought.

Why did she name you Lily?

The lily means birth. When Hercules sucked on the breast of Zeus, the milk flowed heavenward and created the Milky Way. The milk that dripped down to earth formed the lily.

The lily means death. Death camas, poison to any who would eat it. Lilies for a child's grave, for innocence. As an infant you clung to a mother who dripped Schizophrenia onto your skin with each kiss. You couldn't have known it would end in your own destruction.

The pills in the paper cup were black, soft liquid capsules. They would be pills easy to swallow, pills with soothing names. Never mind the drool. That could be wiped away by Agnes with her rough fingers.

I remembered the story my mother once told me.

"She hunted you in your own forest, like you hunted the stag. She was fast upon you. She twisted your dream world so that it no longer belonged to you. It became a labyrinth of nightmares. She took the ground from underneath you. There was no escape."

I picked up one of the pills. I brought it to my mouth. The stars fell out of the sky above. They'd never been stars, really, but flecks of stucco on a too-close hospital ceiling.

"Just as The Nightcatcher was upon you, you cut your shadow from your body. It grew into the shape of a girl, your dark-half with night for hair and eyes. The Nightcatcher seized the shadow, and you were free."

The nurses surrounded me with crossed arms, stomping feet.

"Why are you babbling to yourself? There's nobody there."

"No," I said quietly.

"Speak up," they said. "Stand straight. Your weakness has brought you to this place."

"No."

I dropped the pill, and the paper cup. They fell to the ground without noise.

"No?" they asked, laughing and mocking.

They untied the strings of my hospital gown and tore it away from me. I threw my hands over my bare chest. They tugged at my hair. They pinched my nose until I had to open my mouth to breathe. They threw black pills in my mouth and pushed me backwards. I fell and coughed them up, choking.

"You can't get better if you don't want to get better."

I closed my eyes and tried to remember the demon, her body soft in my bed. I tried to remember her heated kiss, the dark smile. The memories were fading, as if they'd been nothing but chalk outlines on the side of my brain. And yet:

Why did your mother name you Lily?

It was so difficult to think with dirty, calloused fingers trying to pry my mouth apart, slapping my face. A nurse emerged from the dim hallway and pushed a towel-covered cart into my room. She flung the towel aside, revealing a row of syringes.

I remembered the moment in that elementary school auditorium when stories stopped being real, the moment when my mother, haggard and cracked, was banished from her throne of storytelling.

They injected syringes into my back, into the shape of a new spine.

I had seen the poison in a dirty rat girl's eyes. I ran from boiling waters and terror queens and family curses, thinking I was forging my own path, yet I only kept my mother's story alive.

And yet:

Your mother named you Lily because flowers could grow as well as be crushed underneath your feet.

They couldn't take those memories from you. They couldn't wrap them up in a package of insanity. I had left this hospital before. I had walked on ceilings with the billowing black hair of a demon tied around my ankles. I kissed lips that slipped a spider into my mouth. I burned my fingers on the bottom of an ocean, reaching out for pale arms.

I shed my velvet, and the horns remained.

"She's real," I said.

"You're deranged."

I opened my eyes. I stood, naked and cold, jostled from all sides, and held my hands in front of my face.

"What are you doing?" they asked. "This abnormal behavior will be reported."

"When you're asleep, you never know where your hands will be," I said.

In the spaces between my fingers, I saw what Charlie must've seen before he went under the water: a possibility of realities, swirling and crashing into each other. Between my fingers dripped gold and silver, the bleeding tongue of a nurse turning into a snake, the walls of the hospital tearing apart.

It was like bursting through a membrane.

"She's real because I make her real," I said. "Because I made her mine."

I squeezed my hands, and the throne room came back into focus. The dead-thing dress curled back up on my shoulders. The nurses transformed back into goddesses, the dirty mattress into a feasting table.

In my hands I held my hunter's bow, an arrow pointed at The Nightcatcher's throat.

"I'm going to kill you," I whispered.

I could have torn down the entire hush place. I felt it in my fingers, like a muscle I'd exercised only in dreams. I reached up and peeled the tops of the walls apart. Wet and rotting earth spilled through the folds. The gods cowered. A few disappeared. Yes, I'm a monster. I'll be your monster. I grabbed a glass of wine and drank it, then crushed the glass in my fist. The legs of the feasting table came crashing down. Give me your throne, Nightcatcher, I'll unhinge you. You can eat me, but I'll become a rot that spreads across your face.

I stepped off the table and approached her throne. The gods attending her fled.

The empress bled quietly, a pool of blood rising up in her lap. I came before her enormous crystal throne, so big that her small feet were at my eye level. She leaned down, her curls grazing my forehead.

I could take her throne, if I wanted to. And maybe, lifetimes ago, I had. I might have sat there for a long time, wondering why it didn't fit me, wondering why it did not satisfy me to have all the gods she'd captured serve me as I pleased. I probably killed myself out of boredom.

I saw The Nightcatcher was just a child. She held her bleeding stump to her chest, blood running down her golden dress. The fringes of her crown frayed. And she shrunk on her enormous throne, looking at me with a child's eyes.

I let go of the hush place. The walls folded up once again. The table's legs unbent. I placed the hunter's bow at her feet.

"Let's do things differently this time." I said.

I held my hands out toward her. I led her out of the throne room and into the woods.

Thirty-Six

MY WOODS WERE quiet. The river that haunted me for years into a small stream that ran through the middle of the meadow. I no longer smelled machine oil or dead grass.

The Nightcatcher clung to me. She reached with her small child's hands and tried to slice my dead-thing dress away with her sharp nails.

"Stop," I said. "I remember how to do this."

I peeled the dress away from my shoulders. It came apart in a shower of glittering spider legs and beetle's wings. Crystalline insects with iridescent claws scurried into the grass.

Now naked, I bled gray from the wound in my stomach.

The Nightcatcher slipped off, into the trees.

I walked down the path, one halting step at a time, my newborn hooves shaking.

The trees coiled their leaves and retracted their branches. They brushed the weeds and hanging ivy to form a path for me. Their shadows played cool against my skin. Eyes watched me from the trees and the grass. Green eyes, trembling soft. Blue eyes like popped veins. Black eyes, scrying pools.

"Come out," I said.

The grass and the brush trembled.

"I said come out."

The deer came out of the woods first. The Witch's black mastiffs followed. Their eyes changed colors, at once blue, and then gold. Together they followed me through the woods.

Big, black crows flew down from the treetops and landed on my naked shoulders. Their claws gripped my skin hard, leaving red marks. I coughed blood into my hands. The skin of my arms began to unravel. The birds weren't trying to hurt me. They were keeping me from falling apart.

I wanted to laugh, because girls didn't become goddesses every day. Because I'd never again be seduced by hospitals and pills that turned the body into a living gelatin cube. The river would never haunt me.

At the end of the path I came to a grove, and in the center of the grove, sat a stone dais. Blue flowers grew up from the earth around the dais.

The Nightcatcher walked out of the trees, no longer dressed in resplendent gold and headdress, but as naked as me. Unlike me, her skin was unmarred and smooth. In her one hand she clutched a broken piece of mirror. Flecks of cocaine were still smeared across its surface.

"I've been here before," I said. "I've already done this."

"No," The Nightcatcher said. "Never quite like this."

I knelt on the stone. The dogs and the deer encircled me. The birds flew up into the trees and my skin fell apart. I coughed more blood on the dais and lay down in the sticky pool. I spit out the rest of my teeth. There were grooves carved in the dais for my head. My fingertips. I spread my legs and arms.

The dogs and deer tore me apart. They ripped my skin to get to my bones. They cracked my rib cage. They broke my knees.

It took seeing my heart torn out, pulsating on in front of me, to realize this was a ritual embedded into my DNA. I sat on this dais before, my body flushed with warmth, my heartbeat in my head.

I was only a punk girl, a baby child living in the middle of suburbia, trying to survive ostracization at school and an absent mother. I didn't have a chance to remember. A miracle I did at all, really.

Lifetimes ago I must've run away from this place. I remembered. I ran through the forest until the sky grew darker and darker, until I was blinded in the darkness, until the trees dissolved and I tumbled downwards.

I'd trapped my shadow and myself in a dark city. I'd trapped all of us.

But we could be free.

And even though it hurt to speak because my entire body quivered, broken and spilling out, no heart to pump the blood, I spoke.

"I'm ready."

The dogs and the deer came to me carrying blue flowers in their mouths.

They pushed the flowers into my bones. They crushed the flowers in their teeth, into the shape of a new heart, and placed it into my chest. They created a new stomach for me and placed it through the hole in my waist. Wherever I still had nerves to feel pain, they burned.

Then they ran off, as if spooked. The trees rustled as the birds flew away. I sat up, gripping my stomach to keep myself from disintegrating.

At the end of the path, a girl stood with her black hair squirming. She held a headless bird in one hand, and in the crook of her other arm, a black cat with wormwood eyes.

Ke-ke-ke-ke-ke.

I held my arms out, and she came to me.

"I'm dead," I said.

Strips of skin hung down from my arms. I touched my face. It was a ruin of black blood, smoke, and gobbets of gore.

"No," my demon said. "You're glowing."

She let Pluto go and climbed onto the dais next to me. I grasped the demon's hand. She pressed her mouth against my bleeding thigh.

"Good. You feel good," she said.

I offered my wrists to her.
"Eat," I said.
And she did.

Thirty-Seven

THE DEMON LAY in the pool of my skinless body, her lips against my lips, her fingers against my fingers.

The Nightcatcher sewed us together with a gleaming thread made of star shine and a needle made of bone. The thread dissolved inside our veins. The demon breathed into my mouth as The Nightcatcher sewed her cheek to my skull. She was cool in the hollow space of me. I didn't feel the pain of the needle plunging into my skin, sewing into my muscle, sealing the poisonous flowers into my body. There'd been enough pain already.

"I've searched for you for so long," I said.

"I've always been with you," she said. "In you."

"I was so afraid."

"You should be."

Our kiss sealed us together. She clasped my broken, bleeding wrists. I used her lungs to breathe.

This must be what falling in love felt like.

In my skin.

My shadow.

This was almost like the time we did MDMA together, sweetheart. My body slowly slid down into the stone, my brain lit up like a halogen bulb passing through a crystal. We must've shone bright enough to make a new kind of star.

The Nightcatcher plunged the needle into my eye and the thread that passed through my pupil glowed gold. She tugged and pulled. The demon's kiss deepened. Her kiss said I want to make you happy, there's nothing left to live for but your mouth.

I've missed you so much.

The Nightcatcher sewed the demon's ribcage into my empty chest cavity. She braided the demon's hair into my hair, deepening, swirling, snarled against my horns, transforming into a dark, rich red.

We always fit so well in bed sheets, our bodies tucked into each other almost like this. I should've known we fit deeper. How I ached for her, and until that moment never even knew the depths of my need.

She sank into my bone and into the flowers growing like a meadow inside me. The thread sewed our fingers and feet. Her mouth dissolved into my mouth. She sighed, a soft sigh, and it reverberated through my skull.

Then we were whole, and I was alone.

For a long time I lay on the dais, moving my fingers and toes slowly, stretching my new skin. Constellations bloomed on my stomach. Cignus. Scorpio. Ursula. They were brilliant and wild, like neon cutouts on a velvet board. I moved my hand, and watched the shadow of my fingers pass across the stone. My blood and dead organs

Wisps of flowers blew past me. Bits of fluff fell on my mouth and I breathed them away. I didn't think I would be able to stand, but my new skin was more resilient than the old one. It carried a new weight.

I stepped off the dais, and I walked a new path.

New grass bloomed underneath me. I'd never known colors could be like this. I'd been given new eyes. I couldn't really see the world missing my shadow all those years.

The flowers jostled inside my head. My shadow walked the path in front of me, and she kissed the blue azaleas, kissed my bleeding hooves.

Pluto slipped in between my feet, mewling. Her wormwood eyes were a map of the woods. My woods. I followed her through trees. I drank from the water that formed, heavy and crystalline, on cupped leaves. Pluto sipped droplets from my fingers.

It was nighttime at the end of the path, star-time, glowing bright enough to leave a bruise. The woods dropped into deep space. Mercury with her burnt face rose above the trees, her eyes mad celestial marble, her lips made of hot-blooded craters. Mars stood behind her with a frozen crown of twin moons - Phobos and Deimos - vampire asteroids.

The demon promised me a palace of living jewels, but there was more out there than either of us imagined. I didn't need a throne, I didn't need to eat rubies that dripped like juice, or keep slaves that licked at my cuts. Not when I could be the first scientist to float to the edge of the cosmos, picking up planets in my gravity. Maybe beyond the trees I'd find Wormwood. I could chart a new course there and back. I would give its poison to every punk girl, loser, and child murderess, and its secrets could no longer harm us.

And when I opened my mouth, I could swallow the world, cover continents in my saliva. I'd breathe new colors onto the dirty, polluted waters.

I smiled, and the demon inside me smiled.

I kept going.

Phaedra:
A Short Story

IN MY STRANGE GARDEN lives a man-eating tree with limbs of snakes. When I take my midnight walks through the garden, it rears its writhing head above the walls, an oscillating hissing mass of fanged mouths and veined muscles. The tree calls my name in fourteen languages, one for each head.

Phaedra.

Phaedra, let me tell you the things I've devoured today.

I open my arms and the snakes come to me, slithering through dust, through the air, through fuchsia roses I planted years ago that never wither. They sniff my arms and my neck. I throw my head back. Some of them rest their heads on my chest and warm themselves. Their bodies are cool and black, like the membranous bark of a tree's trunk. Others wrap around my legs, my thighs. They embrace me tightly and lift me off the ground. They rock me in the soft cradle.

She is the great Madagascar Tree, the hungry Ya-te-veo of the Mdoko tribe. Ya-te-veo means "I see you already," and she once lived as a goddess in the jungle, thirstier than bloody Kali. Now she lives with me.

Phaedra, you've never known love like this.

I was born in Georgia, but Mama taught me to say I was born in Paris. Mama was thin and always shaking. She listened to French tapes but never learned to say anything except Bonsoir, and Comment allez-vous? And anorexie. The last one means, of course, anorexia.

"Beauty in sickness. You'll understand when you're older," she said, "real beauty is a reptile."

She told me she was a fashion designer in Paris. She nursed me while she fitted children with dresses made of razor blades, crystals, and lace. They were girls as young as twelve, recruited from poor villages in such places as the Ukraine and Estonia. Easier to control that way. Once healthy, now anemic and starved from pressure. When they bent over so Mama could tie them into their dresses, their bones pushed against their skin like angry faces.

"Mama, none of this is true," I said.

"Does it need to be?" she said, and collapsed onto the couch, "bring me another headache pill, my baby."

Headache pill meant codeine. Mama loved her drugs. For a while she even did cocaine with her therapist as some sort of "experimental therapy." She'd come home laughing and sniffing and grinding her teeth together. She talked so fast that I couldn't understand anything she said, except "breakthrough". Another breakthrough. Half an hour later she'd lock herself in the bathroom and start screaming.

She sat on the floor and kicked at the bathtub until the plaster broke.

That didn't last long, because experimental therapy is expensive and the alimony ran out. Back to codeine and klonopin. Downers suited my mother better anyways. She wrapped herself in a towel from the dryer and lay down in front of the television for hours. She looked so warm.

The most important thing Mama taught me was this:

You don't have to be the stupid girl born in dust-choked Georgia. Born in the backseat of a broken-down Chrysler twenty miles away from the city, while your father, or what was left of him, is trying to wave down passing vehicles. You don't have to be the girl who came out of the womb under the eyes of a man who drove up in a tractor. The only man who stopped for you, a redneck with tobacco spit dribbling down into his beard, wearing coveralls coated in dust and grime, chipped fingernails, cancer-spots on his tongue.

He never had to say, "That's going to be an ugly girl someday," when I came out, crying and wheezing.

So when I went to school for the first time, I became the girl from Paris. I didn't know the first thing about Paris, except that it meant elegance - haute couture and coffee shop beignets. It meant I'd slipped into the pulsing center of something significant. I could be a writer, like Hemingway or Gertrude Stein or Sartre. I could model in cold dresses underneath cold cameras, thinning into a sick, scale-flecked beauty. I could be homeless on a street corner, wearing the same thin cotton dress for five years, begging for change so that I could buy a bottle of wine. I could be the wife who sat in the corner of a living room, holding my cat, Miss Margot, knitting sweaters for children that never came. Whatever I chose, I would be safe from the factory smoke of this small town.

From crying during every Father's day.

From becoming my mother.

I drew the outline of who I wanted to be over my door and I forced my body to grow into its shape.

Let me tell you the things I've devoured today.

Once, in middle school, I was applying my mascara in the bathroom when Samantha Hall charged in, slamming the bathroom door.

She was a dark-haired cheerleader. She was a lightning factory, always charged, bursting in and out of rooms and breaking doors. She slipped across the floor in her hurry to get to me and point her finger, with its nail-bitten cinnamon red polish, in my face.

"Stay away from my boyfriend, you fucking Jezebel."

Until that moment, I hadn't given Samantha Hall's boyfriend a second thought. I put down the mascara, but before I could respond, she whirled around and charged for the bathroom exit. Slam. The door swung shut. I heard her stomping down the hallway. I turned back to the mirror and touched my cheek, accidentally smearing mascara on my skin.

I imagined myself a Jezebel. I wondered if I owned the face of a Jezebel - dark skin, rouge cheekbones. I wondered if I could be a princess of Baal, a slut, a whore who danced on the decapitated heads of men. I wondered if I had the eyes for a whore. The lips, pursed. Then slightly parted. Maybe with a vampy lipstick, smoky eyes. I could drift in and out of opium dens and the bedrooms of kings - laughing. Yes. A Jezebel.

The smell of cigarette smoke drifted out from one of the stalls.

"Lily," I said, "give me one or I'm telling."

"Fuck," she said.

I'd known her since we were in preschool - she lived across the street in the haunted house. I used to wish we could trade places, because her mother wore a velvet cloak like a queen and talked to me like an adult. Then her mother went crazy and ended up in the hospital, thought a monster followed her. She tore her cloak apart and grew blisters on her tongue. Lily grew into a dirty kid who smoked too much and hung out with the neighborhood weirdos.

She started fucking the school janitor too. Or, at least that's what I heard.

She passed me a cigarette underneath the stall. I slipped it into my purse and left.

Later at a house party, I found Samantha Hall's boyfriend, drunk on blue Mad Dog. Amateur move. A football player, if you can get any more cliché. Kind of skinny, but with broad shoulders and a broad chest. He had a Georgia peach kind of smile. He stood by the stereo and a broken houseplant, surrounded by his football team friends.

When he went to the bathroom, I waited a few moments and slipped in after him. He was trying to piss, his hand against the wall to steady himself. He left grimy, soaked handprints against the wallpaper.

I sat down on the edge of the bathtub. I took out the cigarette Lily gave me a few hours ago.

"Do you have a lighter?" I asked.

In the mirror I caught his reflection. His eyes rolled back in his head, trying to escape. Strange, how drunken men resembled sick dogs.

"Hey," I said, "I asked you a question."

"I know what you're doing," he said, "I have a girlfriend"

"We're only fifteen," I said. "Do you want to be dead before we're alive?"

It sounded like something a Jezebel would say. In truth I stole the line from Sartre.

He finished pissing. He stumbled a bit, knocking over the soap holder on the counter. Some poor girl's parents were going to ground her for the rest of her life after this party.

"Lighter?" I said.

He moved toward me, trying to zip up his pants.

"So what you're telling me is that this wouldn't be cheating."

"I'm saying you shouldn't care."

"About Samantha?"

"Who?"

The cigarette broke against his chest and pieces of tobacco crumbled and fell down my shirt.

I leaned back to check my reflection in the mirror. Yes, that lipstick would do fine.

Up close his Georgia fuzziness melted away. He was a sharp mass of limbs, all bony elbows and bony knees. He was a bad kisser.

The next day, Samantha Hall came screaming into the bathroom with the rest of her cheerleader friends. She could've knocked over a radio tower with her frequency. She slapped me, and my ears started to ring. A taste, like salt, rushed into my mouth. I fell backwards into the bathroom sink and grabbed the faucet to try and steady myself.

"Fucking slut," Samantha Hall said. "Whore."

"So what? At least I wouldn't be caught dead in that stupid dress you're wearing."

She spit on me. Her friends, like a carousel of skinny, teeth-bared animals, spit on me. They pulled my hair until it tore. I slapped Samantha Hall in the face, leaving a blushing red mark. Another round of curses. Slut. Whore. Like a Hindu mantra, calming almost, as the words lost all meaning.

"We're only fifteen," I kept repeating. "We're only fifteen."

Samantha Hall hit me across the nose. Blood spattered her knuckles. They ran.

I leaned against the sink and spit blood. I avoided looking at my reflection, afraid they'd wiped off my lipstick and mascara, afraid I'd look and see a monster,

Lily came out of a bathroom stall, smelling like weed.

"Wow. That's going to leave a bruise," she said.

I leaned my head against the sink. Cool.

"Is that all you can say?" I said, gritting my teeth, "and you stink. You're not subtle, at all."

I wouldn't cry because I was from Paris. I was the other woman, the dark half thief who could disappear into mirrors, boudoirs. Look at this mouth; I'll eat you alive.

"Let's skip fourth period," Lily said, "I'll take you home."

I wiped the blood off my face with a wet tissue, and we snuck out the side entrance, behind the buses, where the hall monitors wouldn't be waiting. We ran across the street and climbed over barbed wire, into the woods, to take the shortcut home.

We went into my kitchen. I warmed a towel with hot water and pressed it to my face.

"Want any help?" Lily asked.

"No."

"Want any weed?"

"No."

Mama came out of her bedroom, one towel wrapped around her head and one around her body. Her eyes might as well have been Percocet.

"Oh hello, Lily," Mama said.

Mama did not notice the bruise welling up on my face, or my nose crusted with blood.

Miss Margot slunk through the kitchen. She scratched at the door, and before I could speak, Lily opened the door.

"Don't let her out."

Miss Margot dashed out into the garden.

"Oh, stupid. Sorry," Lily said.

I wanted to lash out at her, but I couldn't speak because a blinding pain crushed the bones in my face. I thought that, if I opened my mouth, my jaw might swell and burst my teeth. I went into Mama's bedroom and stole one of her Percocet pills. I swallowed it without water.

While I waited for the Percocet to kick in I went back into the kitchen. Lily pulled a frozen blueberry pie out of the fridge.

"Can I eat this?" she asked.

Without waiting for an answer, Lily sat down at the table and started eating it with her fingers. Her grimy, dirt stained fingers with her encrusted nails. Stupid punk kid, she'd probably go to hell and back and refuse to wash her hands before her next meal.

"Want a glass of milk, baby?" my mama asked Lily.

The Percocet must've started to kick in. I felt trapped behind a warm, rippling mirror. I didn't belong in my life anymore, if I ever did. I could not be the redneck from Georgia, and I could not be the socialite from Paris. I'd built myself up from a simulacrum. I did not know my favorite color or my favorite food. I only knew what people expected me to be. How easily anyone could tear me apart, because I had never really existed.

Mama ran her fingers through Lily's hair.

"Darker," she said, "I think you should go darker."

I went into my bedroom. I slipped off my clothes and climbed into my pajamas. The warm mirror reached up from below and enshrouded me. Every part of my body splintered off into fragments. I not only had one hand, I had six, each one with different coloring, different weight.

I was not a person but a splintering of possibilities. I lost my body and am living as a reflection.

I collapsed into bed. I could see Lily and Mama through the doorway.

Mama started making Lily Pop-Tarts. She wrapped Lily in a soft blue towel. They could have each other. I would be here in the back room, unable to move my head, watching my limbs multiply through waves of distorted time.

Someone rapped on my bedroom window.

"Have you seen my teddy bear?"

I couldn't speak.

"Have you seen my Little B?"

Go away.

Lily tried to eat the Pop-Tart and smeared chocolate frosting all over her face. Mama fetched a towel and wiped it off her mouth. Lily faded in and out of existence. I could see her becoming darker, thinner. Her eyes stretched out and her mouth thinned. She was becoming me.

Percocet shouldn't be making me see these things. Maybe someone switched out the bottle of pills. Maybe I'm going crazy in the way Mama always wished she could have.

The rapping on the window continued.

Go away.

I wanted to get up and wrap my hands around the new Phaedra's throat. I wanted to tell her, it's not worth it to be me. Please go back to who you used to be. We will not be fragments together; I don't even know how to keep one story straight.

Paris would never be like this. Paris would never have me staring out my bedroom door, a purveyor of my own life.

There was a scratching and whining at the kitchen door. It's Miss Margot, and there's sharpness to her mewling I've never heard before. Mama let her in, and she darted through the kitchen and jumped onto my bed.

Her eyes were gone.

I jumped up in bed, my paralysis gone, and I grabbed her. She shook and bled, soft caves cut into her skull, collapsing light. I was screaming. I knew I was screaming because of the tightness in my chest, though I couldn't hear a thing.

I was screaming.

Charlie.

Lily and Mama ran into the room. I wouldn't let them take Miss Margot away from me, not even to clean and care for her. I held her to me and rocked her and kissed her. I fell off the bed, sobbing, and collapsed onto the floor with Miss Margot held tight to my chest. She wouldn't stop shaking. Lily lay down beside me. She tried to tell me things like this happen all the time. I rolled away from her.

I didn't remember much after that day. Everything became static. I dressed. I spoke when spoken to. I fed Miss Margot and I went to school and I kept putting on the dark lipstick, but I ceased to be a living resident of my own body.

I cut out my cerebrum. All of my memories lived in my foreign spine.

They rolled through me like wisps of gritty factory smoke, blown in from the north side of town.

Years passed this way.

It was dark and I was dragging a boy through the dry woods underneath a yellow moon. We rolled through the fog, fog like dry ice in a Halloween machine. We kissed and collapsed into a rotting tree. We were not alone.

I was in the restroom of a gas station with an older man. He told me he was a musician. Then he told me he was a computer engineer. He talked slow, like it was difficult for him to remember the meaning of words. I didn't even feel a pinch when the heroin plunged into my blood.

My father, who I hadn't spoken to in fifteen years, sent me a check for college, in the mail, with a written letter of apology. I tore up the letter. I cashed the check and spent it on a pair of white Valentino heels and a vintage party dress.

I saw Samantha Hall walking down the high school hallway, seven months pregnant, and I started laughing at her because I knew she'd never be pretty again. She looked at the ground and avoided my eyes. If she had looked up, I would've scratched them out.

I went into a party wearing a stolen coat and my party dress. I had marijuana in my pocket and heroin in my boots. I danced in the middle of the floor. No music played, but my heart won't stop pounding. Someone calls me a slut, but in the crowd, I can't tell who it is. I start grabbing people's bottles and smashing them on the ground. I smash the jug of vodka. I smash the glasses. The boys grab my hair and my arms, and I bite someone's neck until blood wells in my mouth. I've never been more bored in my entire life. They throw me out into the darkne and I go.

Spinning.

I wandered through downtown, dru went into the boutique where I bough and they kicked me out. I don't kno but the sales girl screamed, her fa into a ghoul's face. The poundi transformed into a river and t me away.

I went next door to the dollar store. I wandered the aisles of cheap candy and clothes. The cashier followed me. I thought she would kick me out as well, but she remained silent as she stalked me. I pretended not to notice her.

I caught my reflection in a small hand mirror on the shelf. I found dried blood smeared across my mouth and nose, butterfly shaped, an old nosebleed.

I didn't have the energy to run to the bathroom and clean myself. I kept looking through the shop, until I came across her.

She sat on a shelf by herself, in a glossy red pot, her spiked mouths agape. I watched a fly buzz around her for a long time, before landing on one of her green pads. It brushed against her hairs. She closed her mouth. She devoured him slowly, elegantly, no longer a mouth but an eye, the eyelashes brushing against the squirming insect. She was a demure lady, an unfortunate killer. The victim was gone, locked into her center, swimming in secreted enzymes, to never eappear.

Venus Flytrap. Dionaea muscipula. I want to you.

paid for her and took her home.

t home I cleared my desk away and ged a shrine for her near the mesh screen w, near smoky sunlight. In a place where lants died, she grew big and richly colored. As I slept with Miss Margot in my arms, the plant's shadow lay across my bed.

I caught flies for her, slowing them down by placing them in the freezer. Just like feeding a lover drugs, my fingers rubbed raw with their use. My memories came back to me. I stopped going out every night while Mama slept, detoxed from the heroin and the wine. I pulled my reflection back from the mirror.

***

When I slept, my dreams were clear for the first time in years. I dreamt of walking through a thick, ancient jungle, with nothing but a machete and a small girl as my guide. The girl came from a poor village, and yet she wore golden bangles around her wrists and ankles. She wore a red jewel around her throat, and the jewel sang like a bird. Her exposed belly swelled with milk, and her lips were full with blood.

They were given gifts, she said, because they took care of Her.

I hacked away tree limbs and vines that reached out from the woods, dripping with steam, to grab me.

In a clearing we came to Her. The great Madagascar tree with the head of writhing snakes. The small girl clapped her hands. She said, Momma. Momma, I've brought you a gift.

The snakes embraced the small girl. They lifted her up from the dirt, bent her head back as [illegible] in a kiss. They pinched the back of her neck [illegible]ith their teeth. Her body went slack, without a [illegible]h. They devoured her and dropped the red [illegible]el at my feet.

[illegible]hen I woke, Miss Margot was gone. The [illegible]s Flytrap had caught a Daddy Long Legs [illegible] gray legs were sticking out of one of her mouths. Birds were singing outside the window, birds with voices like the red jewel from my dreams.

***

I went looking for Miss Margot in the house, and then in the garage. After she lost her eyes, she often hid underneath shelves or in between the car tires. I did not find Miss Margot, but I found, underneath a tarp next to an unused lawnmower and a rake, a white package of unmarked seeds.

In our yard and backyard, nothing grew except crabgrass and weeds. The Homeowners Association was always trying to knock down our door for not mowing the lawn. Mama would appear in the entryway, stumbling, shielding her eyes from the light.

"I have a medical condition," she said, "I have a rare genetic disorder. I have cysts in my kidneys. Do you think I can mow the lawn?"

They fled.

I pulled weeds and planted the seeds in the backyard, the first time I'd ever done so, in a soft patch of dirt. I raked the dirt back over them with my fingers. I watered them with a ceramic cup.

Inside, Mama was making herself a cup of valerian root tea.

"Have you seen Miss Margot?"

She poured the boiling water into the cup. Her fingers were red and her face flushed with heat. The wallpaper had unfurled above her head and was hanging down, like a reaching hand.

"Mama."

She didn't respond. I realized I hadn't seen her sober eyes in as long as I could remember.

"Miss Margot is gone."

The steam boiled and rose in a plume around her face. It encased her head in a shroud. Underneath the shroud, her skin shifted. My Mama, all these years, was not a human being, but a lizard. The skin was like a bandage to cover the wound, perforated at the edges. The steam had curled her disguise, like it curled the wallpaper.

"Mama"

She turned to me with flakes of green on her face. She was an old lizard and sick, her scales the color of dulled vegetation, left out in the sun to dry. I pulled at my own skin. At my elbows. My fingers. Please, don't let there be tears in this costume.

Please, don't let me be my mother.

"Mama, do you ever think about anyone but yourself?"

The steam boiled in the air. I knew if I touched it, I would burn.

"Mama, have you ever loved me?"

But there was only the sound of her skin tearing. It fell in a pile around her feet. She raised the cup of tea to her mouth.

I knocked it out of her hands. It shattered onto the ground and I immediately regretted it. She fumbled for another cup. She crushed the porcelain underneath her feet, crushed it in a tincture of her own blood.

"I just wanted you to love me," I whispered.

It didn't feel true, even as I said it, but a part of my brain, a lazy, steamy part, believed it so.

I ran out into the street. I ran calling for Miss Margot. I knocked on Lily's door. I'd choke her if I could. If she hadn't come into my house, high as fuck, and opened that door, none of this would've happened. Miss Margot would still have her eyes, I would still know which way was up.

Her mother answered the door. She lurched forward when the door flew open, her body like a hot coiled wire. She smelled musty, an attic thing, her body covered in rags. She wore a gazelle skull mask that hid everything except her eyes, cracked white and wide.

"Where is Lily?" I asked, my throat closing and heart screaming, "I need to talk to her."

She pointed toward the woods.

I ran. Urgency struck at my back. The air pounded at me like an abusive father. It was too early for darkness, but the sun took one look at me and plunged downwards. Hot red streaks of sky gushed from the top of the tree line, like the sun impaling itself below.

"Miss Margot. Miss Margot."

"Lily. Lily."

Even as I called for them, I knew I searched for something else.

For the great Madagascar Tree that took one look at me, its new sacrifice, and ate the child it once cared for and dressed in gold.

For the carnivorous bellflowers that lured rats and birds to their sloping containers of mouths. Promised nectar, and delivered acidic enzymes.

For a garden I'd grow, in which I'd no longer be a splintered mirror. For she could see me for who I was, and there'd be no need for reflection.

I remembered the moment when the mask dissolved. It was not a mask pointing outward, but inward. I thought my facade of painted face and painted eyes was so clever. Instead I wore a costume that only fooled myself.

The woods grew darker. The trees paled in color, the exposed roots, albino, the leaves ivory, as if they'd never seen sunlight. I stopped, gasping. My organs felt too big in my body. I hadn't run that fast or that far in years.

It's quiet here, but I'm not alone.

My shadow turned.

It peeled from my skin

It walked away, and I followed.

Plants with teeth bloomed from the earth. They opened their mouths like oozing sores. They reached for the mosquitoes that landed on my bare hips and ate them alive. My shadow didn't look back to see if I kept following. But I did. Stumbling, acid-eaten, and sore, I followed.

My shadow found Miss Margot on her back in the weeds. She was whining, and scabs covered her legs. I picked her up and cradled her to my chest. She'd thinned. Her ribs were like needles, sharp against my palms.

Moonlight bounced off the grass, and that's when I saw something shiny and wet in the weeds.

An eye. A cat's eye, yellow and white, with a black pulsing center.

Another rolled at my feet. My shadow cupped its hands around it. My cat's shadow batted it like a toy.

The weeds crunched behind me. The trees bent down, moaning. I knew if I looked, my fingers would forget how to make another mask. I'd be naked forever. Self-deception would be a memory.

How did I know this?

Because a Parisian does not find herself in a forest in the southern United States, dizzy, barefoot, and slipping on the soft eyeballs underneath her. Jezebel never stopped cutting off heads to run through the dirt, calling for a sick cat. And she never will.

The trees hissed and the branches lay themselves about my shoulders like a mantle. They were warm and alive. From behind me, someone spoke.

"I can give you."

A familiar voice.

"I can give you something special."

Let me tell you all the things I've devoured today.

A dirty girl sat, cross-legged, among a mound of cat's eyeballs. Her dark hair covered her eyes.

"Lily?"

She'd changed. She picked up an eyeball and popped it with black, sharp fingernails. Her mouth was a piranha's mouth, with sharp rows of fanged teeth. She swallowed the eye.

When she brushed her hair out of her face and looked at me with dark green eyes, a wave of nausea hit me. The air swam thick.

"Lily. What the hell is wrong with you?" I said, my mouth and voice far away, "Are you on drugs?"

"They're under my tongue," she said. "Come have a taste."

"Stop fucking around."

But I know she isn't. The Madagascar Tree stood behind me; I felt her like a guardian angel. Snakes, with leaves buried into their skin, encircled my legs and arms. They flicked their tongues at me, tasting me.

"You never had a chance, Phaedra."

She ate another eye.

"I can give it to you now."

Miss Margot went limp in my arms.

"The ultimate drug. No symptoms, and no comedown. Ever."

She stuck her tongue out at me. It was a tongue made of spiders, and the spiders held, in their limbs, a little red capsule.

"Kiss me."

Kiss me.

You will see what you want forever. Reality as it belongs to you.

Kiss me.

The snakes lured me forward with their black, tree-limbed heads. They lured me down into the wet mud. Miss Margot ran from my arms and jumped into the girl's lap. My chest constricted. I gasped a single word.

"Please."

I inhaled a sharp breath. As I did so, my shadow curled up around me and welded itself back to my skin.

"Please don't let me be my mother."

The girl laughed. The spiders on her tongue clicked.

"That sad little ghost? You could be so much more."

If only I crawled.

And I crawled. Through the eyes, I crawled. I could be more. The tree could be mine. Yes. My limbs would grow into a plant's limbs. So difficult to be human, each generation raised by a tragedy, instead of a parent. I wanted to be more. Let the mask slip. Little Venus teeth were growing underneath.

She took me in her arms. I kissed her soft, cold mouth. I swallowed the pill.

***

I lost consciousness, but when I came to, I was running. Lights flashed behind me, people shouting. The cops. I found myself running in heels and a shredded dress, through a muddy creek. They told me to stop. I knew they couldn't catch me. I was faster than they could ever hope to be. There were muscles in my legs and my head I never knew existed. I flexed them and passed into a parallel world. The trees there glowed. The flowers called my name. I was laughing. I ran without touching the ground. I slipped in and out of realities. I wished for Miss Margot and she appeared in my arms.

I was in all places at once, and at all times.

By the time I got home I'd lost the cops. The doors of the house had blown open and I knew Mama was gone, but I didn't care.

The seeds I planted that morning had grown into my baby. My Madagascar Tree. I lifted my arms. She lifted her arms and took me gently by the wrists. Her snakes clamped down onto my fingers. I didn't need legs anymore.

The backyard had transformed into a midnight garden. The once derelict, broken-down fence became an obsidian wall. The weeds grew into enormous flowers, man-eating bellflowers with red translucent skin.

The mirror that once trapped me, detached itself from my body. The town fell away with its police, high school, and quack therapy in its reflection, leaving me in the garden.

I blew seeds from my mouth and they bloomed into blue roses. I shook my hair and the hair that fell on the ground, grew into cherry trees. The snakes brought me to the tree's center. She could've swallowed me, but I knew she wouldn't dare. I whispered to her, lovingly, teasing, I would be like fire in her stomach. I'd burn a hole straight through her, in the shape of me. I wouldn't allow her to place the golden bracelets on my wrists. Instead, I would collar her snakes with crystal leashes. I'd take them for walks around the garden.

The night would be a long one. Maybe it'd go on forever. I could feel my veins blooming into celluloid walls. Soon vines would overtake my heart and I'd no longer need to breathe with lungs. I'd breathe through my skin.

I touched her trunk and I whispered.

I devoured the pill.

I devoured the mask.

I devoured my neuroses.

I devoured my history.

I devoured the fear, and the shame.

You're in my garden now, and I am your gardener.

About The Author

Autumn Christian is a game designer by day and speculative fiction writer by night. She is the author of **The Crooked God Machine** and **A Gentle Hell**. All love letters, blackmail, and inquiries should be sent to her email address at **axtian@gmail.com**.

She's been a freelance writer, a game developer, a cheese producer, a haunted house actor, and a video game tester. She considers Philip K. Dick, Ray Bradbury, Katie Jane Garside, the southern gothic, and dubstep, as main sources of inspiration. She is waiting for the day when she hits her head on the cabinet searching for the popcorn bowl and all consensus reality dissolves.

Other Books by Autumn Christian

The Crooked God Machine (2011)
A Gentle Hell (2012)

Made in the USA
Charleston, SC
14 June 2014